P9-BYZ-365

WITHDRAWN

THE
GIRL
IS
TROUBLE

THE GIRL IS TROUBLE

KATHRYN MILLER HAINES

ROARING BROOK PRESS

New York

Batavia Public Library
Batavia. Illinois

Text copyright © 2012 by Kathryn Miller Haines

Published by Roaring Brook Press

Roaring Brook Press is a division of Holtzbrinck Publishing Holdings
Limited Partnership

175 Fifth Avenue, New York, New York 10010

macteenbooks.com

All rights reserved

Library of Congress Cataloging-in-Publication Data

Haines, Kathryn Miller.

The girl is trouble / Kathryn Miller Haines. — 1st ed.

p. cm.

Summary: Late 1942 in New York City finds fifteen-year-old Iris helping
more with her father's detective business, as long as she follows his rules
and learns his techniques, but her investigation into her mother's supposed
suicide gets Iris in big trouble—and not just with her father.

ISBN 978-1-59643-610-7 (hardcover)

ISBN 978-1-59643-826-2 (e-book)

[1. Interpersonal relations—Fiction.   2. Fathers and daughters—
Fiction.   3. Private investigators—Fiction.   4. Conduct of life—Fiction.
5. New York (N.Y.)—History—20th century—Fiction.]   I. Title.

PZ7.H128123Gii 2012

[Fic]—dc23   2011031806

Roaring Brook Press books are available for special promotions and premiums.
For details contact: Director of Special Markets, Holtzbrinck Publishers.

First edition 2012

Book design by Alex Garkusha

Printed in the United States of America

10   9   8   7   6   5   4   3   2   1

For G & G and all the mothers

*And for Wynne, who made it possible
for me to become one*

THE GIRL

IS

TROUBLE

1

"DO YOU SEE WHERE HE WENT?" asked Pop.

"Not yet," I said. We were uptown, trying hard to blend into the morning crowd. I had no idea it would be so hard to keep my eye on someone while trying not to be seen myself.

"Look harder."

Boy, howdy—did Pop really think I wasn't looking as hard as possible? I focused the camera on Sixth Avenue and scanned the shops on the first floor. I still didn't see where the man we were tailing had gone, but a display that included a red book with a black swastika on the cover caught my attention. Another twist of the dial and the bold yellow text became clear: *Germany Must Perish!* Above the title, words teased emphatically that this was "The Book Hitler Fears the Most."

"Left, Iris. Look left," said Pop.

I swung the camera left, but it was too late: my mark was gone.

Pop elbowed me in the ribs. "There he is, Iris—by the kiosk. Do you see him?"

I trained Pop's Leica on the newspaper vendor. The man in the black overcoat was flipping through a copy of that day's *Times*. "I've got him," I said. "Now what?"

"When he moves, you move. Make sure there are always at least five people between you and him. Got it?"

I nodded, excitement burning through me. This was it: Pop was finally letting me tail someone by myself. "Where will you be?" I asked.

"The Automat. As soon as you get the picture, you join me. You've got fifteen minutes. If you're not back by then—"

"You're calling the cops and my detecting days are over." I rolled my eyes. "I've got it." I slid the camera into my bag. St. Patrick's Cathedral sounded the hour like the world's most expensive starter pistol: ready, aim, follow that man!

Pop splayed his fingers. "Five people, Iris. If you think he's seen you, run in the opposite direction. Got it?"

Another roll of my eyes. The man wasn't going to eyeball me. I'd probably have the picture and be at the Automat before Pop reached it himself.

Pop started across Fifty-sixth Street. He moved about as fast as you'd expect a man with a wooden leg to move. I cringed as a policeman wielding a stop sign halted traffic so Pop could complete his crossing. Once he was out of sight, I started after the man, who had bought his newspaper and now walked east toward Park Avenue. He paused near a mailbox and lit a cigarette. I paused as well, stopping right by the bookshop window. Looking at *Germany Must Perish!* up close made me even more uncomfortable. I'd seen books like it before, only those had proclaimed that it was the Japanese that we needed to eradicate. Once I'd even spied an awful pamphlet that declared that it was Jews who should be erased.

What would Mama think if she could see this? "This man thinks the only good German is a dead German," she would probably say. "He should know better. *Das Kind mit dem Bade ausschütten.* You don't throw the baby out with the water."

But then she was a good German. And a dead one.

The man started moving again. A group of young men in Air Corps uniforms passed by. I silently counted until five of them were in front of me, then continued on my way.

This was easy-peasy. Pop was worrying for nothing.

We traveled two blocks and then the man turned, just like Pop said he would. He discarded the cigarette on the ground, looked at his watch, then tossed a panicked look over his shoulder, like he could sense someone was behind him.

I slowed my pace and let two women carrying packages from Gimbels get in front of me. One of them wore an enormous veiled hat that did a bang-up job of masking me from view.

Apparently satisfied that he was alone, the man continued

walking until he was in front of a brownstone marked number 19. This was the shot the client wanted: capture the mark entering the building, showing his face *and* the address.

He hesitated as though he were debating whether to approach the building. *Come on,* I silently begged. *Get it over and done with before Pop panics and comes looking for me.*

I pulled the camera from my bag and scanned the street for the perfect place to take the picture. Six feet in front of me was a shrub with the last of the fall leaves clinging to its branches. I slowed my pace.

"Little girl," said someone behind me. A finger tapped me on the shoulder. "Little girl?" I tried not to cringe at the "little" part. After all, I was in my Chapin School uniform, and with the plaid skirt, kneesocks, and the two braids I'd woven my hair into, whoever it was had to assume I was younger than fifteen. I turned to find an old woman, bent with age, looking at me. "Your shoe is untied," she said.

"Oh, thank you." I looked back toward number 19. The man was no longer there. Nuts. Had I missed him entering?

"You'd better tie it," she said. "You don't want to risk a fall."

"I will," I said. "But right now I'm kind of in a hurry."

I tried to walk away, but she put a hand on my arm and held me in place. She had milky-gray eyes and an imposing stare that I was willing to bet had served her well during her long career as a prison warden. "That's the problem with you kids today. Always in a hurry. When I was a girl—"

4

Boy, howdy—was she really going to lecture me?

"You're right," I said. "I'll tie it right now." I returned the camera to my bag, squatted, and wrapped the laces of my saddle shoe into a hasty bow. My skirt was too tight and threatened to bust a button as I crouched. I hadn't worn the uniform in months, not since I'd traded a private school for a public one. "Thanks again," I told her. She narrowed her eyes, but finally seemed satisfied and continued on her way.

I grabbed my bag and attempted to stand back up when a large form cast a shadow over me. It was the man in the black trench coat.

He clamped a hand on my wrist and helped me the rest of the way up. "Why are you following me?" he hissed.

"Excuse me?" I asked. My eyes darted to the left, seeking out the old woman who'd been there moments before. She was apparently faster than Pop, because she'd already managed to move out of my line of sight. In fact, the entire sidewalk seemed to have cleared out, leaving me alone with this man with the very strong grip.

"You've been tailing me since Fifty-sixth Street."

I widened my eyes, hoping that my fear didn't show. Where was Pop? Had fifteen minutes passed yet? "N-n-no," I stuttered. "I'm just looking for my d-d-dog." I reached into my bag and fumbled past the camera until I landed on the object I wanted. Without my eyes ever leaving the man's, I pulled out a leash I'd bought that morning at the five-and-dime.

5

"Dog?" he echoed.

"H-his name's Skippy." Try as I might, I couldn't make my voice steady. Fear had hold of me and wouldn't let go. "We were on our way to Central Park when he got loose. I chased him down Fifty-sixth Street and thought I saw him turn up this way." My eyes blazed with tears. I pushed them away with my free hand. The man must've thought the emotion was because of my missing dog, not my fear of what he was going to do to me, because he let go and fished a handkerchief from his pocket. "T-t-thanks," I said.

"I'm sorry, little girl. I didn't mean to startle you."

"It's o-o-okay." I mopped my eyes and willed my panicked breathing to slow down. The crowd that had seemed to disperse moments before returned, and I took comfort in knowing that at least we weren't alone. If I screamed for help, surely someone would assist me. I offered him the handkerchief. "Do you want this back?"

"Keep it," he said. "Again, my apologies. I hope you find your dog." He turned and moved back toward number 19. I took a deep breath, gathered my things, and crossed the street. I had failed. Not only had I not taken the picture, I'd gotten caught. The jig was up. No matter what I did now, this guy had my number.

What was Pop going to say?

I couldn't stomach the thought of telling him how wrong things had gone. My working for him was new, his conditions clear: I was fated to do desk work if he didn't think I could handle myself out on the street. I should've been grateful that he was letting me help him at all, but answering phones and making occasional calls wasn't what I had in mind. I wanted to be a real detective.

Instead of heading toward the Automat, I pulled my camera from my bag and trained it on the door to number 19. The man's back was to me, making it impossible to identify who was about to enter the building. I hesitated for only a moment before calling out, "Skippy! There you are." When the man turned to observe our reunion, I got my shot, grabbed my bag, and ran like hell.

I HID IN THE FOYER of a building until I was certain the man in the trench coat wasn't following me. There I freed my hair from its braids, traded my too-small plaid skirt for a longer dirndl one, and pushed my kneesocks into a fashionable slouch. I met Pop outside the Automat two blocks away. It was clear he was on his way to look for me. I guess I should've been grateful—he'd at least waited longer than the allotted fifteen minutes.

"Where have you been?" he asked in a hushed tone designed not to draw any attention to us.

"He saw me," I said. I'd made a pact with Pop not to lie to him anymore, and I kept my word. Sort of. Sometimes I stretched the truth slightly, but kept the basic facts the same. "But I got the shot," I said.

He led me inside the restaurant. The place was packed

with servicemen who wanted to see for themselves a restaurant where machines delivered the food instead of people. Of course, it wasn't really like that. While sandwiches and slices of pie waited behind windows for you to drop your coins into a slot and make your selection, women behind the scenes prepared the food just like at any other restaurant.

"I thought I'd better lie low for a while," I told him as I joined him at the chrome-edged table. "But don't worry— everything's aces."

"Did he touch you?" That was Pop's biggest fear and the reason I couldn't be completely honest if I wanted to work on the street again. He couldn't stand the thought of putting me in danger.

"Nope—he asked me why I was following him and I told him he must be mistaken. I was looking for Skippy." Pop's brow creased with confusion, so I produced the leash. The prop had been my idea. If nothing else, the movies had taught me that the only thing a grown man finds more innocent than a little girl is a little girl with a puppy.

"And he bought it?"

"Hook, line, and sinker." And so, judging from his expression, had Pop. If only I felt as confident as I tried to sound. "He even apologized for accusing me of any wrongdoing."

Pop looked pleased. "So if he saw you, how did you get the shot?"

I should've known he'd ask that. "Somebody across the

street shouted and I guess the noise startled him because he turned toward it. I snapped him right then."

"That was convenient."

Boy, howdy, was it—especially since I was the one doing the shouting.

"What could you have done differently?" asked Pop. It wasn't a criticism. Pop always asked the question, as a reminder that sometimes plans didn't go so smoothly and you had to change things on the fly.

"My exit was abrupt," I admitted. "I was pretty rattled when he talked to me." I loved these conversations with Pop. They reminded me of how Mama and I used to sit on a park bench, pick a stranger, and challenge each other to make three observations about their lives based only on their appearance.

"What could have helped?" asked Pop.

"I could've told him I saw the dog," I proposed. "Then I could've just rushed off in the opposite direction."

Pop shook his head. "There's a good chance of tipping your hand there. If he really believed your story and felt bad for accusing you of following him, he might have followed you, thinking you wouldn't be able to catch the dog on your own."

He was right—I'd been lucky. That was the thing I had to keep reminding myself: Pop had been doing this a lot longer than I had. Detecting was in his blood. "Maybe I could've pointed to a passerby, said they were my mother, and gone running after them." I should've used the old lady. Surely he'd seen me talking to her.

Pop pondered this for a moment and nodded. "I like that. Safety in numbers. It would've been good if he thought you weren't alone—just in case." A funny little pang squeezed my chest. Creating an imaginary mother made me miss my real one all the more. "I want you to write up a report of everything you saw today, okay? Just like I showed you." Pop was big on keeping written records of every move he made. It wasn't just to let the client know they were getting their money's worth; he also said the information could be invaluable to the investigation. You never knew what details that initially seemed insignificant might prove important later on. "Good job, Iris."

I should've been swelling with pride, but the parts of the story I hadn't told Pop were still playing in my brain. This hadn't been easy. What if I wasn't cut out for detecting? What if the next time something worse happened?

"Is something bothering you?" asked Pop.

I couldn't tell him my doubts. There'd be no hope of his sending me out on my own if I did. And I needed to be out there, because stuck at home, with little to occupy me, sent my mind in other dark directions. "I saw this book," I said. "In one of the shops on Fifty-sixth Street. The author says we should get rid of all Germans and make it impossible for more to be born."

"And what does he consider a German?"

"Anyone with a drop of German blood."

"That's a rather extremist view," said Pop. "What do you think?" That was Pop for you—he rarely shared his opinions about the war, even when the perfect opportunity presented itself.

If it took only one drop of blood to make you German, that meant Mama wouldn't have been the only one eradicated—I would've been on the list as well. "I think Mama would be mortified."

Pop didn't say anything. He rarely mentioned Mama. I knew he missed her—he'd owned up to that weeks before—but ever since then he'd seemed determined to try to put her out of his mind. I couldn't do that. If I was going to forgive her for what she did, I had to remember the good things about her; otherwise, the way she died eclipsed everything.

"How can someone think every single German is evil?" I asked.

Pop fished change from his pocket. We both approached the enormous glass-fronted Automat machine and lingered in front of the sandwich section as we took in our options for lunch. Pop deposited his money and pushed the button beside the tuna on rye. The door lifted up and he removed his selection, plate and all, while another one slid into place behind it. "I haven't seen the book, Iris, but there is an idea in war that you must paint the enemy with a broad brush. Otherwise, you'll spend so much time worried about whether the person standing before you is the exception to the rule that you'll never fire your gun. That hesitation can cost you your life."

"But he wasn't just talking about soldiers. He was talking about *everyone*."

He passed a dime and two nickels my way. "Sometimes, the enemy doesn't wear a uniform."

I wanted to believe he was wrong, that it was easy to separate good from evil, but experience had already taught me that the people you thought you could trust were the ones you needed to be the most afraid of. Even still, I never imagined in a million years that the person I would come to fear would be my own mother.

2

"SO THEN WHAT DID YOU DO?"

"What else could I do?" I said. "I ran." My best friend, Pearl, and I were entering P.S. 110 together. I'd spent the walk to school recounting my job with Pop while Pearl listened in silent awe.

"But you got the photo?"

"I guess. I mean, Pop didn't show it to me after he'd developed it." I hadn't asked to see it, either. I knew better.

"I wish I could've been there," said Pearl. Ever since Pop had agreed to let me work with him, Pearl had been dropping hints that she wished she could do it, too. Part of it was boredom, I'm sure, but I also thought Pearl had a predilection for detection. Not only was she observant, but she knew how to get information and use it to her advantage.

One of these days I'd mention her skills to Pop. But not yet. Not when I was still trying to figure out if I had what it took to get the job done.

13

A girl walked by us, her face a mess of running makeup and bleary red eyes. "Her brother?" I asked Pearl.

"Yep," she said. "Guadalcanal." No further words were needed. The fighting on that tiny island in the South Pacific had ramped up the last few weeks, and more and more casualties were being reported. I saw the numbers on the front page of the newspapers, but, like Pop, I avoided the detailed lists of dead and wounded that populated the inner pages. Pop did it because he feared there would be friends and former colleagues listed. I'm not sure why I did.

Pop used to be in Naval Intelligence, a job that had allowed him to continue his family's legacy of detection while serving his country. It's also the reason he was at Pearl Harbor on that fateful day and lost his leg, which was why he was now willing to accept my help on cases.

Pearl Harbor. The name of that once inconsequential Hawaiian landmark smacked me in the face wherever I looked these days. The posters were everywhere at P.S. 110:

Remember *PEARL HARBOR!*

Commemorate the one-year anniversary
of our entrance into the war

SCHOOL-WIDE CONVOCATION
Monday, Dec. 7, in the Auditorium

Immediately following lunch

December 7 was only a week away. Had it really already been a year since Pearl Harbor? How had the date snuck up on me so quickly?

"Hi, Pearl," said a boy from across the hall. Pearl gave him a tentative wave before bidding me farewell. I stopped at my locker to exchange one cumbersome textbook for another. The boy who had greeted Pearl lingered, even after she was gone.

"Are you Iris?" he asked.

I looked him up and down, trying to place him. He was my height and wore a heavy pair of horn-rimmed glasses that were at that moment sliding halfway down his nose. He pushed them back into position without ever leaving my gaze.

"Yes," I said.

"I'm Michael Rosenberg. I'm a friend of Pearl's."

I nodded, uncertain what, if anything, I should say. Pearl's halfhearted wave hardly spoke of an intimate friendship with Michael.

"Well . . . I mean I'm a friend of her brother's. But I know Pearl, too." He lowered his voice and leaned toward me. He smelled vaguely fishy. "I hear you're good at finding stuff out."

"I'm not sure I know what you mean," I said.

He cocked his head toward the row of lockers across from us. I caught his meaning, let's continue this conversation over there, though why he thought it was more discreet I couldn't begin to guess. "Paul said your old man is a detective. He said you work for him."

Boy, howdy—so that cat was out of the bag. Not the detective thing: everyone at P.S. 110 knew what Pop did for a living after he'd helped track down a missing student earlier that year. But Pearl was the only one who was privy to what *I* was doing. My role with the agency was supposed to be on the Q.T.—Pop's rule, not mine. There were a lot of reasons for that, not the least of which was that I was only fifteen years old.

"You heard wrong," I told Michael. I started to walk away, but he snagged the sleeve of my sweater to keep me from going. I looked at where he touched me and he released his hold like I was on fire.

"Sorry," he said. "It's just . . . I'm desperate." He made another attempt to push his glasses up his nose. Cat fur clung to his sweater vest. "I found this in my locker the other day." He passed me a folded piece of paper. "Read it."

I opened the note, then closed it just as quickly. That's all the time I needed to read the words: "Kill the Jews Before They Kill Us."

"I'm not the only person who got one. Another member of the Jewish Student Federation got one, too."

I gave him back the page. "I'm sorry, but you're barking up the wrong tree. My pop's a detective, not me."

"I can pay you," said Michael. The bell rang, signaling that we had five minutes remaining to get to our first class.

"This isn't about money. I've got to go."

Michael said something else, but his words were lost as I disappeared into the crowd of students rushing to get to their homerooms.

"I'M GOING TO KILL YOUR BROTHER," I told Pearl over lunch.

"What did Paul do now?"

"He's got a slow leak. He's going around telling everyone I'm working for Pop."

"Oh." She immediately looked guilty. "I told him a long time ago." She meant before I actually *was* working for Pop. There was a time when I was a little flexible with the truth with everyone. After all, I was the new girl at P.S. 110. I would've said just about anything to keep people from thinking I was a drip. "I'll tell him to stop." Pearl made a move like she was going to march over to his table right then and read him the riot act.

I waved her off. "It's too late now. And besides, what are the odds he'd actually listen to you?"

Someone walked by our table humming the melody to "Remember Pearl Harbor." Pearl turned beet red.

A year ago, right after the event that would make all of us aware of that Pacific landmark, everyone at school started calling her Pearl Harbor. In their eyes she'd become a bit of a sad sack after the death of her oldest brother, Peter, the kind of girl whose doom and gloom could make the lights dim when she entered a room. No one ever called her that in front of adults, who would've found it shamefully inappropriate no matter how they tried to explain it.

And the truth was, Pearl *was* strange. I don't know what she was like before Peter died, but in the time since I'd known her she'd been an odd duck who talked to few people other than me, and then only if it was absolutely necessary. Paul used to coddle her, but he'd passed the torch to me in the last few months, probably because his girlfriend, Denise, preferred it that way.

There were times when it seemed like Pearl would rather disappear than be seen, that the discomfort with being in her own, increasingly pudgy body was so immense that she would rather be invisible than face her awkwardness for another minute. I understood her impulse even if I didn't feel it for the same reasons. After all, none of us were happy with ourselves. That was the nature of being fifteen. But while I was starting to understand that I would grow and change and get beyond who I was now, Pearl seemed certain she'd be trapped as the same person in the same uncomfortable package for the rest of her life.

Another boy walked by, imitating the sound of a bomb striking its target. Pearl receded further into herself. I gently kicked her under the table and shook my head at her once I had her attention. *Be strong*, I silently urged. *Don't let them get you down.*

"I'm going to be so glad when this anniversary has come and gone," said Pearl.

"You and me both." Pearl Harbor would always mean more to me than anyone else I knew. It was the day Pop lost his leg. A few short weeks before Mama did the inexplicable and killed herself. The moment my entire life was turned upside down. I changed the subject. "Who was that boy you waved at this morning?"

She frowned for a moment, trying to remember who I was talking about. "Oh, that's Michael Rosenberg. He's the head of the Jewish Student Federation. His dad owns the A and P on Delancey." The federation was an after-school club for Jewish students. Both Paul and Pearl belonged. They'd tried to get me to join as well, but I told them from the get-go that I wasn't interested. "Why do you want to know?"

"He's the one Paul squealed to. He cornered me right after you left this morning."

"Well, he's a nice guy, despite the company he keeps." She rolled her eyes toward where Paul was sitting with Denise Halloway. "Did he say what he wanted?"

I told her about the note he'd shown me. She gripped her fork until her fingers turned red. "Did he tell the principal?"

"I didn't ask."

"I can't believe someone would do that, and right before Hanukah, too." The mention of Hanukah stirred guilt deep in my stomach. Pop had changed our surname from Ackerman to Anderson years ago and we had never been an

19

observant family. That changed last year, right after December 7. I don't know if it was the United States entering the war or hearing that Pop had been hurt, but Mama and I lit our candles for the eight days of Hanukah, blindly believing that religion could make everything better.

When it didn't, it was easy to discard it again.

"You're going to help him, right?" asked Pearl.

"I don't know how," I said. "What am I supposed to do—analyze the handwriting? Check the paper for fingerprints?"

"We could stake out the lockers. If two people in the federation got notes, I'll bet there are more coming."

Her "we" didn't escape me.

From across the cafeteria, laughter rang out at the table the Rainbows occupied. They were a gang of fast-living upperclassmen who, if gossip was to be believed, were behind everything that ever went wrong at P.S. 110. It was easy to see why everyone thought that. The girls in the group wore tight sweaters, bright lipstick, and a knowing grin that would've made a nun blush. And the boys slicked back their hair with Brylcreem, wore their wallets on waist chains, and peppered their speech with the latest slang straight out of Harlem dance halls. I used to be friends with them, until they found out I was trying to get information for a case for Pop. I'd made peace with some of the group, but the rest of them still wanted nothing to do with me. Or Pearl. Once a rat, always a rat, I guess.

Pearl continued to ramble on with her scheme for

catching whoever had left the notes, suggesting that I talk to the other person who received one and see what time of day they'd been discovered. I only half listened to her— the rest of my attention was directed at the Rainbows' table, where Benny Rossi, an Italian boy with black eyes and a sixty-watt smile, was telling a story with so much animation that I felt like I was there with him.

Benny. Looking at him made me weak in the knees, quite a task when I was already sitting. We'd spent an unforgettable night together dancing at the Savoy in Harlem. Sometimes I thought I could still feel his hand on my waist and the gentle touch of his lips on—

"So what do you think?"

I snapped to attention. Pearl was waiting for an answer to a question I hadn't heard. "I think it sounds like a swell plan."

"Great. So you'll ask Michael who else got the notes and interview them, then I'll find out where the other federation members' lockers are." She pulled out her composition notebook and pencil and jotted down our list of tasks. If Pearl was anything, she was organized. That was part of the reason she was allowed to work in the attendance office during study hall.

"Maybe you should interview them," I said. "I mean, you know them, right?"

A strange look came over Pearl's face that I couldn't begin to read.

"What's the matter?" I asked.

"I'm kind of not in the federation anymore."

"Why not?"

"They kind of . . . um . . . kicked me out."

"For what?"

She wouldn't meet my eyes. "They said I didn't seem very committed to the group anymore. They seemed to think I'd rather be friends with you than them."

I still wasn't getting it. Were they jealous that Pearl and I spent so much time together? That seemed . . . weird.

Pearl pulled a cookie from her bag and snapped it in two. "Paul told them that you're not practicing."

"Oh."

"It's not a big deal," said Pearl. "I'd much rather spend time with you."

She offered me half of the cookie and I took it. It wasn't sweet like I was hoping. Mrs. Levine must've been short a few sugar ration tickets. "Michael said he was your friend," I said.

"Oh, Michael's swell. He would've been happy for me to stay. It's the other people who weren't so keen on me."

I still didn't get it. I looked at the table where Michael was sitting with Paul, Denise, and several other people who I suspected were in the federation. "Denise isn't Jewish," I said. "How come Paul's still in the group?"

"Because Denise isn't Jewish," said Pearl.

Ah. It was one thing to be a gentile who didn't know any better. It was quite another to be a bad Jew.

"Why do you want to help them so badly?" I asked.

Pearl shrugged. "Because this is wrong. I may not like how they treated me, but that doesn't mean we shouldn't help them."

And maybe Pearl hoped it would help both of us get in their good graces.

AFTER LUNCH I SAID FAREWELL to Pearl and stopped in the girls' restroom off the cafeteria. Ordinarily I would've waited to use another restroom, since this particular one was taken over as a smoking lounge by the female members of the Rainbows. But with so little time left before we had to return to class, I had no choice.

They tried to cover up what they were doing when I walked in, but once they realized it was me, they resumed blowing smoke circles while touching up their hair and makeup. Rhona and Maria did what they did best and ignored me. Only Suze smiled my way and offered me a greeting. "Hi, baby girl."

"Hi yourself," I said. A few months before, talking with Suze had felt forced and awkward, but time had taught me that Suze was a good egg. All of them were, really, though Rhona and Maria liked to pretend that talking to me was taxing.

"How's tricks?" asked Suze.

"Good," I said. This was as friendly as our conversations got these days. It made me sad, but I understood: I had betrayed the Rainbows' trust, and while they were willing to let bygones be bygones, they weren't going to let me get close again.

"We gotta blow, Suze," said Rhona as she stubbed her cigarette out on the counter and then tossed it down the drain.

"I'll be out in two ticks."

The other two girls exited, leaving Suze and me alone. She studied her reflection in the mirror, erasing a stray line of lip cream with her fingertip. "He saw you watching him, you know."

"What's that?"

Her mouth quirked into a smile. "Benny. You were playing cat to his canary during lunch."

I burned with embarrassment. "I wasn't—"

She winked from the mirror. "It's okay, baby girl. He didn't mind. I just thought you should know he noticed." She snapped her pocketbook closed and hung it on her arm. "See you later, alligator."

"In a while, crocodile," I said as she walked out the door.

What was I supposed to make of that? Benny knew I was watching him? And he didn't mind? Did that mean there was still a chance? I grinned at the mirror, imagining for a moment that it was his eyes I was staring into instead of my own. And then I left the restroom, having forgotten what I'd gone there to do in the first place.

* * *

24

I COASTED THROUGH THE AFTERNOON on fumes of hope. Instead of hunting down Benny at the end of the day, I caught up with Michael Rosenberg after school. It wasn't hard to find him; the federation was scheduled to meet that afternoon in the journalism classroom. I lingered outside the door as members of the group arrived. Most of them ignored me, except for one girl who put the name to my face and offered me a sneer.

"Can I help you?" she asked in the kind of imperious tone that I hadn't heard since we'd moved from the Upper East Side.

"I need to talk to Michael."

She raised an eyebrow but didn't respond. Instead, she disappeared into the journalism room. Thirty seconds later, Michael appeared.

"Iris! Have you changed your mind?"

"Pearl changed it for me."

He removed his glasses and cleaned them with the edge of his cardigan. "I had a feeling she would. How much will it cost?"

"Nothing, if you can get the federation to take Pearl back."

He paled slightly. Or at least I think he did. It was hard to tell, given that his normal skin tone was on the spectrum between vampire and cave-dwelling amphibian. "Oh, I see. Look, I wish I could, but there are some real hard-liners in the group. I don't think it's going to be possible." He reapplied his glasses and checked the air behind me to make sure no one was lingering to eavesdrop. "You must understand: the others . . . they think we need to band together. With everything that's been going on in Europe, our commitment to our faith is more important than ever. I agree it isn't fair to Pearl, but our group is a democracy and I must follow what the majority says."

We had heard stories about what was happening to Jews in Europe: pogroms, ghettos, yellow stars pinned to coats, and much, much worse things that, so far, hadn't been verified. It was so much easier to hear about these awful things when you'd fooled yourself into believing they had nothing to do with you.

"But Pearl is committed to the same things you are," I said. "You couldn't ask for someone more dedicated."

It was like Pop said: you had to paint your enemy with a broad brush to protect yourself. Maybe you used a much more narrow one to define your allies for the same reason.

He looked toward the classroom door again.

"This isn't just about Pearl being friends with me, is it? Something else is going on here."

He took me by the elbow and led me away from the door. "Look, this isn't me talking, okay? I like Pearl just fine. But the others find her . . . weird."

"So?"

"Like I said before, this is a fragile time for us. We need

the group to band together. People are looking for excuses to drop out."

"So let them. Pearl's worth all of them put together."

"While I might agree with you in theory, it's not just the other members of the federation who are the problem. If Pearl gives everyone at school the heebie-jeebies, and they know she's in the group, they might start to take us less seriously, too. We can't afford that right now."

Poor Pearl. Did she suspect this was what was really going on? I found it hard to believe that she could know what they thought of her and still want to help them.

I certainly didn't.

"Maybe you should talk to Principal DeLuca about the notes," I said.

"The principal's office couldn't care less. They think we're a nuisance. They love us when we're working on the school paper and editing the yearbook, but when we congregate and try to encourage dialogue about Jewish causes, they think we're being too political."

"I thought the Lower East Side was more open-minded than that."

"Maybe more than where you come from, but no one wants us to flaunt our faith around here, either." It was still an improvement. On the Upper East Side, you didn't even *talk* about being Jewish. "That's why we need your help," said Michael. "No one else is taking this seriously."

I crossed my arms. "Pearl and I are a team. We work together."

Michael cleared his throat. "And you still can. The others don't have to know she's helping you."

"Forget it." I turned to go.

"She's going to want to know why you said no," he said.

I stopped in my tracks and once again faced him.

"When she does, what will you tell her?"

I knew where he was headed: Pearl wanted me to help them. If I told her I'd decided not to, she would want a reason, and objecting to her being removed from the group for being my friend wasn't likely to satisfy her. Could I tell her the truth? How would she take being told that all of these people got together—including her own brother—and kicked her out for being a weirdo?

Michael steepled his hands, and I had a strong sense of what he would look like when he was a much older man. "So, will you do it?"

I said yes, because I didn't feel like I had any other choice.

3

MICHAEL SAID he'd talk to the group that afternoon about the investigation. I gave him Pop's office exchange and asked him to call me as soon as the meeting was over. Now that I was working for Pop, I was always in a rush to get home after school. As I rounded the corner to Orchard Street, I saw a man lingering in front of the house. When I reached the steps to the front stoop, he lit a cigarette.

I couldn't tell if he was waiting for someone there, or just pausing for his smoke. There wasn't a bus stop nearby and he didn't look familiar. It wasn't unusual to see people loitering on the Lower East Side, but given how cold it was and how darkness was fast approaching, his presence gave me pause. I offered him a quick smile as I passed and hurried up the steps to Mrs. M.'s.

"You must be Iris," he said as I reached the stoop.

I paused, and turned back to him. "Do I know you?"

"No. I'm a friend of your father's. Tell him Stefan says hello." And then, without saying another word, he turned and left.

I went into the house and made a beeline for Pop's office. He wasn't there, but a number of tasks for me were, each with instructions penned in his nearly indecipherable chicken scratch. There were case notes to type up, calls to return, and a set of picklocks he wanted me to practice using. AA Investigations wasn't booming by any means, but in the weeks since I'd started helping Pop, business had definitely picked up, probably because he knew, with my help, he could take on more work without fear of getting in over his head.

"Iris? Is you?" Mrs. Mrozenski, our landlady, popped her head into the office. "You are hungry?" she asked. In her hands was a bowl of soup so hot the steam wavered in the air above it.

"Sure," I said. Mrs. M. could make the most delicious soups out of nothing. They didn't stick with you, but they did a fine job of tricking you into thinking you were no longer hungry.

"You have nice day?" she asked.

"It was fine, thank you."

"Good, good." Her eyes danced over the desk, taking in the work that Pop had left for me. Each page of instructions had been laid out parallel with the edges of the desk, each stack of paper meticulously straightened. When Pop first got home from Pearl Harbor, he seemed determined to leave every detail of his time in the Navy behind, going so far as to leave his bed unmade and his shoes unshined. Over the course of the year he had slowly been returning to the rigidity of military life. Nowhere was that more evident than in his office.

"Where's Pop?"

"He go to the bank, he say. And to mail letters." That "he say" was important. Pop always gave Mrs. M. a cover story in case anyone was looking for him. When you made a living investigating often unsavory people, you sometimes crossed the wrong person, and he wanted to make sure Mrs. M. was never held accountable for anything he did. So he deliberately kept her in the dark. She preferred it that way. While she didn't seem to mind being lied to, she wasn't comfortable with doing the lying herself. If he gave her false information about his whereabouts, all she was doing was passing on what she'd been led to believe was the truth.

"Your father, he leave interesting work for you?" She knew I was working for Pop, though I'm not sure what she thought about it. Mrs. M. wasn't the kind of person to make her opinion known.

I looked at the notes waiting for me atop the desk, but a quick glance didn't tell me much of anything. "Hopefully."

She put the soup on the desk and worked her hands into a ball. "There is something I want to talk to you about."

Anxiety tugged at my shoulders. Mrs. M. was much more than a landlady—she'd become a dear friend to both Pop and me. As our friend, she was more than patient when it came to things like late rent and light envelopes. I thought Pop was doing better—he seemed to be making more money, anyway—but what if that wasn't the case and Mrs. M. had finally had enough?

"What's that?" I asked.

"Tomorrow is when Hanukah starts, yes?"

I think the relief must've shown in my face. Boy, howdy—*that's* what she wanted to talk about? "Right."

"You don't celebrate, though."

Apparently, the word was out: Iris Anderson was a bad Jew. The relief I'd felt moments before was eclipsed by a knot in my throat. "Not really."

"Every year I have tree." She gestured toward a window in the parlor, where blackout blinds obscured the lamplight from the street. "Is okay with you?"

She was asking me for permission to have a Christmas tree? Seriously? "Sure."

"And your father?"

"Pop won't mind a bit," I said.

She smiled, and the lines that had crisscrossed her forehead when her query first began grew shallow. "Is good. You will share a meal with us on December 25? I make big feast."

I said yes, even though agreeing to it only increased my

guilt. If we celebrated Christmas, did that mean we were no longer Jews?

She left me and I sat down and tried to put questions of faith out of my mind. The desk was littered with the usual banal tasks, save one: *Call the following hotels and find out if a Mickey Pryor is staying there or has recently stayed there. On the Q.T.* Most of Pop's work involved tailing spouses suspected of infidelity. He spent a lot of time calling and visiting hotels, hoping to catch a glimpse—and hopefully a photo—of the couple together. His instructions, though sparse, were clear: come up with a story to use when calling the hotels that will convince the desk clerk to pass on what is considered confidential information.

I cleared my throat before picking up the phone and asking the operator for the first hotel's exchange. Two rings later and I was greeted by a chipper woman at the hotel's switchboard.

I put on my best little-girl voice, full of rounded vowel sounds and a lisp that softened the attack on all of my words. "Mr. Pryor's room, please."

There was no Mickey Pryor staying there.

Nor was he at the next ten hotels on the list.

I filled the time waiting for each receptionist to respond by practicing opening a series of locks Pop had mounted on a board for me. I had the hang of getting them open with the picks, but my speed wasn't particularly impressive. This, he kept telling me, was the most important part of gaining entry to forbidden places. You had to get in fast so you could get out fast.

By the time I called the twelfth hotel, I was growing weary with both the calling and the lock picking. But I soldiered on, determined to complete the task set before me. After being greeted by the switchboard operator, I again stated my query in the same juvenile tone.

She told me she would check the register. When she came back on the line, she hesitated before telling me, "I'm sorry, there's no guest here by that name."

I took a chance. I was pretty sure that pause of hers wasn't a coincidence.

"But . . . but he said this is where he would be." My voice shook with imaginary tears as my fingers deftly opened a dead bolt with three turns of the pick. Instead of hanging up on me, the clerk pulled the story behind my emotion out: we'd received one of the telegrams every family dreaded, announcing that my older brother, Bud, was missing in action. "Mama won't get out of bed," I told the sympathetic operator. "I don't know what to do. I thought if I could find Uncle Mick, he might be able to help."

"Look," the woman on the phone whispered. "I could get in a lot of trouble for this, but he *was* here. He and his . . . uh . . . wife checked out about an hour ago."

I breathed a sigh of relief. I'd found him. "Oh. Then he must be on his way home. I'm sure Mama will come around." And with that I hung up.

I wrote up a paragraph describing everything for Pop, finished up my notes from tailing the man over the weekend, and then did the little bit of filing and typing he'd left for me. As I was completing my tasks for the day, I heard the front door open and close. I left the office to greet Pop and found Betty Mrozenski instead.

"*Bonjour,* Iris."

"Hello." Betty was Mrs. M.'s daughter. She was in her twenties and worked as a salesgirl at Macy's. She usually came over once a month, always toting some little gift for her mother as a surprise.

"*Comment allez-vous?*"

"Fine, thank you," I said. One of the reasons Betty got her job was because she spoke several languages, a fact she was always happy to demonstrate whether you wanted her to or not. Unfortunately, while she had a knack for learning languages, she lacked the same skill for learning proper accents, a failing that amused me and my one year of private-school French to no end.

"You look surprised to see me," she said, mercifully reverting to English.

Did I? I certainly didn't mean to. Betty had just joined us for Thanksgiving the week before, so I suppose I didn't expect her to show up so soon after that visit. I liked her well enough, but there was something about her presence that I found off-putting. Maybe it was just that she changed things among Mrs. M., Pop, and me. When it was just the three of us I could pretend we were family, but when Betty was there, it reminded me that Mrs. Mrozenski wasn't mine.

"Oh, I just didn't know you were coming is all," I said. "Is everything all right?" Betty had a brother in the Navy who Mrs. M. spent far too many hours worrying about. I'd never met him before, but after hearing about him for so long I began to worry for her whenever the phone rang at odd hours or the Western Union courier was spotted on our street.

"*Tout va bien*. Ma invited me for dinner and I couldn't say no. The Christmas shopping season has me too pooped to cook." She must've come straight from work. She wore a smart gray suit with a fitted jacket and pencil skirt. Underneath the jacket was a crisp white blouse and a string of pearls similar to ones I'd inherited from Mama. Her hair was in an updo, her lips colored a deep red that matched her nails. She had an impressive figure that I knew was helped out by a girdle. (I'd borrowed one from her once upon a time, though she didn't know it.) She was softer and rounder than Mama had been, but nothing like her own mother, whose large girth demanded waistless dresses. It wasn't hard to predict that she'd be just like her one day. You could see the older woman trapped inside her, just like I could see a glimpse of the young woman Mrs. M. must've been every time she smiled. "Plus I brought her this." She had the newest issue of *Screen Album*, with Lana Turner on the cover. "Is your pop here?" she asked.

"He will be. Soon." My eyes danced back toward the office. Would it be rude to leave her?

"Is he out on a job?" She lowered her voice when she asked it, like there were spies about whom she didn't want to clue in to what Pop did for a living. Usually I enjoyed people being impressed by what Pop did, but coming from Betty it annoyed me.

"Nope, he went to the bank. And the post office."

"Probably for a case, huh?" She picked up the photo of Mama that sat on the radio. The glass had been broken out of it months before and we still hadn't replaced it. "She was so pretty," she said.

"Yes," I said, because what else was there to say?

"You're going to look just like her."

I shrugged. What was the point in agreeing with her when I knew it was a lie?

"I never thought to ask you. Do you speak German, too?" she asked.

"Nope."

"Such a shame. I've been dying to find someone to practice with. Ma refuses to help me until I learn to speak Polish, and that's not likely to happen anytime soon. And you can't just break out the German with any old person without seeming suspicious, you know?"

The office phone sang its shrill song.

"Oh, don't let me keep you," said Betty. "I'll see you at dinner."

I left her and answered the phone with a chipper "AA Investigations."

"Iris?" It was Michael Rosenberg. I settled into Pop's chair and again worked the picklocks. As I listened to Michael apologize for not calling sooner, I could hear Betty flipping through magazines, fiddling with the radio dial, tapping her nails on the side table, humming along to the music underplaying a Chock Full o' Nuts commercial. It unnerved me. Why? Betty was a perfectly nice person. She had every right to visit her mother as often as she wanted.

"Anyways," said Michael, "the group was very enthusiastic about you helping, especially since two more of them received letters today." I put aside the picks, got out pen and paper, and jotted down notes as he told me about what he'd learned at the meeting.

There were now four people who'd received the anti-Semitic notes: two boys and two girls. Two of them had found them in their lockers after lunch, and both Michael and the most recent victim had found them at the end of the day. They had been pushed through the locker vents, so anyone could have placed them there. The notes were similar in content, except for the most recent one, which included a newspaper clipping with the headline "Slain Polish Jews Put at a Million. One-third of Number in Country Said to Have Been Put to Death by Nazis."

"Is that true?" I asked after he'd read me the headline.

"Yes," he said, a note of disbelief in his voice. "The

38

number might actually be much larger." How had I not known that? "So what else can I tell you?" he asked.

It was hard to concentrate with the image of all those dead people dancing in my head. "Were all of the notes on the same kind of paper?"

"Yes. Lined, with no distinguishing marks." In other words, the same paper every high school student used.

"And the handwriting and ink color?"

"Identical."

I forced myself to focus. "What about the locations of the lockers? Are the people who received the notes near one another?"

"No. Two of us are in the upperclassman hall, two in the lower."

"Then I guess the next steps are to interview the other three people who got the notes and do a stakeout on the lockers of those who haven't gotten any."

Michael gave me the names of the as-yet-unaffected members and hung up.

I called Pearl and gave her the scoop. She'd used her time in the attendance office that afternoon to identify where each federation member's locker was located. She suggested we do our first stakeout before school started the next day.

"Meet me at a quarter after seven, okay?" she said.

I promised her I would.

As I hung up the phone, the front door opened and I

heard the unmistakable sound of Pop entering the room. His wooden leg always lagged, creating a momentary drag that was like the walking version of a lisp.

"Look who's here," he said to Betty. I moved so that I could catch sight of him as he came into the parlor. "Everything all right?"

"Yes." Her eyes flickered toward me before returning to him. "I hope you don't mind, Arthur, but Ma invited me to dinner. I think she's worried I'll starve to death if left to my own devices."

"You and me both," he said. He removed his fedora and hung it on the hall tree. Pop was a handsome man, with the kind of good looks that used to make my friends insist they'd seen him in a movie before, only they couldn't remember which one. He'd aged a lot in the past year, but even though he looked older than his years, he still managed to turn heads wherever he went.

"Would you like to sit?" asked Betty.

"Thanks," said Pop. Of course he wanted to sit. He'd been walking around on an ill-fitting prosthetic all day. And who was she to offer him a place in the parlor? It wasn't her house. We should be the ones inviting *her* to sit down.

Why was I getting so upset about this?

"I'm glad you're here. I tried telephoning you this afternoon," said Pop.

"Oh, really?" said Betty. She tossed another look my way. Pop followed her gaze and suddenly increased the

40

distance between the two of them. "Iris! Why are you hiding in there?"

I left the desk and came to the doorway. "I'm not hiding. I'm working."

He raised an eyebrow. "No need to get defensive. It was a joke. Why don't you come out here? We have company."

I left the office reluctantly and offered a forced smile to Betty.

"It's fine," she told Pop. "Iris had work to do."

Why had Pop tried calling her? "What did you do this afternoon?" I asked him.

"Errands. Got the mail." Ah, of course he wasn't going to tell me what he had really been doing. Not in front of Betty. I raised an eyebrow to let him know I knew he was lying. In response, he tapped a stack of envelopes sitting on his lap. He had a P.O. box for client mail, and for those occasions when he needed an anonymous address to help track down a lead without tipping his hand that it was a detective behind the inquiry.

"I could file it if you like," I said.

"No need. Actually, there are a few checks in here. I should probably stick them in the safe before I forget. If you'll excuse me, ladies."

Pop went into the office and opened the closet at the rear of the room. There was a safe stored on the floor there, recently purchased after a break-in convinced him that more sensitive documents—and money—should be a little bit more difficult to get access to. I could hear the tumblers click as he spun the dial. He'd never shown me what he kept in there and I'd never asked, though I'd be lying if I said I wasn't curious.

"Finish your work?" asked Betty.

"Just about," I said.

"I guess you're helping your pop out now, huh?"

"Here and there."

"It's exciting stuff, working for a detective."

"Sort of," I said.

"Just don't let it get in the way of your studies."

"I won't."

She looked around the room like she was hoping to find the next topic of conversation hidden among the throw pillows. "Have you seen *You Were Never Lovelier?*"

I'd been dying to see the flick starring Fred Astaire and Rita Hayworth but there wasn't money for movies. "Nope."

"You should. It's great. Fred Astaire is just dreamy in it."

Part of my discomfort with Betty had to do with how close we were in age. She was only a few years out of high school. Sometimes, like when she was talking about which movies she'd seen, her youth showed, and yet other times, like when she told me to mind my studies, she acted like she was the same age as Pop. I found it very confusing—was I supposed to treat her like an adult or a friend?

"Is ready." Mrs. Mrozenski came into the parlor, wiping her hands clean on her apron. A cacophony of scents wafted in from the kitchen: onions, beef, cabbage, tomatoes. My stomach growled with approval. She peeked into Pop's office. "Is ready, Arthur."

I could hear Pop struggle to get back on his feet. I don't think it occurred to him when the safe was installed that putting it on the floor was the least convenient place possible for a man with one leg. But then there were days when I thought Pop was surprised to wake up and find his leg was missing. Just like there were days when I awoke and expected to find Mama in the parlor.

We all piled into the kitchen and filled the chairs at the round table. On Thanksgiving we'd eaten in the dining room, but it was apparent that that was a once-, maybe twice-a-year treat and that the rest of our meals would take place, like this one, in the overly hot kitchen. The air was hazy from the stove, which belched coal every time it heated up. The icebox leaked a steady drip of water that filled moments of silence with a soothing tap that I often unconsciously mimicked with my fingers on the tabletop.

"You have good day, Betty?" Mrs. M. asked her daughter as she passed around the platter for us to serve ourselves from.

"Busy. My dogs are barking."

"I thought you'd be here sooner. You get off at two, yes?"

There was tension in the air. Betty seemed determined to stare at her plate. "I had to work late. One of the girls had to take her kid to the doctor, so I stuck around for her."

"You get paid for this?"

"I do for them, they do for me."

"You make sure that happens. You don't want to be taken advantage of."

Betty finally looked up from her food. "Trust me, Ma—ain't no one going to take advantage of me."

Over dinner the adults talked about the recent happenings at Guadalcanal. Betty seemed flushed as she sat across from Pop at the table. I wasn't the only one who noticed it.

"You are getting sick," said Mrs. Mrozenski. "Your face is like tomato."

"It's hot in here. I'm fine."

"Eat more. You're too thin."

Betty rolled her eyes. "I'm filled to the gills, Ma. Any more and I'll have to retire this skirt."

Mrs. Mrozenski wasn't taking no for an answer. She left her seat and proceeded to scrape another stuffed cabbage roll onto Betty's plate. "This won't keep. You don't waste," she said. "There are starving children in Armenia."

"And Poland and England and who knows where else," said Betty. "Let them eat your overcooked cabbage. I said I'm full." She pushed her plate away and stared down her mother. She suddenly looked very young. I half expected to see her stomp her feet and begin a tantrum.

"I'll take it," I said, even though I'd also reached the point that I was going to bust a button. I was embarrassed for Betty. And a little sickened at the idea that we had so much while

44

so many had so little. But mostly, I was mad for Mrs. M.'s sake. Who was Betty to criticize her mother's cooking?

"Is overcooked?" asked Mrs. Mrozenski. Betty pushed her plate my way, the petulant look never leaving her face.

"Not to my mouth," I said as I scooped up the limp, colorless cabbage onto my fork.

We finished the meal in silence.

When the food was done, Betty cleared the plates and started washing up. I probably should've offered to help, but after eating far more cabbage than I should've, I was feeling worse for wear.

Instead, I followed Pop into the parlor to listen to the news.

"Is it true, what they're saying about the Jews who've been killed in Poland?" I asked him.

I half expected him to ask what I was talking about. It would've been a relief, honestly, to know that I wasn't the only one who hadn't been paying attention.

"The sources seem to be reliable," said Pop.

"How can we let the Nazis get away with that?"

Pop lit a cigarette and stared at the radio. "I don't think we're letting anyone do anything."

Moments later laughter escaped the kitchen. Then singing. A Polish folk song escaped in bits and drabs.

"They made up," I said.

Pop shook his head. "Mothers and daughters."

I looked toward the picture of Mama on the radio. When

she and I squabbled, it was usually because she was trying to treat me like a little kid. If she'd lived, would that have changed? Would our arguments have become about curfews and boys and my failure to write thank-you notes promptly?

I left the picture and took in Pop. He was absentmindedly rubbing his leg where the stump met the prosthetic. Usually he took it off after a day out and about. I had to imagine he left it on because Betty was there.

"What else is bothering you, Iris?" asked Pop.

I didn't want to talk to him about Mama, so I reached for the next available topic. "There was a man here when I came home. In front of the house. He told me to tell you hello."

"Any idea who he was?"

"I'm not sure. He said, 'You must be Iris,' and when I asked if I knew him, he told me to tell you Stefan says hello."

Pop sat taller, his back rigid. "What else did he say?"

"That was it."

Pop's hand found my arm and squeezed. "He knew your name?"

"Yes, he knew my name." He was grabbing me as hard as the man I'd tailed on Fifty-sixth Street. "You're hurting me, Pop."

"I'm sorry." He released me and put a hand through his hair.

I rubbed his handprint off my wrist. "Who's Stefan?"

"Just a client."

46

"Then why are you upset that he knew my name?"

He forced a smile and slumped his shoulders. He wasn't fooling me: I knew a put-on when I saw one. "I like to keep business and personal separate, is all. My clients don't need to know who you are. And they certainly shouldn't be talking to you when I'm not here."

"Oh." It was that old chestnut: Pop couldn't stand the idea of my possibly being in danger. And let's face it: his clients were hardly the kind of people you wanted hanging around your fifteen-year-old daughter, whether she was working for you or not. "It's not like we had a conversation. I barely said two words to him."

"Good. In fact, in the future, if there's anyone you don't know lingering about, don't even give them those two words. Just keep on walking and go someplace where there's a telephone and call the house. All right?"

"All right."

Betty entered the room and paused at the coat tree. "*Bonne nuit,* Iris. Arthur. It was lovely to see you both." She began to bundle herself into a smart winter coat.

Pop rose to his feet. "I'll walk you. It's too dark for you to be out there by yourself."

"Are you sure?" asked Betty. Her eyes momentarily lowered to his leg.

"Absolutely," said Pop. "And that will give us a chance to talk." With more vigor than he usually had after a long day on his feet, he retrieved his coat and hat.

47

I told Betty goodbye and then returned to the office to see if there was any work I'd forgotten to do. My report on the calls tracking Mickey Pryor still sat neatly on top of the other folders. Pop hadn't even looked at it yet. There was also the small pile of mail he'd brought with him from the P.O. box. Two were invoices he needed to pay—the phone company and the printer he used for his stationery and business cards. I put them with my notes. Two other envelopes had been sliced open and their contents neatly removed. A third one had also been opened, but the check in it was still shoved deep inside. Pop must not have seen it.

I pulled it out and was about to leave it on the desk, when it occurred to me that he might be more likely to see it if I left it on the safe. As I went to put it there, I pulled the safe's lever out of habit. Instead of remaining barred, it slid easily to the left.

The safe was open.

4

EXCITEMENT TAP-DANCED DOWN MY BACK. Pop must not have secured the safe before dinner. I could've closed it and spun the dial, but something stopped me. I pushed the edge of the heavy door with my fingertips, daring it to stay almost closed under my light touch. If it did, that would be that—I wouldn't go any further. But it didn't. The door creaked open and the contents lay before me. There was a gun, which I'd always suspected Pop had, even though he'd denied it, several folders, and an expandable envelope that held checks awaiting deposit.

I added the check I'd found on the desk to the envelope and told myself to close the door, but I couldn't. I didn't like being in the dark about anything, not even something as seemingly insignificant as Pop's other cases.

I strained for sounds of Pop returning. How long had he been gone now? Surely not enough time to walk to the subway station and back.

I picked up the first folder. The tab was labeled "Rheingold Accounting" in Pop's hurried hand. There wasn't much in it—just notes in handwriting I didn't recognize and several photographs of a man taken at a distance. Was this the man I'd helped him tail? I couldn't tell. I set the folder aside, planning to read his case notes if I had time.

The second folder held photographs of me, all of them taken from a distance.

Irritation made me slump. Had Pop been tailing me to make sure I wasn't skipping school? Or was this part of some exercise about surveillance to which he was going to introduce me?

I didn't have time to ponder it, not if I wanted to see what else was in the safe.

The third folder appeared to be full of personal papers: my birth certificate, Pop's passport, his marriage license, his discharge papers.

I exchanged this folder for the last one.

That was a mistake.

It was also full of a series of eight-by-ten photographs, only these weren't of me. I stared at the one on top. At first I couldn't figure out what it was depicting, but as the image came into focus, recognition dawned on me: it was a bed made up with sheets decorated with a bold modern design. No, it wasn't a design; it was blood. A lot of it, splashed onto the wall beside the bed and spilled onto the floor beneath it.

Mrs. Mrozenski's stuffed cabbage fought its way back up

my throat. I swallowed hard and closed my eyes long enough to quiet my nausea. *Easy, Iris. This is crime. It isn't pretty. But you have to get used to it if you want to be part of Pop's world.* Once my stomach was settled, I flipped to the next photo and caught the same room at another angle. More blood spatter. My head felt like it might float away if it wasn't tethered to my body. I took slow, deep breaths and forced myself to keep looking at the photo. A pillow had been moved to demonstrate where blood had pooled, presumably beneath the victim's head. The top sheet had also been moved, making it clear that some of the blood had landed on an object that had been removed from the room, but whose outline remained courtesy of the tremendous amount of liquid that had spilled around it.

I looked at the other things in the photo, searching for clues as to what I was really seeing. The furniture was plain, the room barren. A hotel, maybe? Out the window I could see a church steeple in the distance and other buildings whose height made it clear that wherever this picture had been taken, it wasn't on the first floor of this particular building.

I flipped to the next photo. Oh, God—there was a body in the picture. A naked woman whose head was turned toward the wall, her face obscured by a mound of hair and blood. This was a person. A real person who was murdered. Stop, I told myself. Think about this objectively, not emotionally. But try as I might, I couldn't distance myself from what I was seeing. All those dead Jews in Poland were people, not numbers. They were parents, children, wives, and husbands. And whoever this woman was, she was a person, too, not a fact for me to skim over because I didn't want to have to think about what her death meant. Those arms had once held a lover. That hair had been tied into pigtails. Those legs had wobbled unsteadily on high-heeled shoes. Who was she?

It was this question that forced me to look at the next photo, where her face was turned toward the camera.

Not a stranger's arms. Not a stranger's hair. Not a stranger's blood spilled across a bed. Mama. Oh, God—it was Mama.

HOW LONG DID I STARE at her picture? Ten years? Twenty? All I know is I would probably still be sitting there, my heart ripped in two, if Pop hadn't come home.

"Iris? What are you doing?"

There was no point hiding the folder from him. It was too late. Instead, I lifted it toward him as though it were Mama's body in my hands and he had the power to revive her.

"Put those away," he said quietly. "Shut the safe and spin the tumbler." His tone made it clear that I had no choice but to do what he was telling me. I returned the folder to the safe, closed the door, and spun the dial.

"You left the safe open," I said.

He nodded, clearly accepting the blame for what had just occurred.

"Why do you have those?"

"Iris, we're not going to talk about this. Not now, not ever. Understand?"

Maybe I would've demanded otherwise if I'd had my wits about me, but I was so stunned by what I'd seen that all I could do was nod.

"I want you to go upstairs and go to bed. That's an order."

I did as he said, but I knew there'd be no hope of my sleeping. If I closed my eyes, she would be there waiting for me, and I couldn't bear to see Mama like that again.

I wanted to retch. I wanted to sob until the sound blended into a seamless wail of grief that would rival the sirens of fire engines headed to a call. But for some reason, I couldn't. Pop had been so calm, as though it were perfectly normal to have pictures of his dead wife in his safe. Surely I was misunderstanding what I had seen. I'd been told that Mama took too many pills the night she died. Perhaps the pills had been a story all along, meant to cushion the knowledge that she'd killed herself by assuring me she'd done it in a peaceful way when the truth was she'd shot herself. Yes, that had to be it. She shot herself and Uncle Adam, Aunt Miriam, and Pop couldn't bring themselves to tell me, so they invented the pills, hoping it would make the fact of her death a little bit easier.

But then why would Pop have pictures of it?

He'd still been in Hawaii when she died, recuperating from his Pearl Harbor injuries in a naval hospital. They couldn't delay her funeral until he made it home. That would've required embalming her, which, like her suicide, was a violation of Jewish law. Instead, Adam paid for Pop to listen to the service by telephone and invited him to speak a few words in her memory. The connection was lost before he could do that, the dial tone ringing through the synagogue like the bells that tolled in Whitman's poem, the one we'd read in school about Abraham Lincoln's funeral procession.

Maybe that's why Pop wanted the photographs. He hadn't been there when she died, nor when she was buried, and he needed the chance to see, for himself, what her last moments had been like.

Yes, people did strange things in their grief. That had to be it. I was looking at this all wrong. What had I really seen?

Mama dead in a hotel room, just like they'd said. Walls splattered with her blood. Sheets stained with the same. They hadn't told me that part. And the weapon she had used to end it all? Why hadn't I seen a gun?

If this was suicide, where was her weapon?

I swallowed hard, trying to stop the vomit once again. No, I'd been right before. This was a murder scene. And if I knew that, Pop had to know it, too.

How could he lie to me? All the energy I'd wasted on

54

being angry at her, all the sleepless nights I'd spent wondering how she could be so selfish without giving us any sign until now—all of that was for nothing. My rage had been directed at the wrong person. And as for her selfishness, I had indicted her without evidence.

Mama hadn't wanted to leave me. In fact, it was probably the farthest thought from her mind.

That was it—I couldn't hold back my tears. Pop be damned. Let all the Lower East Side hear my grief. I wrapped my arms around my legs and rocked to the rhythm of my sobs.

Oh, Mama, what have they done to you?

I didn't know yet, but I was going to find out.

5

I WAS EXHAUSTED BY THE TIME I arrived at school the next day. I'd thought about feigning illness and staying home, but the idea of being trapped in the house with those pictures propelled me out the door. I couldn't face Pop or Mrs. M., and so I left before either one was up, leaving a note explaining that I had left early to study for a test.

It was a cold, drizzly day. In the distance trains blew their whistles in a mournful way that never seemed duplicated on sunny days. I thought about skipping school entirely, but the weather convinced me that this wasn't the time to do that. Instead, I took a long, meandering walk to kill time, traveling streets I hadn't been down before, past unfamiliar houses marked with stars that signaled that sons and fathers had gone to war. I abandoned using the umbrella halfway through my journey. I wanted the frigid rain to fall on me and bring me out of myself.

When I arrived at P.S. 110, Pearl was on the front steps

huddled beneath her umbrella with an impatient look on her face. "Where have you been?" she demanded as I made my way to her. "I had to do the stakeout by myself."

"I forgot," I said, and followed her into the building. The floor was a mess of water and mud tracked in by everyone who'd entered ahead of us. I realized for the first time that I was soaking wet.

"Why didn't you use your umbrella?" asked Pearl.

"I forgot," I said again, not really hearing her question. "I need to dry off." I ducked into the nearest restroom with Pearl fast on my heels. We weren't alone. The mirrors were clogged with girls repairing their hair before their first class began.

"What do you mean you forgot? How do you forget to use an umbrella?"

I shrugged and removed a towel from the dispenser. I blotted myself dry as best I could while Pearl watched me. Based on the look on her face, you would've thought I was skinning an animal alive.

The bell rang and all around us people gathered their things and began heading toward class. I turned to do the same, when Pearl stopped me. "What's wrong with you? I thought you were going to help me today. Yesterday you said you were happy to help out the federation."

I was. But finding out Mama hadn't committed suicide eclipsed everything. Who cared if someone was writing hurtful things and shoving them in people's lockers? My mother had been murdered, and for some reason nobody cared. "I just have a lot on my mind. Pop dropped a big case in my lap last night."

"But you'll still interview everyone who got the letters, right?"

"Sure," I said. "We'll talk about it over lunch."

The worry left her face and was replaced with relief. "Great," she said. "I'll see you then."

I HAVE NO IDEA how I made it through that morning. Clearly I went to each class, sat in my assigned seat, and did a fine job of looking like I was paying attention, but the only things I saw were the photos of Mama burned like an imprint of the sun on my eyes, the only things I heard were Pop's words echoing through my head like a song I couldn't shake: "Iris, we're not going to talk about this. Not now, not ever."

Not now, not ever.

Not *now*, not *ever*.

By the time lunch arrived, I thought I was going to lose my mind.

Pearl was in our usual spot, dividing her attention between her sandwich and her pencil and paper. When I arrived she smiled up at me, then instantly changed her expression. "What's the matter? You look awful."

"I lied before. About Pop giving me a case. I found out something about my mom last night. Something really upsetting."

"About the affair?"

The affair; I had forgotten about that. There'd been rumors that Mama was having an affair in the days before she died. That the affair might have been the reason behind why she killed herself. Pop had told me not to listen to the Upper East Side women who spread these tales—it was just idle gossip. But now that I knew he'd lied about how she died, I had to wonder if he wasn't lying about why she died, too.

"Iris?" said Pearl. "Are you there?"

Before I could lose my courage, the whole story came pouring out of me. Pearl's mouth hung open as I talked, her entire body still, as though she were worried that one single movement could cause her to miss something I said.

"Oh, Iris, I'm so sorry," she said when I was done. "But why would he lie?"

"To protect me, I guess." And from what? Did he honestly believe suicide and murder weren't equally awful?

"Who killed her?"

"I don't know. I don't know if anyone knows. All he had were the crime-scene photos." It wasn't just the shock of learning that Mama had been murdered and that Pop had lied that unnerved me; I now knew nothing about how she met her end beyond what the photos told me.

"Where did she die?"

I didn't know that, either. I'd been told a Yorkville hotel, but I had no idea if that was another fabrication. "I'm not sure."

"But you're going to find out, right?"

The task seemed insurmountable, but it didn't have to be. Pop wasn't the only one with information. If Mama had been murdered, there was a police file on the case. Newspaper articles written about it. A death certificate that provided the details about where, when, and how.

"How could I see her death certificate?" I asked Pearl.

"The Department of Health and Mental Hygiene. Vital Records is there. They have all the birth and death records for the city."

"And anyone can see it?"

"Sure."

"Then that's what I'm going to do first."

Strangely, making a plan made me feel better. Once I had more information, perhaps it would become clear why Pop had wanted to protect me and why he was so determined not to talk about it.

"So tell me about the stakeout," I said to Pearl.

"We don't have to talk about that if you don't want to."

"No, I want to help. I promised you I would. I need to focus on something else right now."

Pearl picked at the crust of her bread. "There's not much to report. I watched the lockers in the upperclassman hallway this morning, but no one other than the owners approached them."

"Maybe after leaving four notes, our suspect decided to lie low for a while."

"Do you think you'll still be able to interview everyone who got the letters?"

"Of course. I talked to Michael yesterday, so he's done. Harriet Rosenstein is in my Geography class, so I'll talk to her then. And my locker is right by Ira's, so I can grab him after school. Who's left?"

Pearl's gaze shifted to where the federation sat during lunch. "Natalie."

I followed her line of sight to the girl who'd greeted me so snootily outside the journalism office the day before. "I met her briefly yesterday. She seems like a real cold fish."

"She's not so bad," said Pearl. "You just have to get to know her."

I doubted that would change my impression. "Should we do a stakeout of the lowerclassman lockers this afternoon?" I asked.

"Probably . . . or we could go to the health department and see the death certificate."

"You'll go with me?" I asked.

"Of course."

Natalie got up to deposit her empty tray in the bin.

"No time like the present," I told Pearl.

I left her side and joined Natalie at the counter, where she was placing her dirty dishes on the conveyor belt that would ferry them back to the boy enlisted to wash them in the kitchen. Her face was slightly pinched, as if she were smelling something rotten and unpleasant . . . which she probably was since we were standing by the trash can.

"Hi. Remember me?" I said.

"Pearl's friend. The detective. Michael said you'd be talking to me." While I should've been grateful that he'd prepared her for our conversation, I was too caught up in the way she'd said "Pearl's friend," like it wasn't a casual connection, but a shocking political affiliation. I wasn't friends with someone who used to be her friend; I was a Fascist. Or a Nazi.

"That's right," I said, matching her tone for tone. "You got a minute?"

"Just one." She crossed her arms over her chest. I tossed a look back toward Pearl, who was picking up the remains of her own lunch off the floor. Someone had knocked into her and sent her meal flying. Poor Pearl.

"Looks like someone had an accident," said Natalie.

I ignored her. "When did you find your note?"

"Yesterday after lunch," she said.

"And what did it look like?"

"It was written in blue ink on standard notepaper. Didn't Michael tell you all of this?"

"I like to hear it from the horse's mouth. Is there anyone you might've upset lately? Someone who would have a reason to leave the note?"

"Of course not."

While I might've agreed that the content of the note

could never be justified, I doubted that Natalie's record was clean when it came to upsetting people. In fact, something told me that she was the driving force behind getting Pearl kicked out of the federation.

"Are you dating someone?" I asked.

"That's hardly any of your business."

"It kind of is. I mean, if you just broke up with someone, that might prompt them to do something like this."

Her jaw went rigid. "I go steady with Ira Rosenblatt."

He'd received a note, too. "For how long?"

"Almost a year."

"And before then who were you seeing?"

"A boy in my congregation who doesn't go here."

"And Ira? Did he ever go steady with anyone else?"

"Not really. Just a date here and there."

"Who do you think might want to hurt the federation?"

She raised an eyebrow. "Isn't that what we hired you for?"

Cold fish didn't begin to describe her. This fish was dead and had begun to rot. "Yes," I said, "but it strikes me that you're pretty astute. If you have any theories, I'd love to hear them."

"I told Michael this was pointless. In case you haven't noticed, being Jewish isn't exactly a bragging point around here. We're an embarrassment. But wait—you already know that, don't you?"

Ouch. So that's why she thought I wasn't practicing? Because I had given in to peer pressure?

I decided it wasn't worth arguing with her. It was clear that nothing I said would appease her, though part of me was dying to say *Last night, I found out my Jewish mother was murdered, so your snotty attitude is* really *appreciated.* "Has this note made you rethink being in the federation?"

"It might have, but after Ira got his, I realized how stupid it would be to drop out now." She looked at her watch. "Are we done?"

"For now. I might have other questions later on."

She rolled her eyes. "If so, you know where to find me."

I MADE IT TO GEOGRAPHY a few minutes early to talk to Harriet. She was always there before anyone else, textbook and notebook in hand, just in case the lecture started early, which it never did. But Harriet was one of those kids who was obsessed with good grades. She was the top girl in our class, and you could already tell she was fixated on the thought of being our valedictorian three years down the line.

"Hi, Harriet," I said. She was absorbed in writing a page of notes that looked like an exact match for the notes she'd already written. "What are you doing?"

"Rewriting my notes. It's a study technique I use that helps me better absorb the information."

As dull as the activity was, it did give me a chance to observe her handwriting. Her letters were wide and crisp, with the sort of flourish that would take me hours of practice to imitate. It definitely wasn't the messy scrawl on the locker notes. I had a feeling Harriet couldn't do anything sloppily.

"I was wondering if I could talk to you about the note you got?"

"Paul mentioned you might have questions for me." She didn't stop what she was doing. Unlike Natalie, she wasn't exactly being rude; she just clearly had more important things on her mind. "Go ahead."

"When did you receive it?"

"After lunch yesterday. I usually go by my locker before returning to homeroom, but I wasn't able to yesterday." The way she said it, you could tell she considered this an unforgivable error on her part.

"Why not?"

"I . . . um . . . had . . ."—her voice dropped to a whisper— ". . . cramps."

I felt for her. I'd spent many a moment between classes suffering through the same thing. "Is there anyone you know who might be angry at you who could've done something like this?"

Unlike Natalie, she didn't rush to a no. She actually thought about the question as, I imagined, she thought about everything. "Dale Cornwell might."

"Why's that?"

"He and I are currently jousting for top of the class. Perhaps he thought if he upset me, it might affect my studies."

It was hard to imagine anyone being that serious about academics at P.S. 110. Oh sure, at my old school, where everyone fought to get into a good college, it was common to see little acts of sabotage in hopes of improving your class ranking, if not by your brains then by your brawn. But those girls came from wealthy families who could afford college tuition. Perhaps that was the point. Harriet and Dale knew if they had any hope of furthering their education, they needed to be at the top of the class to attract scholarship money.

Of course, if the war was still going on by the time we graduated, Harriet wouldn't need to worry about Dale at all. He would hardly need a scholarship if he was fighting in Europe.

"I'll take a look at Dale," I told her. The rest of the class was filing in and taking their seats. "One more question: Did getting this note make you consider dropping out of the federation?"

Harriet returned to her writing. "Absolutely not. I refuse to be defeated by something so cowardly."

IRA'S LOCKER WAS ONLY two away from mine. I found him there after school, searching the innards of a textbook page by page.

"Hi, Ira," I said.

He looked up just long enough to see who it was, then returned to his searching. "Ah, yes—Natalie said you might have questions for me."

His tone was considerably more welcoming than his girl-friend's, not that that was saying much. German shouted over a megaphone was more pleasant than Natalie. "Is now a good time?"

"Sure, sure." More searching.

"What are you looking for?"

"My geometry notes. Ah, there they are." He plucked a piece of notepaper from the book. Bright blue ink and barely legible writing bled across the page. "So what are your questions?"

"When did you find your note?"

"Yesterday afternoon. About this time."

"And you didn't just have a note, right? There was also a news clipping?"

"Yes, from the day before's *Times*. I confirmed it when I got home."

"Why do you think they decided to give you the clipping and not the others?"

"Perhaps whoever it was wasn't satisfied with the response to the other letters, so they thought that by adding the article they might get more of a jolt out of me."

"Did it work?"

He shrugged, though it didn't seem like he was dismissing the question. "Not really. I mean, I had read the article before, so its content was no more disturbing than the first time I saw it." He spoke like a middle-aged man. I couldn't imagine how Natalie and he had gotten together. She was the epitome of a snooty high school girl, and I would expect her to be so khaki-wacky that she spent every free moment looking for soldiers, not slumming with this poindexter. "Of course, it did alarm me that whoever this was was doing their research. It's one thing to say anti-Jewish things out of ignorance, but cutting out that article seemed to imply that they really meant the things they said."

I hadn't looked at it that way, but he was right. This wasn't casual racism that simply echoed the thoughts other people might have because they didn't know any better. This person went out of their way to educate themselves about Jewish issues.

"Is there anyone you know who might have a grudge against you, or any of the other federation members?"

He closed his locker and tucked his textbook beneath his arm. "Michael and Natalie might not have been willing to come out and say it, but I will: your friend seems like the most likely suspect to me."

"My friend?"

"Pearl. She's obviously mad that we kicked her out of the group. That's the one thing that all of us who received the notes have in common, isn't it? Sometimes the most obvious suspect is the right suspect. Anything else?"

I shook my head, too startled to know what to say.

"Then if you'll excuse me, I have a piano lesson to get to."

I went to my own locker and gathered my things. Poor Pearl. Why did she want to be part of a group like that?

Michael seemed like a good egg, but the rest of them could go soak their heads as far as I was concerned.

"Are you ready to go get the death certificate?" Pearl appeared behind me, her arms full of the books she was planning to tote home.

"Are you sure you want to go?"

"Of course. And it's not far. I looked up the address during study hall. It's on Worth Street, off Lafayette."

That was good. I had a feeling that Pop wouldn't look too kindly on me if he found out I'd left the Lower East Side for this little mission. Not that he was going to find out either way. We headed outside, where the brisk fall air made us both reach for hats we'd stuffed into our pockets. I pulled on a soft wool beret. Pearl tied on a maroon snood.

"How did the interviews go?" she asked.

"Okay, I guess. I didn't get much out of them." I told her about Harriet's competitor for top of the class and Natalie's ex-boyfriend.

"I don't know who Natalie dated, but I think you can rule out Dale Cornwell."

"Why do you say that?"

"He's like the male version of Harriet: very studious, very serious. I can't see him carrying out a plan like this, not if there was any chance he could get caught and jeopardize his class standing."

"But if the principal doesn't care about the notes, maybe Dale wouldn't have anything to fear?"

We passed an open garbage can, where the putrid scent of old food greeted us, despite the newspaper someone had placed on top of it. Pearl lifted the paper and wrinkled her nose. "SCHOOLS TO OBSERVE PEARL HARBOR ATTACK; Moment of Silence Monday to Honor Armed Forces," blared the headline. Instead of reading it, she returned it to the can. "I think Mr. DeLuca would start to care if there was evidence of who was behind this. And I'm telling you: I know Dale. No matter how competitive he may be, he wouldn't do something like this."

"Fair enough. I'll strike him off the list."

"What about Ira?"

I wasn't about to tell her that he had named her as a suspect. "He seemed a little cagey. And I eyeballed his handwriting. I don't know if it's a match, but he could make a killing drafting ransom notes."

"Do you want me to get a sample of his writing?"

"Let's hold off. It's a lot more likely it's someone outside the federation than someone in it." If only Ira had seen that logic himself.

"What did he say when you asked him if this would make him leave the federation?"

"I didn't ask him. I forgot."

We turned down Broome, then crossed Canal Street. The sun was going down faster than I would've liked, so we quickened our pace. We arrived at the massive building at a quarter to five. Inside, we scanned a sign that indicated

70

which office was located where. The building was packed with all sorts of divisions with peculiar names that dealt with health and welfare. Some were so new that descriptions were tacked beside them to explain what they did. "Nurseries for working women," said one. "Nutrition during rationing," said another. "Services for slow children," read a third. The sheer number of offices made my head spin.

"Here it is," said Pearl. "Second floor." I followed her upstairs and around a corner until we arrived at a door marked "Office of Vital Records." Directly beneath the title of the office was a hand-scrawled note that said, "We close promptly at 5:00 p.m. No exceptions."

"Can I help you?" asked a woman so old I was surprised her own death certificate wasn't among the drawers of files behind her.

"I wanted to get a copy of my mother's death certificate. Her name was Ingrid Anderson."

"Fill this out." She passed me a form and a pencil. The form asked for the decedent's name, birth and death dates, and city where the death took place. I scribbled quickly, constantly aware of the massive clock ticking away the minutes above her desk. "Here you go."

She took the form and put it into a metal basket, where a stack of filled-out forms waited for her attention.

"We can wait," I said.

"Not in here, you can't. The certificate will be mailed in one week."

"A week?"

She fanned her arm behind her, where row after row after row of file cabinets stood. "There are more in the basement. One week, maybe two, and then you'll have your certificate."

I did the only thing I could think of that might sway her in that moment: I started to cry.

6

MY TEARS DIDN'T MOVE HER. We left dejected. The only thing that had helped me make it through the day was the thought that at least part of the mystery of what happened to Mama might be cleared up. Waiting a week— possibly two—seemed absolutely intolerable.

"What about the library?" said Pearl.

I mopped my eyes with my scarf, though that did little to stop the flow of tears. The wetter I got, the colder I got, which made me shiver through each sob. "They don't have death certificates there."

"No, but they do have newspapers. They would've published information about her murder, right?"

In the days after Mama's death, I couldn't recall seeing a newspaper, not that that was so unusual. It was Pop who helped develop my interest in current events. Before then, newspapers were things street vendors wrapped food in.

The Seward Park Branch of the New York Public Library was on East Broadway, across from the park that gave it its name and only about five minutes from where we were. We rushed in that direction, uncertain what time the library closed. Fortunately, they were having a book drive, so their hours were extended beyond the norm. We hurried inside the massive redbrick, Renaissance revival building, which was alive with people checking out books, reading newspapers to catch up with that day's war news, and donating their own worn copies of fiction and nonfiction titles to be sent to our boys overseas. Pearl pointed up the marble staircase, toward the reference desk. I followed her, taking the steps two at a time. As we reached the librarian stationed there, I decided to let Pearl do the talking. This was her domain, not mine.

"Can I help you?" asked a friendly-looking woman with a port wine stain on her neck.

"We're doing a school project for the anniversary of Pearl Harbor," Pearl said. "We were hoping to look at the newspapers from January 1942, to get a sense of the way the war was received in those early days so that we can compare it with the coverage going on for the anniversary."

"You wish to look at every day from that month? And every paper?"

"Oh no," said Pearl. "Just the beginning of the month. Say, between New Year's Day and January 10. And only the

74

New York papers. We want to see what the coverage was like after the holidays."

She nodded, clearly impressed that we were taking on such an ambitious project. She wasn't the only one. "Have a seat. I'll get you what I can."

We sat across from each other at a reading-room table and waited for what seemed like an eternity for the newspapers to arrive. I was starting to worry that this librarian would, like the woman at Vital Records, appear and declare that our task had a standard waiting time of two to four weeks. Fortunately, just as I was giving up hope, she appeared with an assistant. Together they deposited two stacks of newspapers on the table in front of us.

"Read in good health, girls. What you don't get through today, we can set aside for tomorrow."

We thanked them and quickly zeroed in on the issues from New Year's Day to January 2. There was nothing in the January 1 papers, but on January 2 Pearl hit the jackpot toward the back of the front section of the *Times*. I moved to her side of the table and read over her shoulder.

WOMAN FOUND DEAD IN YORKVILLE HOTEL ROOM

A woman was found dead on New Year's Day at the White Swan Hotel, East 86th Street, Yorkville.

THAT WAS IT. There was nothing else. We combed the next few days' worth of papers until we found a follow-up article.

YORKVILLE BODY IDENTIFIED; VICTIM ENDED OWN LIFE

The body discovered on January 1 at the White Swan Hotel has been identified as that of 36-year-old Ingrid Anderson. Mrs. Anderson, of the Upper East Side, committed suicide sometime on December 31, 1941, by taking an overdose of sleeping tablets. Mrs. Anderson, who was distraught at the news of her husband's injury at Pearl Harbor, checked into the hotel on December 30. According to police, Anna Mueller, a chambermaid, discovered Mrs. Anderson after entering room 3C to clean it. Mrs. Anderson was the wife of Arthur Anderson, a Naval Intelligence officer.

I couldn't breathe.

"Iris? Are you okay?" asked Pearl.

"He didn't start the lie," I whispered. I should've realized he couldn't have. After all, Pop was thousands of miles away when Mama died. How would he have coerced Uncle Adam and Aunt Miriam into telling me she'd committed suicide? He most likely didn't know about her death until after I did. So who was the first one to call it suicide? And why?

"Maybe the papers got it wrong. We haven't seen the death certificate yet. Is it possible they changed their minds and decided it was a murder later on?"

Anything was possible, but the idea sounded far-fetched to my ears. "If they did, it probably would've been in the paper."

"Girls, we'll be closing in five minutes," said the librarian who helped us.

I hated the thought of leaving there with even more questions than I'd started with. It wasn't fair.

"It could have been a trick," said Pearl.

"What do you mean?"

"Maybe the police called it a suicide to get her murderer out into the open. By making them think the case was closed, the police might've been hoping the killer would've slipped up and said the wrong thing to the wrong person."

She was clutching at straws. That wasn't a theory: it was the plot of a movie starring Humphrey Bogart. But I was grateful for her efforts all the same.

"We'll find out what's going on, Iris. I promise."

"Maybe that's why Pop didn't want to talk to me about this. Maybe he hit one dead end after another, too."

"This isn't a dead end," said Pearl. "It's just a roadblock we have to go around."

I didn't have the heart to tell her that sometimes they were the same thing.

I ARRIVED HOME and found Pop's office door closed. He was on the phone, cajoling some poor hourly worker into giving him information for one of several cases he was working on. I wondered if it was a job he'd intended me to take on after school and then decided to do himself when I failed to show up.

Frankly, I kind of hoped that was the case.

I dropped my books with a boom onto the cocktail table. As the sound faded, Pop's door opened. "Where have you been?"

"The library," I said.

He still had the phone in his hand, the cord stretched to its maximum capacity. "No, she's here," he said to whoever was on the other end of the call. "Thanks for the offer, though." He limped back to the desk and put the receiver on the cradle. "What's the rule if you're going to be late?"

"To let you know."

He charged the doorway once again. "Did that slip your mind?"

"Kind of." I stared him down, trying to force him to read my thoughts: *Sorry for not calling, Pop, but I was a little preoccupied by the news that my mother had been murdered and that you weren't the only one who insisted on calling it a suicide.*

He receded, slightly, into the office. "Don't let it happen again."

"All right."

He tapped his fingers on the jamb, seemingly debating whether to say more or leave it at that. "I'm giving you a pass tonight, because I know you've had a shock, but you only get one pass. Tomorrow, everything's back to normal. Same rules, same everything." He turned away.

"It seems to me I've earned at least two passes."

He froze. "What was that?"

"Nothing." What was the point in egging him on? It wasn't going to solve anything.

He faced me again. "I'm going out for a while."

"All right."

He frowned. "Are you okay? You look pale."

"I didn't sleep well last night." I hadn't intended to make another dig at that *thing he wouldn't talk about*, but I could tell he took it that way anyway.

"Try to go to bed early tonight. You don't want to get sick."

"Okay."

He left the house and I lowered my head onto my lap the way we'd been taught to do for air-raid drills. Only it wasn't blows from above that I wanted to protect myself from; it was the ones that were coming from inside my head that worried me.

"Iris? Is okay?" Mrs. M.'s voice brought me back to myself. I shot up straight and offered her a stiff smile.

"Just stretching."

"Good. You give me scare."

"Sorry."

"You are sure there is not something more?"

"Nope." The office phone rang. "I better get that," I told Mrs. M. I made it to the desk on the fourth ring, and breathlessly announced that the caller had reached AA Investigations.

"Iris? It's Michael Rosenberg."

"Hi, Michael."

"I heard you did the interviews today."

"Yep."

"Is this a bad time?"

"Um, kind of." I wasn't being fair. Just because Mama was on my mind didn't mean Michael didn't deserve my attention. "I mean no. It's fine."

"Are you sure?"

"Absolutely."

"Were you able to do the stakeout, too?"

"Pearl did one this morning, but we weren't able to do it this afternoon." My gaze passed over the contents of Pop's desk. The stack of bills he needed to pay was still there, the corner of each invoice neatly lined up.

"Then I guess you missed it."

"Missed what?"

"Whoever put the note in Saul's locker."

Oops. "Apparently so. What did this one say?" I opened

Pop's drawer. There was nothing in there but a few pens and pencils and some paper clips.

"'If the Germans can't get rid of you, maybe I should.' And there was a yellow felt star in the note with Saul's name written on it."

"Wow." I closed the drawer and something caught my eye. A piece of pink stationery was facedown on the floor as though it had drifted out of a folder without Pop noticing. I bent down and picked it up.

"I know," said Michael. "Our writer is making direct threats now."

"How did Saul take it?" I picked up the page and turned it over. It was a note to Pop in pretty, feminine writing.

Art,

Kommen Sie häufig hier?

Are you impressed? I've been practicing!

Looking forward to this weekend,

Betty

"Iris?"

"Hmmm?"

"Are you there?"

"Yes. I'm listening." But I wasn't. All I could think about was that note. Why was Betty leaving Pop notes, in German, no less? And what were they doing this weekend?

I copied the German phrase onto another piece of paper and returned the original to the floor.

". . . tomorrow, right?" said Michael.

"What?"

"You're doing the stakeout tomorrow, right?"

"Yes. Absolutely. And I'll talk to Saul."

"Good. We're counting on you, Iris."

"I know. I'm sorry, but I've got to go. I'll see you tomorrow." I hung up and went into the kitchen, where Mrs. M. was stirring a pot steaming on the stove. "That smells good," I told her.

"Is krupnik. Barley and vegetable soup with a little meat. Good on a chilly day."

"You sure do know a lot of Polish recipes."

"Is not just Polish food. I know Russian and German recipes, too."

I was grateful for the segue. "You speak German, right?"

"A little."

"Can you translate this?" I passed her the German sentence, written in my hand.

"What is?"

"Something I heard a woman say at the library tonight. I'm not sure I spelled the words right."

"No. Spelling is good. A woman, you say? Are you sure?"

"Pretty sure. Either that or it was a very pretty man."

She smiled and held the piece of paper away from the steam. "I ask because this is—" She struggled to find the word. "You know, when a man wants a woman to go out on a date with him."

"You mean like a proposition?" I said.

"Yes! Is proposition. It means: Are you coming here frequently?"

I finessed her translation: Do you come here often?

"This is why I ask if you hear woman say it. Is a man thing to do, yes?"

"Maybe she was quoting someone else," I said. "She laughed right after she said it." I took the paper back and shoved it in my pocket.

"Ah, to be young again and told these sorts of things by men." Mrs. M. shook her head sadly. "Is anything else I can help you with?"

"No, thanks," I told her. She hadn't cleared anything up for me, but I wasn't about to ask her why her daughter was propositioning Pop.

I TOSSED AND TURNED THAT NIGHT, too many new facts battling one another for me to have rest. Mama had been murdered, but officially it was called a suicide. Pop was in possession of a letter from Betty Mrozenski in which she wasn't just flirting with him; she was outright hitting on him. In German. And apparently they had a date for this weekend.

What did it all mean?

Had Pop figured out why they had declared Mama's

death a suicide? The presence of those photos in the safe made me think he hadn't. Was he still trying to solve the case, or after a year had he decided to move on?

And if he had, was Betty Mrozenski the reason why?

That would explain why she was at the house so much and why, even when exhausted, he offered to walk her to the subway station. Maybe it was also why he was so adamant about not talking about the photos with me: he was ready to leave them in the past and move on with his life. And he needed me to do that, too.

How could he be so selfish?

Mama deserved to have someone pursue what had happened to her. If the police declared her death a suicide, they clearly weren't interested in finding out the truth. And if Pop was ready to move on with his life, he wasn't game for it, either. So who was left?

Me.

7

PEARL WAS WAITING FOR ME at the corner of Orchard and Delancey the next morning. Her cheeks were red from the cold, her hand shivering as she struggled to hold her umbrella steady. Snowflakes danced between the raindrops, a hint of the weather to come. The first snow of the year used to excite me, but this year it was depressing. Winter was here. A year had passed since everything had gone so terribly wrong. And what did we have to show for it? A whole year without Mama. A whole year of doing nothing while the trail to her killer might've gone cold.

"There was another note," said Pearl by way of greeting.

"I know. Michael called me last night. How did you know?" I closed my umbrella and joined her beneath hers.

"Paul, of course. He couldn't wait to tell me that you and I had missed another one. Was Michael mad?"

"Not really." Was he? I was so distracted for most of the conversation, he could've been busting my chops and I'm not sure that I would've noticed. "I told him we'd stake out the lockers this morning and I'd talk to Saul as soon as I could."

Pearl had spent the evening looking at her maps of where the lockers were and trying to pinpoint where the note-writer would most likely strike next. There was no clear pattern. He wasn't alternating male then female or lower-classman then upper. Nor could Pearl find any other connections that might make his next attack easy to predict.

"I think the best thing for us to do is to split up: you take the upperclassman hallway and I'll take the lower," she said, passing me the map of the lockers for my designated spying location.

"All right."

For the first time since we'd met at the corner, she took me in. "Are you okay?"

"I still have yesterday on my mind." I could tell she was embarrassed that she hadn't thought to ask me about it since launching into her theories about the lockers. "I'm starting to think that Pop has moved on and doesn't care what happened to Mama."

"Why?"

As we passed onto school property, I told her about the note that was plaguing *my* household. "I think Pop is seeing someone. Romantically."

"Who?"

"Betty Mrozenski."

Pearl knew Betty. She used to babysit Paul and her. "Wow. Betty's . . . um . . ."

"Awfully young," I said.

"Nice, I was going to say nice."

Yeah, I thought, but I knew what you were thinking.

"How do you feel about it?"

"Not good. Mama hasn't been dead a year. And for all we know, her killer is still out there."

"Just because he's seeing someone doesn't mean he's given up on her," said Pearl.

"I'm not so sure about that." I took a deep breath, worried that if I didn't pause for a moment, I would find myself in the same dark place I'd been early that morning. "I think our next step is to go to Yorkville and visit the hotel where she died. I have to talk to the chambermaid who found her. Anna Mueller. I have to find out if the lie started with her."

"Who says this Anna Mueller even works there anymore? This was a while ago."

Two men struggled to bring a ladder into the front doors of the school, maneuvering their way through the morning crowd. Michael appeared and helped to direct them down a clear path. We squeezed past them and watched as a third man joined them, toting a large box. "We won't know until we go there, will we? Besides, I want to see the place with my own eyes."

"We can't go there," said Pearl.

"Why not?"

"We just can't."

"That's not enough of an answer."

"We can't because . . . there are Germans there."

"My mother was German."

"Not that kind of German. You know what I mean."

I did, unfortunately. Pearl wasn't willing to travel, as a Jew, into a predominantly German neighborhood, where certain ideologies lingered in the shadows like rats looking for homes inside walls. Where someone like our note-writer would feel at home.

"We'll go during the daytime," I said.

"That won't matter."

"We'll be together. Please. Think about it."

"I'm sorry, Iris. I just can't." Her eyes watered. I knew her fear was real, but that didn't make it any less frustrating. "Please don't be mad at me."

I wasn't mad, I was sad. It appeared the only two people I could rely on had completely abandoned me.

NOTHING HAPPENED DURING our divided-up stakeout. I watched the lowerclassman lockers until right before the last bell rang, but no one except the proper owners of those lockers ever appeared. I wasn't surprised. With the men installing what I learned was fire prevention equipment, there were far too many witnesses for our note-writer to risk striking again.

During my first period—Personal Hygiene—Mr. Pinsky,

our saliva-stricken instructor, lisped that a representative from the American Social Hygiene Association would be giving a presentation entitled "Hygiene During War," a topic that set off a titter of whispers that the real topic was venereal disease. We weren't the only class that would be listening to the lecture. Several others would also be congregating in the auditorium.

As we gathered our things and marched toward the hall, my frustration reached its breaking point. I couldn't spend an hour sitting still in an auditorium, not when there were so many questions swimming about my head. Who cared about the stupid war when Mama had been murdered and nobody cared?

Pop may have given up on her, and Pearl might be too afraid to help me, but that didn't mean I couldn't do this on my own. And if I was going to do it, I better do it now, before I lost my nerve.

As we passed the girls' restroom, I took the opportunity to duck inside the door. I waited for someone to call out my name, demanding to know where I was going, but the rest of the class passed without noticing me. I half hoped I'd find Suze inside there, killing time with a cigarette, but the room was empty. I waited until the hall was silent, then left the restroom and rushed toward the main doors of the school—

Where a hall monitor was standing.

"Um," I said, as soon as he eyeballed me. "I'm turned around. Where's the auditorium?"

He was sitting beside a small table with a stack of tardy notices to hand out to anyone who arrived once first period started. He barely looked up from the *Archie* comic he was reading as he pointed me in the right direction. I thanked him, followed his finger, and turned the corner out of his sight.

There was another entrance to the building, at the rear of the school, where a series of crash doors let students leave but kept them from returning the same way. The only problem was that it required going past either the auditorium or the front office. I started toward the lesser of two evils, only to find that Mr. Pinsky was stationed just inside the auditorium doors, smoking a cigarette. I tiptoed toward the doors. The auditorium lights were down and a projector whined as a film filled the screen at the front of the room.

"GERMans are the Enemy," read the screen as bacteria goose-stepped in formation.

Mr. Pinsky coughed and turned my way. I moved back to my starting place just in the nick of time.

There would be no getting past the auditorium. He'd spot me for sure.

I doubled back and started toward the front office. A sour-faced woman in a tiny hat stood with her hand wrapped around a lanky boy's collar. I couldn't hear what she was saying, but the boy blushed a deep purple as the woman railed at the secretary about something that required effusive gesturing with her free hand. I couldn't have asked for a better distraction. Whatever the woman was talking about, the secretary couldn't take her eyes off her.

I ducked down so that if they did look my way, they wouldn't see me. I was almost past them when—

"Shouldn't you be in class, young lady?" a deep voice in front of me asked.

Nuts—the jig was up. I began to straighten and tried to think of a story that could get me out of this predicament.

But it was no teacher calling out to me. It was Benny Rossi.

"NO, STAY DOWN," he whispered. He waved me his way and I continued my strange half crawl, half walk until I was past the office. We turned the corner toward the upperclassman lockers and I was finally able to stand up. "You should've seen your face," he said.

"That would've required a mirror." I tried to continue on my way, but he stopped me.

"Relax. I'm not going to sing. I'm skipping classes, too, dig?"

"I know. It's just I've got places to be."

"You sore at me?"

Were we really having a conversation about this now? "Actually, if memory serves, you're the one who's mad at me. I'm the detective's lying daughter, remember?"

"If Suze can forgive and forget, so can I."

"Thanks." Any other day I would've been thrilled to hear this. Any other day standing alone with him, leaning in close so we could hear each other's whispered words, would've thrilled me. But this was the day I needed to find out what happened to Mama.

"So what's your story?" asked Benny.

"I have to use the restroom."

"Tell me another one while that one's still warm."

"I've got to be somewhere."

He seemed to understand that this wasn't something he should continue to bug me about and dropped the eager beaver act. "Well, you can't go that way." He nodded at the exit I was headed toward.

"Why not?"

"There are poindexters at every entrance. Principal DeLuca's got it bad for tardies and truants."

"I thought that door only opened from the inside."

"Somebody figured out how to make it open from the outside." He winked at me. If he wasn't the someone in question, I'd eat my hat. "But don't worry, there's another way. Come on." He took me by the hand and, before I could register where we were going, pulled me into the boys' restroom. As the door closed behind us, he put his finger to his lips and gestured for me to stay where I was. Then he checked the stalls and the long trough against the wall that I thought was a sink until I saw that there were actual sinks in another part of the room. "The coast is clear."

"Great, but your plan isn't. Am I escaping through the sewer?"

He pointed toward a small window above the radiator. "It's a tight fit for me, but you should have no problem getting through. It's a rough drop on the other side, so I'd better go first to catch you."

Before I could respond, he climbed onto the radiator and pulled himself through the tiny opening. He was right about it being a tight fit. As the window reached his waist, he turned and wiggled with the ease of someone who had done this many times before. His legs slithered through the opening and I heard a thump as he landed outside.

"Okay," he said. "The coast is clear."

I didn't think about what I was doing, or how I'd reverse the process when I wanted to return to school later that day. I just climbed up on the radiator and pulled myself through the window, hoping someone wouldn't choose to come into the restroom as my skirt-clad rear headed north.

Benny waited on the other side, reassuring me that he'd catch me and help me to the ground. It wasn't a long drop, but it was an awkward one. A door opened behind me, and I slid through the window and into Benny's arms just as someone entered the restroom.

"What the—?" said a voice. With me still in his arms, Benny flattened against the side of the building so anyone looking out the window wouldn't see us. It worked. Whoever it was retreated back into the bathroom and Benny gently set me on the ground. He took two steps to the right, then stopped himself. I saw the problem at the same time he did: there was a police car curbside. The officer inside would spot us for sure. Rather than risk it, Benny backed up, took me by the hand, and pulled me in the opposite direction, across the waterlogged baseball field. The rain had stopped, but its damage was done. Thick mud threatened to swallow my saddle shoes with every step.

Finally, we reached the edge of the school property where only a chain-link fence separated us from freedom. In the shade provided by the baseball bleachers, I turned to thank him. "That was swell of you. Thanks."

"Thanks aren't necessary, but payback might be."

"I guess that's fair. What's your price?"

"You can start by getting your friend Pearl Harbor to find a way to excuse my absence for the morning."

I cringed at his use of Pearl's nickname, but I didn't correct him. "All right."

He removed a pack of cigarettes from his pocket and tapped one out. He offered me the package and I declined with a shake of my head. "So where you got to be?"

Why not tell him? It's not like Benny would squeal. "Yorkville."

"Huh?"

"It's a German neighborhood on the Upper East Side."

He lit the cigarette one-handed like he'd been doing it all his life. "I know where Yorkville is, Nancy Drew. I'm just wondering why you want to go to someplace like that."

"Don't call me Nancy Drew," I said.

"Relax. It's just a joke." He exhaled a circle of smoke. "So what's with the destination?"

"It's where my mother died."

"Where she killed herself?" Had Suze told him that, or did everyone at school know my strange, sad story?

"Maybe."

His eyebrow lifted. *Did you lie about that, too?* he seemed to ask.

I shrugged. Who cared if anyone trusted me anymore? I certainly didn't.

"You look like you've got the weight of the world on you," he said.

I took the cigarette pack from him and pulled one out for myself. They were Lucky Strikes, the ones in the green package that signs on the subway declared had gone to war. I'd never smoked before, but at that moment I desperately wanted to, as though the warmth it provided could take away the chill that settled in my bones the night before. Benny lit it for me and I held it at an awkward angle close to my face so I could feel its heat without inhaling its smoke.

"My pop has a safe," I said. "He left it open a couple of days ago and I found some photographs. Of my mother." The whole story spilled out. Benny listened in silence, all traces of skepticism wiped from his face. He didn't move as I told my tale, not even taking time to ash the cigarette that dangled from his lips and threatened to drop to the ground.

When I finished, he was silent for a beat, though you could see the gears in his head jumping into action.

"You have to go to that hotel and talk to that maid."

I wished Pearl was there to hear his conviction. This was the kind of help I needed. "I know. That's my plan."

"You can't go alone," he said.

"Are you volunteering for the job?"

"I might be. For a couple of hall passes."

"Okay," I said. "It's a deal." I finally took a pull from my own cigarette and immediately regretted it. The acrid smoke filled my lungs and made me want to vomit.

Benny took the butt from me and tossed it onto the damp grass. "Maybe stick to one violation a day," he said. "Today, you skip school. Tomorrow, you can add cigs to the mix."

8

"IS THIS WHERE YOU LIVED?" asked Benny. We were on the Upper East Side, my old stomping grounds. Up until the spring this had been my neighborhood, *my* home one of the large apartment buildings with a doorman who greeted you by name, *my* school the one where all the girls wore plaid skirts and crisp white blouses.

"Near here," I told Benny.

He let out a low whistle that I could guess at the meaning of. To someone who had nothing, it had to seem much better to have once been rich and lost everything than to have never had anything to begin with.

I hadn't expected for us to lose all of that when we lost Mama. I had imagined my life would continue pretty much the same as it always had, only with Pop in the role that Mama had played. But the transition proved to be more difficult than that. Somehow the money we'd relied on to maintain our lifestyle had disappeared when Mama died, a reversal of fortune that had never been explained to me. And rather than trying to continue carving out a life he knew we couldn't afford, or relying on his brother, Adam, to provide it for us, Pop had abandoned the Upper East Side entirely, banking on a fresh start being preferable to remaining where we would constantly be reminded of everything we'd lost.

He'd been right, I guess. Staying on the Upper East Side would've meant confronting Mama's absence every single day. In our new place it was possible to pretend she'd never existed rather than being faced with the memory that this was a space she used to occupy. She'd never been in Mrs. Mrozenski's home, never sat on her sofa.

Or at least I used to think that. Now Mrs. M.'s house would always be the place where I'd learned that Mama had been murdered.

"So where's the hotel?" asked Benny. I hadn't bothered to check for the address. This whole scheme had come upon me so quickly that I hadn't had time to plan.

"East Eighty-sixth Street."

"That's a long street. You got a number?"

I shook my head. "There wasn't one in the article. All I know is that it's called the White Swan."

Benny held up a finger, telling me to wait, and ducked into a phone booth. I half expected him to emerge in costume, like Superman, but when he came out he looked exactly the same, save the directory page he clutched in his hand. "Got it," he announced as an old man walking past us sent a frown our way.

"Public phone directories should not be vandalized," he barked.

"Tell someone who cares, geezer," said Benny as he pulled my arm and quickened my pace.

"Hooligans!" the man said into the wind. I blushed. Was that who I was now?

We continued on, eventually reaching East Eighty-sixth Street and weaving our way into the neighborhood called Yorkville.

It was one of Manhattan's many ethnic neighborhoods, only instead of being home to Eastern European immigrants and Italians like the Lower East Side, it was the Germans who had settled here. There was a time, Mama told me, when the streets were alive with German music and the scent of sauerbraten and other national delicacies wafted through the air. The German flag flew beside the Stars and Stripes, and the majority of the words that crammed the shopkeepers' windows or were shouted from the newsstands were in the residents' native tongue. English was infrequently spoken; this was a haven for those who had moved here from abroad, where they didn't have to force themselves to assimilate but could recede into their own culture for a while and rest.

"It's creepy, huh?" said Benny.

"What do you mean?"

"This place. Look at it. It's like they're trying to hide who they are." He was right. The war had changed Yorkville. How couldn't it? Anything German began to be viewed with suspicion; even the food underwent a sort of patriotic makeover by being assigned American names (no more sauerkraut—instead, enjoy liberty cabbage). The German-language newspapers could still be purchased at the kiosks, but more and more people opted to buy the ones in English, as though to reassure us that they weren't reading anything subversive. The flags were gone—at least the German ones—as were any other proud signs of German nationalism.

And yet, for all the attempts they'd made to tone down the foreign flavor that had once distinguished this neighborhood from all the others, Benny was right: there was something about Yorkville that felt . . . well . . . creepy. I knew that was why Pearl didn't want to come here. Hitler may never have walked these streets, but it still felt like we were marching into his lair.

"What would you rather they do?" I asked. "Wear armbands that declare that they support Hitler?"

"At least we'd know then. By hiding who they are, it makes you wonder if everyone here is a Nazi," said Benny.

"Because they're German?"

"Sure. Why else?"

"My mother was German. I'm German. All it takes is one drop of blood."

"Yeah, but you're not like them."

"But going by your logic, how do you know for sure?"

He didn't respond. As we walked East Eighty-sixth Street, searching for the White Swan Hotel, Benny and I eased closer and closer, until we moved as one. We seemed to be watched as we walked, "outsider" stamped on our foreheads even though, to my eyes, we looked like everyone else (perhaps they were wondering if we should be in school, I reassured myself, but no—those stares seemed to imply something else).

Maybe it was just that we knew what had happened here. A woman had been murdered, and for some reason no one had done anything about it.

Benny pulled the directory page from his pocket and handed it to me. I focused on checking the building numbers. This was it—the address for the White Swan Hotel, only the building that stood there was vacant. The door was chained, the windows boarded up. A sign hanging in front of it had had its letters removed, though the sun had left behind a shadow of what had once been the eponymous bird beckoning travelers to stop here for the night.

Pearl was right. This was a wild-goose chase.

"It's closed," I said. "I'm sorry I dragged you all the way up here."

"What else was I going to do today?"

The familiar burn of tears threatened to overtake me. *Not now,* I pleaded with myself. *Not in front of Benny.*

He approached the building and tried the doors. "Iris,"

he stage-whispered. He waved me toward him. One of the windows was open. Did we dare? The street seemed oddly vacant, the way the city always got just before a storm hit. Benny waved again. Then, losing his patience with me, he climbed over the windowsill and disappeared inside. He landed noiselessly and let out a low whistle. "You've got to take a look at this place," he said. "Come on now—don't be chicken."

Boy, howdy—I had no choice now. With a quick glance to make sure we weren't being watched, I followed him inside. On the other side of the window was a dusty couch that had softened his entry. I coughed as months of disuse floated into the air, and attempted to clean the residue off my backside before moving on.

It was dim inside, but not too dark to see that we were standing in the lobby. The furniture was threadbare but alluded to a time when it had been grand. Not last year when Mama was here, but some years before, perhaps when the White Swan first opened its doors and being located in Yorkville wasn't viewed as a disadvantage to a business.

We gravitated to the lobby desk, where a guest ledger stood open as though someone still expected people to check in to the place. Almost everything was covered in the same dust that coated the furniture, except for the corner of the desk where the phone and a stack of papers sat. I picked up the receiver and confirmed that the line was still live.

"Someone's still working here. Or living here or something," I told Benny.

"Interesting." Benny opened drawers, setting off a rattle of dried-out fountain pens and broken pencils.

I rifled through the papers. There were newspapers and typewritten pages piled into a hasty stack. All were in German. From the formatting of the typing, the pages appeared to be a flyer announcing something. "Amerikadeutscher Volksbund," it read, followed by what looked to be a date.

"Anything?" asked Benny.

"Just a bunch of stuff written in German. You?"

"Rusting paper clips. Let's go upstairs," he said.

I hesitated. "If the phone is still being used, whoever's using it might be up there."

"If we run into someone, we'll tell them we came in to get out of the storm."

I looked toward the window we'd climbed through. "It's not raining."

"No, but it was. Relax. We haven't done anything wrong except a little breaking and entering. If there's someone up there, I'll handle it."

That didn't reassure me. "Oh, a little breaking and entering. Is that all? What if the someone up there is armed and dangerous?"

"Don't bust a button. You may not get another chance to get in here. You want to see where she died, right?"

"I guess."

"Then come on."

There was an elevator that clearly wasn't operating, and a stairwell whose door had been left ajar. We weren't the first uninvited people in here. Someone else had been through the building, no doubt looking for anything of value they could take. There was no lighting in the stairwell beyond the little bit of sunlight that leaked through the boarded-up windows. We both held on to the banister for dear life and followed the stairs up two flights.

We exited the stairwell and entered a sparse lobby. Dents in the carpet told of furniture that used to be there to offer a momentary respite for guests waiting for the elevator or for a friend, and darker strips of wallpaper hinted that there used to be paintings, mirrors, and sconces on the wall, all of which had been taken down in the days since the White Swan had closed.

Rooms fanned off in all directions. Some of the doors were removed from their hinges, others closed. There seemed to be no rhyme or reason to which rooms were accessible and which weren't. Through the open doors we spied bare, stained mattresses, broken furniture, and more signs that things that used to be there weren't anymore.

"This one," I said. I stopped before a closed door marked 3C, the room number that had appeared in the newspaper article. Benny took hold of the doorknob and turned. It didn't budge. I scanned the hallway and found two nails still in the wall, though the pictures they'd once held were gone. I pried them free with a thumbnail, then inserted them with shaking hands into the lock for room 3C. It took some effort, but eventually my improvised picklocks landed in the right spot and the lock clicked open.

"You're too much, Nancy D.," he said.

"I asked you not to call me that," I replied.

Like the other rooms, 3C had been ransacked. Benny touched my shoulder and pointed at the mattress. A rust-colored stain that someone had attempted to scrub away told the tale of a pool of scarlet liquid that had once sat there. It was on the walls, too, though the sun had done a better job fading it from the peeling wallpaper. Either Mama died here, or the hotel had a history of very bad things happening inside it.

"Oh, God—I'm going to be sick," I whispered.

Benny took me to the window and pushed the pane up until the fresh air rippled through my hair. That was better. The acid that rose in my throat began its descent. I stuck my head out the window and took a deep breath.

"That's it," said Benny. "Breathe slowly."

"This was a terrible idea. We shouldn't have come up here."

"It's okay."

But it wasn't. That was Mama on the bed, on the walls, on the floor. I squeezed my eyes shut. "I can't look at it again."

"You don't have to. Keep your eyes closed. Take my hand and I'll guide you out of the room. Okay?"

I did as he instructed. I only made it two steps before a metallic click stopped me.

"Und es sieht aus wie ich habe unbefugten Zugriffen." My eyes popped open. There was a man with a gun standing at the door to room 3C.

HE GESTURED US AWAY from the windows. I couldn't tell if it was because he didn't want to shoot the glass, or if the light was bothering his eyes, but I hoped it was the latter.

"Gibt es nicht mehr von ihnen?" he said.

"What?" asked Benny.

"Are there any more of you?" the man said with a thick German accent—Mama's accent—coloring his words.

"There's no one else, just us," said Benny. He was remarkably calm, as though he encountered men with guns all the time. He still held my hand. As he spoke, he put his other arm around my waist and pulled me close to him.

"Today is not your lucky day. My friend across the street sees you break in and he calls me. I'm tired of you people coming into my building and thinking you can walk away with whatever you want. Empty your pockets," said the man. I produced a subway token and my house key. Benny uncovered an identical token and the wallet he connected to his waist with a chain. "What have you stolen?"

"Nothing," said Benny.

"So I stopped you in time?"

"We're not here to steal," said Benny.

"A likely story. Then why have you come?"

Standing in the room my mother died in, with a gun pointed at us by the man who could've been her killer, I felt no urge to come clean about our true purpose for being there. I tried to think of a reasonable lie, but the combined forces of his gun and Mama's blood (it was hers, wasn't it?) rendered me completely mute.

Fortunately, Benny hadn't lost the gift of gab. "Promise me you won't tell her old man," he said.

Pop? Was he really going to bring Pop into this?

"I don't believe you're in the position to make demands of me," said the man.

Benny squeezed my hand reassuringly, silently asking me to trust him. "I know. It's just . . . look, if he finds out we were together, that's it. I'll never see her again."

The man lowered the gun, but he didn't speak.

"We shouldn't have broken in. That was dumb. But we needed someplace to be alone."

The man's eyes crinkled with amusement. "Some place with a lot of beds, eh?"

Benny looked down, doing a bang-up job of being bashful.

"And what do you have to say for yourself, Juliet?" the man said to me.

Nuts, I thought this was Benny's scene. I didn't realize I was going to have to act in it, too. "Please don't tell," I whispered. "Pop will send me away. He's already said as much."

He slid the gun into his jacket and I finally felt like I could breathe again. He was going to let us go. The danger was past. "This is no place for young lovers. It's dangerous here, eh? Your girlfriend deserves better than rats in the walls and stained mattresses."

At the mention of the mattress I went woozy.

"Your girlfriend doesn't look so good."

Benny attempted to steady me. "It's that bed. She thinks it looks like blood on it. We heard a rumor that someone was murdered here."

He smiled, showing us a mouth missing half of its teeth. "Murdered? No. Killed themselves. My girl is the one who found her."

Anna Mueller. He was talking about Anna. "Your wife?" I asked.

"Not anymore. When business gets bad, she gets out, says she'd rather wait tables at the Biergarten than clean rooms for me. Her loss, eh? Now get out and don't come back. Next time maybe I'm not so nice about it."

Benny led me from the room and back down the stairs. "You okay?" he asked as we reached the window through which we'd entered the building.

"I think so."

He flashed that brilliant smile of his. "Good, then we're off to the Biergarten, whatever that is."

IT TURNED OUT THAT THE BIERGARTEN was a combined social hall and restaurant in the heart of Yorkville. I vaguely remembered Mama telling me about it, or places just like it. It was the kind of joint Pop and she used to go to in the early days of their courtship, sharing each other's life story over mugs of warm beer and plates of fried potatoes and pickles.

As we entered the building, I thought of the two of them huddled together at one of the picnic-style tables while a band played music from the stage, forcing them to yell above the music to be heard. "The music was so loud," Mama once told me, "your papa doesn't hear my name right. That whole first night he thought I was called Enid. It was only when he asked if he could see me again that I corrected him."

We took in the room where a smattering of people ate their lunch. Waitresses toted large platters of food and beer on trays they hefted high above their heads. None of them wore name tags—this was the kind of place where the clientele most likely knew their names and when to use them.

One passed by us with an empty tray she slammed onto a counter.

"Excuse me?" I said.

She raised an eyebrow. This was my invitation to go on.

"Is Anna Mueller working today?"

"Who wants to know?" Her accent was as heavy as the tray she'd just dropped.

"My mother is a friend of hers and she asked me to stop by and say hello."

The eyebrow stayed raised. "What is your mother's name?"

"Ingrid Anderson. They knew each other at the White Swan."

She made a noise like a snort. "The White Swan? There's a memory to dredge up. I'll see if she's busy." She walked away. Instead of going into the main hall where the other waitresses were, she disappeared behind a door marked "Private."

"What was that all about?" asked Benny.

"Your guess is as good as mine."

Barely a minute passed before the waitress returned. "She'll see you. Through the door and up the stairs."

I went cautiously through the door, half expecting to find another man with a gun waiting for us. There was no one there. At the top of a dark staircase was another door, this one open. A blond woman was seated at a desk, typing figures into an adding machine.

As we entered, she stopped her work and stared at us. "So she was right: you really are a couple of kids. What business is Ingrid Anderson of yours?"

"She was my mother," I said.

Though her accent was lighter than the other woman's, there was no denying her heritage. "So this wasn't a lie?"

"Of course not."

She cocked her head toward Benny. "And who is he?"

"Her boyfriend," Benny said. Just like at the hotel, he wrapped a protective arm around my waist. A blush burned its way down my face.

"How did you find me, daughter and boyfriend?"

"We went to the White Swan. There was a man there who said he was your ex-husband. He said you were working here as a waitress."

She removed a cigarette from a wooden box and lit it. "A waitress? The swine is still charming as ever. Someday he will open his eyes and realize that all this is mine, no thanks to him." She tweaked her mouth to the right and exhaled a stream of smoke. "So why are you here?"

"Because the papers said you were the one who found her," I said.

She continued smoking, showing no sign of saying anything in reply.

I dug my nails into my hand, hoping the pain would give me courage. "I've seen the crime-scene photos. And I've seen the room it happened in. There was blood everywhere. That was no suicide."

She stared at me in silence for so long that I started to think she was never going to respond. Then, "No, it wasn't."

My face twitched into a momentary smile before the joy at finally hearing the truth was overtaken by the enormity of what she was saying. "Then why did everyone say it was?"

"When your mother checked in, she was with a man. I never talk to them, but I see them come and go." She flicked ash into a silver beer stein. "When I find her dead, I call the police. They come and so does the man. He takes me aside and explains to me that I need to forget everything I saw in that room. To help forget he will give me money."

"Who was he?"

"I don't know and I don't care. He paid for my ignorance so I did not ask."

"So he bribed you so you would lie to the police?"

She laughed and a stream of smoke escaped her nose. "I'm not the only one who got fat pockets that day. Make no mistake about it."

I'd never felt like hurting someone before, but right then, I wanted to hurt Anna Mueller.

"Easy, Iris," Benny whispered in my ear. The arm around my waist grew tighter, holding me back.

"I'm sorry if that upsets you, but Ingrid Anderson was not a good person. That is why I take the money."

"How can you say that? You didn't know her."

"No, but I know her kind." She stabbed the air with her finger. "We all do. And it may be hard to hear, but no one cares how she died, they are just happy that she did. We don't need people like her here."

Finally, I understood what she was saying. Pearl was right: Yorkville was nothing but a hotbed of anti-Semitism. This woman, the police—everyone thought that Mama's faith justified her murder.

No wonder Pop didn't want to talk about it.

"Get me out of here," I whispered to Benny.

"Why are you so angry?" asked Anna. "You know what she was, don't you?"

I met her, cold stare to cold stare. "No. Why don't you tell me?"

I braced myself for her to declare that Mama was a Jewish pig. But she surprised me.

"Poor little girl, don't you know? Your mother was a Nazi."

I DON'T REMEMBER leaving the Biergarten. The time between when Anna declared Mama a Nazi and when I found myself on the street, crossing the imaginary line between Yorkville and the rest of the Upper East Side, vanished.

"She was yanking our chains," said Benny.

"Of course she was," I said, though I didn't feel nearly as certain as I tried to sound. On the surface, it was a crazy accusation, but in some strange way it made sense. Of course the police didn't care that she had been murdered. Wasn't one less Nazi a reason for rejoicing?

But then why claim it was suicide? To protect her killer?

"It was probably just a rumor," Benny said. We reached the subway but he seemed hesitant to go through the turnstile, as though we needed to resolve the truth about Mama before we left the Upper East Side and went home. "You know how rumors are. Once they start, they've got legs and there's no stopping them, even if there isn't a whiff of truth in it."

He was right. We were in high school, after all, we knew how rumors began. All you needed to do was wear a tight sweater or a different shade of lipstick or skip class with a notorious Italian hoodlum and suddenly your reputation was being questioned.

But would one German say that sort of thing about another? It was, I had to imagine, the worst possible thing you could claim. To call another girl easy because of the way she dressed was one thing, but this? Was this really the sort of thing you would tell someone—total strangers at that—without evidence? What could Anna possibly gain by doing so?

And was there evidence? The worst part of Mama's

death was how incomprehensible it seemed. Everything had been so normal until Pearl Harbor. Mama had seemed so happy. She had always been independent—she had to be with Pop being gone for months at a time—and it wasn't unusual for her to go out at night. Although she left on her own, I assumed she didn't remain that way—it wouldn't have been proper for a woman to walk the streets by herself. She had lots of friends, including a number of German ones who she often spent hours talking to on the phone in her native tongue. And she received mail from Germany, from family members who still lived abroad. Those were in German, too, of course, so I never knew what they said and relied on the brief translations she shared with me. I'd never had any reason to doubt the explanations behind the phone calls or the letters, but it's not like I could've questioned her honesty. I didn't speak the language, after all, and there was no Mrs. M. back then to translate it for me.

"Iris?" said Benny. I snapped to attention. He dropped his token into the turnstile and waited for me to do the same. "You going to be okay?"

I forced a smile. Why was I even allowing myself to ponder this? "Of course. I know my mother wasn't . . . there's no way she could've been . . ." I couldn't even say the word. Maybe that was why Pop told me he didn't want to talk about the photos: he figured thinking she had killed herself was much better than learning what some people thought she had really been up to.

We boarded the train. It was standing room only so we huddled together at a pole, sharing an easy intimacy that, on any other day, would've thrilled me. As we barreled toward home, I took in the crowd around us: businessmen on their way back from lunch, mothers heading to and from appointments, soldiers enjoying the city before they shipped out to places unknown, immigrants hoping they'd guessed at the right train to take them to their destination. As cautious as Pop always encouraged me to be, I never thought I was at risk when I roamed around the city. But now I wondered who else was lurking in the shadows created by the subway tunnels.

What was it Pop had said? The enemy didn't always wear a uniform.

We arrived on the Lower East Side and I followed Benny as he took a roundabout path designed to avoid truant officers and anyone else who might be able to make things difficult for us if they saw us out and about. We entered the school property the way we'd left: through the chain-link fence.

I glanced at my watch. It was almost 12:30. We would be able to sneak into lunch and seamlessly rejoin our day. I could ask Pearl to take care of the attendance records for us. No one would have to know that we'd left school.

"Come on," he said as he approached the window we'd exited from.

"I can't," I whispered.

"It looks higher than it is. I'll give you a boost."

"No. I can't go back in there. Not now."

He nodded, finally understanding what I was saying. There was a scream forming somewhere deep in my abdomen and I was worried that once it started, it would never stop. Until I found some way to quell it, I couldn't sit in a classroom and pretend everything was all right.

He looked up at the window, almost longingly, before returning his focus to me. "Can you go home?"

I could. I could tell Mrs. M. I was sick and spend the rest of the day in bed. She would call the school for me, her voice a low murmur on the phone so she wouldn't disturb my rest. But that would require lying to her, and I didn't have the strength to do that. Nor could I bear to tell her the truth because that would mean saying it out loud. *No one cares that my mother was murdered. You probably don't, either. After all, the only good German is a dead German.*

"No," I told Benny. "I can't go home. Not like this." The tears were starting. What had held them at bay until now? I didn't know. All I knew was that once they started, it would be many hours before they stopped.

"Come on. I know a place." He took my hand and led me away from the school and down a series of streets until we arrived at an apartment building. We didn't go inside. Instead, he led me around back, where stacks of sandbags leaned against the rear wall. In the center of them was a cave made of corrugated metal. Still holding my hand, he ducked inside it and led me into a space that was larger than its exterior implied. He released me just long enough to turn on a kerosene light. It revealed a barren room lined with wooden benches.

"Where are we?"

He barred the door. Daylight illuminated the edges. "Air-raid shelter."

Of course. We had one on our block, though I'd never been inside it. There were supposed to be drills to teach us what to do if bombs started falling from the sky, but somehow our part of Orchard Street hadn't had one yet. "Are we allowed to be in here?"

Benny shrugged. "No one's told me otherwise. I come here sometimes. You know—to think." A small pile of spent cigarette butts testified to how many times he'd been here before. He dipped into the shadows and emerged with a blanket and a box of animal crackers. "Here. It gets a little cold in here, but it's not so bad."

"Thanks." I let him wrap the blanket around me and took a cookie when he offered it. He sat close enough that I could feel the heat radiating off his body. It was the kind of space that should've terrified me—after all, it was designed for us to pass time in the worst of circumstances—but I found it oddly cozy. For a moment it was like we weren't even in New York anymore, but in some prehistoric cave in another time and another place that had never heard of Nazis.

Stop it, I told myself. *Don't think about that. It doesn't deserve space in your head.*

"Do you live in this building?" I asked him.

"Top floor."

"Where are your parents?"

"My old man's probably asleep."

"And your mother?"

"Died four years ago."

"I'm sorry."

He shrugged. Did that mean my apologies were unnecessary or that in light of the reasons behind my own mother's death, losing his mother was nothing to dwell on?

"What does your pop do?"

"He used to deliver the mail until they found him passed out drunk on his route. So now he spends his days sleeping and his nights drinking."

Suze had once told me that Benny's dad wasn't exactly Spencer Tracy. "What will happen when he finds out you skipped?"

"He won't find out, not if I want to walk again."

I'd seen evidence of his father's temper. The night we'd gone dancing in Harlem, Benny had come home late enough to get beaten black and blue. Suze had taken him in that night, and in the wee morning hours, as he got ready to sleep on her bedroom floor, he'd told her how much he liked me.

But that news hadn't had the impact on me that Suze

predicted. She told me the same day I'd heard the rumors that Mama had been having an affair.

"Have you slept here?" I asked because I wanted to think of anything but Mama.

"A few times when the weather was warm. There's a heater in here, but I didn't want to use it, you know, just in case."

What he meant was just in case there really was an air raid.

I thought about the Jews in Poland and how many cold and terrifying nights they'd spent in rooms like this one, of all the reasons the Jewish Student Federation had banded together and wanted only the most devoutly religious in their ranks. What would they think if they heard the rumor that my mother had supported the people who coined the rhetoric written on the locker notes?

What would Pearl think?

"Iris?"

Pearl. She had to have been worried when I didn't show up at lunch. She could never know about any of this. I'd swear Benny to secrecy, and I'd put my heart and soul into finding out who was behind the notes. I'd start going to synagogue, too. I'd become the best damn Jew ever, so that if word ever did get out about what my mother was (maybe!) up to, no one would accuse me of sharing her twisted ideals.

"Iris?" Benny was staring at me. I returned his gaze,

though he had to see in my eyes that I'd heard nothing else he'd said. "Do you want to talk about it?" he asked.

"No." I gulped hard. If it required only a drop of blood to make you a German, how many did it take to make you a Nazi? "Promise me you won't tell anyone about what we learned today."

"You don't think it's true."

"No. Of course I don't." A new stream of tears started its journey. "But other people might. People who didn't know her."

"I promise, Iris. I can keep a secret."

"Because if anyone found out, I'd die." The tears came faster, and I was finding it harder and harder to breathe. No wonder Pop walked around the Orchard Street house with the weight of the world on his shoulders. How could he ever be happy when the woman he loved had been accused of something like this?

Benny put his arm around me and pulled me into his chest. "I won't let that happen," he said.

I buried my face in his sweater and let the wool soften my sobs. Eventually the darkness enveloped me and I slept.

I'M NOT SURE WHAT ROUSED ME. I awoke to find myself still in Benny's arms. He was awake, one hand tangled in my hair, where it was gently rubbing my scalp.

"Hey there, Nancy Drew," he said as I looked up at him. "Feel better?"

It took me a moment to remember where I was, and what had happened. "I guess." I was so comfortable in his arms. While it should've felt strange to be so close to a boy, it reminded me of being a little girl and waking up from a nap in Mama's bed.

Mama.

Rain pattered on the corrugated roof. The little light that had leaked around the door was gone. If it wasn't for the kerosene lamp we'd be in complete darkness. "What time is it?" I asked.

He strained to see his watch. "Just past five."

Oh no. I'd missed the entire afternoon of classes, missed out on interviewing Saul and helping Pearl with the afternoon stakeout. And now I was probably worrying Pop and Mrs. M. to boot. "I've got to go." I untangled myself from Benny, shocked to find how cold the shelter was when my body wasn't up against his. I gathered my books and purse and was surprised to find Benny behind me with my mackintosh at the ready. As I slid into it, I could feel his breath on the back of my neck.

"I'll walk you. You shouldn't be out alone after dark."

But I wanted to be. I needed some time to sort out my thoughts before I saw Pop again. "I'm supposed to meet Pearl at school," I said.

"Then I'll walk you there."

It was obvious he wasn't going to let me out on my own. He led me from the shelter into the increasingly dark evening. The rain that had pounded the roof all afternoon had started to freeze. I winced as needles of ice hit my face. As I took my first tentative steps onto the sidewalk, I discovered it was slick with sleet. Benny caught my elbow just before I tumbled to the ground.

"You okay?" he asked.

"Fine," I said as I straightened up.

We slowed our pace and I grasped Benny's arm to help me keep my balance. Dusk was quickly deepening as the sun set. The streetlights that should've clicked on remained dark as part of the mandatory blackout the city was under. Just as we were about to clear the building and cross the street, a voice rang out in the rain, "Benicio!"

Benny turned to the sound and I turned with him. I could just make out an older man waving from the main door to the building.

"Shit," said Benny under his breath. "What's he doing up already?"

"Get over here, boy!" said the man. I could feel his temper. Even in the icy downpour it managed to radiate heat.

"Go," I said. Had the school called Benny's dad? I hated to think so. After all, if they'd called him they might've called Pop, too.

"He's going to be mad whether I come now or later," said Benny.

"Go," I said again.

Reluctantly he released me and trudged toward the door

123

of the building. I watched as he reached his father and the man grabbed him by the ear and pulled him inside. Then I continued on my way before anything else that was my fault escaped into the frozen night.

I trudged homeward on a sidewalk that grew even more slick and treacherous. I did my best to stay steady, but as the sleet fell harder and I grew colder, I picked up my pace and grew less cautious. As I reached my turn, my feet slid out from under me and I landed ass-first on the ground.

The cold seeped through my skirt and stabbed my legs with dozens of tiny pins. I struggled to my feet and cleaned off my backside with a hand, only to find that I'd torn a hole in my skirt when I landed. Try as I might to stay calm, tears forced their way out of my eyes, and by the time I got home I was full-out sobbing.

What I wanted more than anything else in the world was to find Mrs. M. waiting for me with a warm cup of cocoa and a roaring fire. What I got instead was Aunt Miriam.

10

POP AND UNCLE ADAM STOPPED SPEAKING right after we moved to the Lower East Side. Things were admittedly tense before then. In the months between Pop's return from Pearl Harbor and his recovery and rehabilitation, I'd lived with Uncle Adam and Aunt Miriam and tried to maintain the life I'd had before Mama's death—going to Chapin, hanging out with my wealthy friends on the weekends, and attending synagogue with my decidedly devout aunt and uncle.

Something went wrong, though. Very wrong.

As soon as Pop was well enough to come home, he'd announced that we were moving to the Lower East Side. Within days of our settling into Mrs. M.'s house, Adam and Miriam stopped by with a proposition for him: Pop could work with Uncle Adam at *his* agency for a fifty-fifty split. Pop said no, and that was the last time my uncle ever came around. I had seen Aunt Miriam once since then, and, thanks to her, Pop found out I was somewhere I wasn't supposed to be. I was awfully steamed when it happened, but given how it caused Pop and me to finally be honest with each other, it probably wasn't such a bad thing after all.

Not that I would ever tell Aunt Miriam that.

"Iris," Aunt Miriam said as I arrived on the front stoop. "I'm so glad to see you. I rang the bell, but no one answered. I was just getting ready to leave you this." The "this" in question was a bag of brightly wrapped presents. I would bet my right arm they were Hanukah gifts. "I suppose your father's not home?"

"I think he's out on a case," I said. Odds were good Pop had spied her out the window and decided not to answer the door.

"Have you been crying?" she asked.

I wanted to lie, but after the awful day I'd had, I couldn't. Not about that, anyway. "I fell on the ice," I said.

"Oh, you poor thing. I was hoping you were holed up at school until the storm passed." She looked out on the ice-streaked sidewalk. I hadn't seen a car go past since I'd left Benny's. Of course, that wasn't unusual now that gas and tires were being rationed, but it certainly didn't bode well for Aunt Miriam making an easy return trip home. She had to be cursing her decision to come out here today. "Are you hurt badly?"

"I'll be okay," I said. Here was the thing about Aunt Miriam: I liked her. I'd always liked her. Mama did, too, as

126

a matter of fact. I have no idea how I would've survived the first awful months after Mama's death without her. But I was also fiercely protective of Pop. If he didn't want to talk to his brother or sister-in-law, I had to believe there was a good reason for it.

But that didn't mean I was going to send my aunt out into an ice storm. "Would you like to come inside? I could make us some tea or something."

She nodded, picked up her bag of presents, and followed me in.

I'd been wrong that Pop was hiding inside. The lights were off, the house frigid from the plummeting temperature. I clicked on the lamps, got Aunt Miriam settled in the parlor, and peeked into the kitchen to verify that we were alone.

The phone began to shriek. It was the house line, not the office one, thank goodness. Aunt Miriam wouldn't exactly be happy if she knew I was working for Pop. I caught the phone on the third ring. The line crackled with static that foretold of an evening without phones at all. I could just make out Pop's voice, so distant I imagine two tin cans strung together would've gotten better reception.

"Iris? You're home safe?" he asked.

"Safe and sound," I said.

"Oh, thank goodness. I've been trying to reach you for over an hour. I'm trapped uptown for the time being. I'm not sure when I'll make it back home. Is Mrs. Mrozenski there?"

"No."

"She's probably stranded, too, then. She went to a funeral this afternoon. I'll see if I can't track her down and make sure she's safe. Until she gets there, stay inside. All right?"

I heard music in the background. Wherever he was, he was indoors at least. "Where are you?" I asked.

"Not to worry, I'm at Betty's apartment. I can stay here for the night if things don't improve, but I'll try to make it home if I can."

"Okay." He was at Betty's? The crackling ceased. "Pop?" The line was dead. With it went any possible explanation for why he'd journeyed to Betty Mrozenski's.

Not that I needed one.

I hung up the phone and put the teakettle on the stove. While I waited for it to whistle, I made a few pieces of toast and spread them with jam.

When I returned to the parlor Aunt Miriam was standing in front of the radio, holding the framed photo of Mama.

"I made us a snack," I said as I placed the tray of tea and toast on the coffee table.

"That was very kind of you, Iris. Thank you. Was that your father on the phone?"

"Yes, he's stuck uptown." Even though her face made no query, I offered an explanation anyway. "He's at a friend's, so I guess he has a place to stay if things keep up like this."

She returned the photo to the radio, turning it so Mama could be included in our conversation. "What happened to the glass?"

Pop broke it one morning, or rather his prosthetic leg did. I thought it was an accident at the time, but now I wondered if he might've done it out of frustration for what she'd been involved in. How much did he know? He was a good detective. He had to know at least what I did, though the odds were good that he knew more. "I was goofing around and knocked it over," I said.

"I wish I'd known; I would've gotten you a new frame." She pushed the bag of presents my way. "Go on and open them."

There were at least eight packages in the bag, maybe more if she'd brought things for Pop, too. "It's only the second night of Hanukah," I said.

"We'll be a little unorthodox this year. That way I can enjoy you opening things." As she said it, I could see her eyes scanning the room, looking for a menorah. A little unorthodox was right.

"I . . . I didn't get you anything," I said.

"Nor do you need to. Hanukah is for children. Go on now."

I picked up the smallest package and peeled away its paper. A small velvet jewelry box was inside. I pried open the clamshell and found a pair of pearl earrings.

"To match your mother's necklace," said Aunt Miriam.

"Thank you." I hadn't worn Mama's necklace since I'd tried to pawn it several weeks earlier. I thought Pop needed the money more than I needed the bauble, but my efforts had been waylaid. I'd been grateful at the time—what had I been thinking, trying to get rid of the one memento I had from Mama—but now I found myself itching to get rid of anything associated with her.

I closed the box with one hand, surprised by the force of the hinges. "Thank you."

"You don't look very happy with them. I could take them back and get you something else if you like." She reached for the box.

"No," I said. "They're lovely. It's just . . ." I tried to think of a good excuse for my mood. Such a nice gift. While Miriam and Adam had money, certainly more than we did, the earrings still felt like a bribe. What was she hoping? That I'd see the gift and tell her Pop was wrong to stop talking to them?

"I don't really have anyplace to wear them," I said.

"Not yet, but you will."

"I mean here, on the Lower East Side. People don't really dress up."

She nodded, like the idea hadn't occurred to her until I'd given it voice. "Life is different for you, isn't it?"

"It's not so bad," I said. I didn't want to talk about my life now. I wanted to talk about life a year ago but I wasn't sure how to broach the subject. I hadn't really talked to anyone but Pop about Mama, and up until the night I found the photos our conversations were more about what we didn't say than what we did. Oh, Aunt Miriam had been there when I'd been told the awful lie about how Mama met her end and held me as I'd cried. And she'd comforted me when my Chapin School friends' curiosity got the better of them. But beyond telling her how much I missed Mama, I'd never told her how much Mama's death hurt. When I believed it was suicide that had ripped Mama from us, it was just too inexplicable to put what that loss meant into words. After all, it wasn't just about Mama dying, but about Mama preferring death to being with me. And Pop.

"Are you still mad at me for that business last month?" she asked.

"No," I said. "I mean, I wasn't happy about it, but it's fine."

"I hope you understand why I did it. I was just so concerned when you told me you were working for your father. I had to know for myself that it wasn't true." And it wasn't. *Then*. Now? What Aunt Miriam didn't know wouldn't hurt her. "And I was so relieved. I knew your father wouldn't put you in danger like that. Not after—"

"After what?"

She had been caught in something and she knew it. Lying didn't come easily to her. I knew that. "After your father was injured," she said. "He must know better than anyone that danger comes when you least expect it."

Nice one, Aunt Miriam. "Pop wouldn't let me get hurt," I said. "Not physically anyway." The words were out of my mouth before I had time to register what I was doing.

Her face became a rigid mask of concern. "Has your father said something to upset you?" she asked.

"No. Pop wouldn't do that. It's just hard with the anniversaries coming up."

"I worried about how all of that might affect you."

"One minute I'm doing fine, but the next minute my mind goes back there. Wondering."

"Wondering what?"

I hated feeling like I was playing Aunt Miriam, but there was no way to outright ask her anything without tipping my hand. If she didn't know what Anna Mueller had accused Mama of, I certainly didn't want to tell her what I'd heard. And if she did . . . well, it would have to be her choice if she wanted to tell me more. "Why Mama did it," I said. "She seemed so happy about Pop returning. I just can't imagine why she'd choose to leave him at a time when he needed her so badly."

Her lips were set in a thin, straight line, though I swear I caught tiny ripples that hinted there was something she wanted to say.

"Every time I try to justify what might've occurred, I just confuse myself, you know?"

"Maybe it's best not to think about it at all," said Miriam.

"But I can't help it. Don't you wonder why she did it?"

Again there was a ripple of hesitation. "No. There's no point in doing that, Iris."

She wasn't going to budge. If she knew something—and

I was almost certain she did—she had no intention of letting me in on it. "I hate her," I said.

"You don't mean that."

"It's unforgivable what she did, not just in our eyes but in God's." I was pushing all the right buttons and I knew it.

"You shouldn't judge your mother."

"Why not? God will. I'm sure he already has. Suicide is a sin, after all."

"You can't know what was in your mother's mind. I'm sure there were circumstances beyond her control. You don't know."

"I do know. I know that she was a selfish bitch who didn't think of anyone but herself."

Before I could register what was happening, Aunt Miriam slapped me. Tears flooded my eyes and I clasped my injured cheek. I had wanted a reaction out of her, but this was completely unexpected. For both of us.

"I'm sorry, Iris." Aunt Miriam threw her arms around me and held me so close it was a struggle to breathe. "I just couldn't bear to hear you talk about your mother like that."

My tears kept flowing. It wasn't just Aunt Miriam's slap that brought them on. I had stated for the first time that I doubted my mother's motives. As horrible as all the thoughts I'd had about her over the past day had been, actually saying something like that out loud seemed ten times worse. That wasn't who she was. It couldn't have been.

Mama was one of the most loving people in the world. She would've done anything for me, I was certain of it.

Aunt Miriam pulled away. Her makeup ran in a steady stream down her face. "She was a good woman." She brushed away my tears.

"Then why did she do it?" I whispered.

"Things aren't always what they seem."

"Then tell me how they really were."

She pulled a handkerchief from her pocket and dabbed at her eyes. "I wish I could. All I can tell you is that the woman I knew loved you and your father with all of her heart. She would've done anything for either one of you." I didn't respond. I couldn't. How could Mama be both that and a woman considered so contemptible that the police didn't bother to investigate her death? "She was smart, she was kind, she was brave."

"How?" I asked.

"How wasn't she?" asked Miriam. "She came to America and started over. She spent all those years without your father, raising you. She never let anything stand in her way."

She wasn't going to tell me any more—that was clear. Whatever she knew was hers alone. "What happened to her money?" I asked.

"What?"

I hadn't thought much about that one strange piece of the puzzle until then. We'd been comfortable in the years before Mama's death, but the life we lived wasn't just because of a naval officer's salary. Mama had money—an inheritance—that helped provide for the Upper East Side address, the private school, the allowance for treats. When she died and we moved, at first I thought it was simply Pop's way of putting the past behind us so we could move on, but it became clear that we were just scraping by, depending on Mrs. M.'s kindness for those months when AA Investigations could barely pay its phone bill.

"Mama's money," I said now. "What happened to all of it? That's why we moved, right? Why you and Uncle Adam offered to pay for Chapin? The money was all gone."

"I . . . I'm not sure what happened to it. She must've made some . . . unwise decisions." She ran her hand through my hair and tucked a lock behind my ear. "Are you going to be all right, Iris?"

"I don't know," I told Aunt Miriam. "I just feel so lost."

"I know you may not want to hear this, but at moments like this, I feel like the best thing I can do is turn to God for strength."

I didn't open the rest of my gifts.

11

THE NIGHT MOVED SLOWLY. I built a fire and we moved our chairs close to the fireplace for warmth. As the ice storm continued, the lights flickered on and off as the power lines grew weighted down. I found myself wishing I was still with Benny in the air-raid shelter. As cold as it had been there, it seemed even colder here, where secrets ripped the warmth from the air and left Aunt Miriam and me grasping for pleasantries to fill the silence.

It was obvious she was going to be stuck there that night, and I only hoped that Mrs. M. would be able to miraculously make it home and break up our little party.

Aunt Miriam called Uncle Adam and let him know that there was no chance she would be able to get a cab in this weather. While she was on the phone, I spun the radio dial trying to find anything other than static to listen to. I could hear Miriam's low voice as she talked to my uncle. What she said was indistinct until:

"It was my decision and I'm not going to waver from it. We're family. That's what family does."

So Adam didn't like that she had come to see us. He probably hadn't been thrilled that she brought us presents, either. I abandoned my search for a clear radio station just as Miriam ended the call.

"Your uncle Adam says hello," she said cheerfully. I smiled, not sure how to respond. "You know, Iris, we would love to have you come stay with us. Anytime. I know your uncle would love to see you."

It didn't sound that way to me. "It's hard with school and everything."

"You could come over a weekend. In fact, this weekend would be wonderful. That way we could celebrate Hanukah together."

The idea of staying with them just like I had last year at this time didn't sit well with me. I tried to think of a way to explain that to Aunt Miriam, but I was worried that if I did, everything else I was thinking would come out in a rush of words.

"You don't have to answer now," she said. "Just think about it. How about I make us some dinner?" I gave her the tour of the pantry and icebox and then told her I had homework to do and disappeared into the parlor.

Ten minutes later, Pop's phone rang.

I went into the office and in a muffled tone answered the AA Investigations line.

"Iris?"

"Yes?"

"It's Pearl." My momentary confusion at hearing her voice on the office line disappeared. "Thank goodness you're okay. I was so worried when you didn't show up at lunch. And then with the storm and the early dismissal, I didn't know what to think."

"Why are you calling Pop's office line?"

"I tried the house line, but I got a busy signal." Miriam had been talking to Adam, no doubt, when she'd called. "So you're okay?"

"Fine," I said, though my voice was anything but. "There was early dismissal?"

"They canceled afternoon classes and let us out at one-thirty because of the storm. Where did you go?"

I should've told her everything, but with Miriam within ear's reach I had a perfect excuse not to. "I can't really talk right now. My aunt's here."

"Oh. Gotcha. You missed a scene this afternoon, let me tell you. There was another note in one of the federation members' lockers and Paul got jumped on the way home."

"Is he okay?"

"Bruised and bloodied, but he's going to be fine. He lost a tooth, though. Dad's on fire about how much that's going to cost to fix."

"So what happened?"

"These two random boys followed him home, asked him

138

if he was a Jew, then just started hitting him while telling him the war was all his fault. They were by Kamiskey's butcher shop and I guess Mr. Kamiskey himself came out and chased them away."

"Does anyone know who the boys were?"

"Not a clue. Denise was with Paul and she said she'd never seen them before. They're pretty sure they don't go to P.S. 110."

"They didn't hurt Denise, did they?"

"Not a chance." She lowered her voice. "She insisted on coming home with Paul. She's in the parlor with him now, waiting on him hand and foot. Oh, nausea!"

"So do you think these two boys have anything to do with the notes?"

"Iris?" I snapped to attention. Aunt Miriam was standing at the office door, a bewildered look on her face. "What are you doing?"

Boy, howdy—I knew how it looked: me, in Pop's office, on his phone, asking the kinds of questions detectives usually asked. "Just talking to a friend."

"Dinner's ready. You can talk to your *friend* later."

To the phone I said, "I've got to go, Pearl. I'll see you tomorrow, okay?" I put the receiver down before she uttered her own farewell. Aunt Miriam had gone into the dining room, where she was lighting a single candle.

"I couldn't find a menorah, but your landlady has lots of candles. Come join me." I stood beside her, and in a low, rich voice she began to recite the three blessings. The flame danced to her words, threatening, as her timbre rose, to go out completely before once again growing fat and strong. I closed my eyes and thought about the year before, when it was Uncle Adam reciting these words. Mama, Aunt Miriam, and I had been there with him, and though Pearl Harbor was very much on their minds, mine was wondering if this brief return to religious tradition meant that I might be getting presents for the next eight nights.

I did, though with what followed, I couldn't remember what I'd been given if my life depended on it.

Mama had chanted "Hanerot Halalu" that night, her voice turning the words into less of a thank-you for past miracles, and more of a plea for a new miracle: Let Pop's injuries be more benign than we'd been led to believe. Let our entry into the war be brief, the death toll small. Let us find comfort in our families.

Instead, Mama had died. Pop came home without a leg. The war dragged on and Pop exiled us from Adam and Miriam.

I opened up my eyes. Aunt Miriam began to sing "Maoz Tzur," a Hebrew song praising God for helping us to defeat our enemies when our strength failed us.

I didn't bother to join in. A better plea would've been for God to show us who our enemies were to begin with.

* * *

WE WENT TO BED SHORTLY after dinner. Miriam slept in my room and I stayed on the parlor sofa, just in case Pop came home in the middle of the night. An hour after we turned in, when I was just beginning to accept that I wasn't going to be able to sleep, I heard the familiar rattle of a key in the lock. I clicked on the lamp as Mrs. Mrozenski came inside.

"Iris. You are safe. I'm so glad."

I left the sofa and helped her pull off her drenched coat. "Were you stuck at the church?"

She sat on the bench by the front door. "Ten hours I was there. I should get a pass for a month of Sundays. Where is your father?"

I took her discarded boots and put them in the closet. "He's uptown. At Betty's."

"Betty's?"

I shrugged. Did she have any idea what was going on between them? If she didn't, I wasn't sure I wanted to be the one to tell her. "That's what he said when he called. Any idea why he would be there?"

"No. But at least he's somewhere warm and safe." Her eyes fell on the coffee table, where Miriam's teacup and mine still sat. "You have company?"

"My aunt's here. She's sleeping in my room."

"It's good to have visit from family."

I wasn't sure if she was asking a question, so I nodded.

"You look sad," she said.

"Just tired. I was dozing off right before you came home."

"You can have my bed. I sleep down here."

"No, I'm fine. I want to be able to hear Pop when he comes home."

"All right then. Good night." She hesitated, then planted a kiss on top of my head. "Happy dreams, Iris."

I don't know how, but I eventually fell into a fitful sleep. Pop arrived in the early morning hours. He tried to be quiet as he came into the house, but every footfall was a gunshot to my ears.

"Pop?"

He froze at the sound of my voice. I turned on the lamp, as I had when Mrs. Mrozenski arrived, and he straightened up at the sight of me. "Why aren't you in your bed, Iris?"

"I couldn't sleep."

"Me neither," he said. "I was worried about you, all alone in the house. Did the lights go out?"

"No. The phones never stopped working, either."

"Then things are better here than on the west side." He plopped onto the sofa beside me and released the harness that held his leg to his stump. He could do it one-handed now, where before it had been a two-handed task. "Did Mrs. Mrozenski make it home?"

"A few hours ago."

"Good. You'd better head up to bed. I don't think you

can depend on school being canceled today." He turned on the radio and found, as I had earlier, that everything was static.

I hesitated just long enough for him to look up at me questioningly. "I can't sleep in my room. Aunt Miriam is in there."

He raised an eyebrow but didn't reveal the shock I would've expected.

I nodded toward the bag of unwrapped presents still sitting by her chair. "She came by to bring me Hanukah presents but got trapped by the weather. Uncle Adam didn't seem very happy about it," I said.

"I'm sure he wasn't." Pop retrieved the clamshell jeweler's box and opened it. "These look expensive."

"I told her I didn't have any use for them."

He snapped the box closed. "Come now—women always have use for pretty things." It was funny how Pop wielded that word. Sometimes I was a woman to him, sometimes a little girl. "Your mother had a pair like this," he said. "I wonder what happened to them?" He opened the box again. "I'll bet Miriam knows."

Maybe that and so much more, I wanted to say. "So why were you at Betty's?"

He continued looking at the pearls. "Happenstance. I was working a case when the ice started. I knew she lived nearby, so I called her and she was kind enough to give me a place to weather the storm."

"What case were you working on?" I asked.

"Mickey Pryor. His wife has decided she wants photographs to document his infidelity. Bad for Mickey, good for our coffers."

For the first time since I'd found the photographs, things were starting to feel normal. Pop was talking to me, even if he wasn't talking about the things I wanted to talk about. Maybe it would be okay. Maybe I could do as he asked and forget about what I'd seen and things could go back to normal. Would that be so terrible?

"Did you get what you needed?" I asked.

"Nope. The storm threw a hitch in my plans and most likely his, too. I'll try again in a few days." He closed the earring box and tossed it my way. I caught it handily and put it back on the table.

"I could help you," I said.

He looked at me head-on. "I think you need to take a break from the business, Iris."

It was the last thing I expected to hear from him. "Why?"

He held my gaze. "I'm not sure your skills are where we need them to be. First you got made during the tail—"

"I covered that up," I said. "I got the picture."

"And now I've heard from his wife that Mickey Pryor knows someone was calling around asking about him." I'd been too abrupt with the hotel clerk. She must've realized what I was really up to and warned him. "Maybe later, when you've had a little more time to practice, we can reconsider putting you out in the field, but I think it's best if I go it alone for now."

Did he know that I tried to get Mama's death certificate? Had he found out that I'd been to Yorkville? "I could still file and answer the phones, right?"

"Arthur?"

Pop looked toward the stairs, where Aunt Miriam was poised, ready to come down.

"I thought I heard your voice," said Aunt Miriam as she started her descent. "It's good to see you."

"You, too," said Pop. How much of our conversation had she heard?

"Has the ice stopped?"

"Yes. It's warmed up a bit, too."

"Good." She arrived on the first floor and wrapped her arms around herself as though she needed to ward off a chill. "Do you mind if I use your telephone to call for a cab?"

"You don't have to leave now, Miriam. It's awfully early."

"Not for your brother. And you know Adam can't fend for himself." Translation: she didn't want to make him any angrier than necessary. "I brought gifts."

"So Iris told me. That was very kind of you."

"I had such a lovely time with Iris last night. It's so nice to see her."

"You're welcome to visit anytime, Miriam. You know that." She also knew what he didn't say: the same invitation would not be extended to my uncle.

"And Iris is certainly welcome in our home. I know Adam would love to see her. But she seemed hesitant about the idea."

"Did she?" said Pop.

I don't know why I did it. Maybe I was mad at Pop for telling me I couldn't work for him anymore. Maybe I was irritated at the way he'd shut me out over the photographs. Or maybe it was the disappointment in Miriam's eyes. But I spoke up right then and said, "Actually, I've reconsidered. I'd love to spend the weekend with you."

"What?" said Pop.

"Aunt Miriam invited me to stay with Uncle Adam and her this weekend. If it's okay with you."

I expected him to say it wasn't. I was depending on it, in fact. That way I wouldn't look like the bad guy and he could give me some hope that he still wanted me around. But hope, it appeared, was in short supply that morning. "It's fine by me. In fact, I think it's a great idea."

"You could come, too," said Aunt Miriam.

Pop put his free hand on my leg. "I think you know that wouldn't be a good idea. But it would be nice for Iris to get away for a few days. Celebrate Hanukah with your congregation."

"It would?" I said.

"You should spend the whole weekend, if Miriam thinks it's all right."

She brightened at the suggestion. "Of course it is."

So he really was pushing me out. And why? So he could retreat to Betty's love nest?

"Wonderful," said Aunt Miriam. "I'll take a cab to your school on Friday afternoon. That way we can make it to the Upper East Side before the Sabbath begins. You could invite a friend if you like. I know the idea of being all alone with your aunt and uncle must seem terribly dull."

"You should ask Pearl," said Pop. "I bet she'd love to spend the weekend uptown."

"All right." I swallowed hard to keep from crying. Pop wasn't just shutting me out. He was sending me away.

12

POP SENT ME TO BED and told Miriam he'd call her a cab. When I woke a few hours later, Miriam was gone and Pop was on the phone in his office. He gestured as I passed his open door, asking me without words to close it for him.

I pushed it a little harder than was necessary.

I finished getting ready and ate a piece of toast for breakfast. Then I headed for school without bothering to tell him goodbye.

Let him stew on that, I thought. Let him know how it feels to be shut out.

Pearl was waiting for me just outside Mrs. M.'s house.

"Hi," I said, startled to find her there.

"So what's the scoop?" she asked. "Why was your aunt there last night?"

Pearl knew that Pop didn't speak to Aunt Miriam and Uncle Adam. She also knew Miriam had gotten me in trouble several weeks before. It hadn't occurred to me how strange and mysterious my claim that Miriam was in the house must have seemed when I had to abruptly hang up the phone the night before.

"She brought Hanukah gifts," I said.

"That was nice." She looked disappointed. She was expecting drama and all I had to offer were seasonal tidings. "I thought maybe something bad had happened to someone in your family, you know, and that's why you left school early. I'm glad that's not the case."

Now that she had no reason to be worried, I could see irritation creeping into Pearl's face. After all, I'd abandoned her yesterday. She deserved an explanation.

"Can you go to my aunt's with me this weekend?" I asked. "She invited me and a friend to stay with them."

"Seriously? Sure. I mean, I'll have to check, but I don't think my parents will mind."

"Good." It would be easier with Pearl there. It was going to be awkward enough spending an entire weekend with them; having someone to distract me from dwelling on what Pop was doing during his time without me would make things much, much easier. "Is Paul better?"

"He seems to be. He's coming to school, anyway. Probably wants to show off his war wounds so he can be a big man on campus." I could tell she was biting back the urge to demand to know where I'd been the day before. I relented before she exploded.

"I went to Yorkville. With Benny."

She couldn't have been more confused if I'd just said I'd journeyed to the moon with F.D.R. "Huh?"

"That's where I was yesterday. I went to find Anna Mueller."

Her mouth flapped uselessly like a puppet's. There were just too many disparate elements for her to assemble. "And did you?"

I slowed my pace, recognizing that this was a story that was bound to take longer than the walk to school would allow. As Pearl listened in silence, I told her about my trip to Yorkville, accompanied by a boy who I didn't think wanted to talk to me, much less help me with something like this. I described the run-down hotel and the terrible room still stained by my mother's blood, the man who'd held us at gunpoint, the ex-wife who had allowed her silence to be bought, and the strange, sad afternoon we'd spent in an air-raid shelter.

I told her everything. Everything except that my mother was, according to Anna Mueller, a Nazi. As far as Pearl knew, the story ended as soon as Anna admitted that she'd been paid to lie that Mama had committed suicide.

I just couldn't bring myself to say the words out loud. And the story was strange and awful enough not to need that meaningless twist. Wasn't it enough to know that Mama had been murdered?

"So Anna confirmed everything. What about the police,

though? They must've known that it was a murder, not a suicide. You said there was blood everywhere."

"Anna said the man bribed the police, too." Despite my attempts to slow our pace, we'd arrived at school.

"But who was he?"

"That's the thousand-dollar question. Anna said she saw him going into Mama's room several times. Whoever it was couldn't have been a casual acquaintance."

I stopped walking. Why hadn't I thought of this before? Anna's accusation had so blindsided me that I hadn't realized that Mama's real crime was staring me right in the face. "Oh, God. It must've been true."

"What?"

"The rumors about the affair."

I was going to be sick. That was why Pop felt no shame about starting a new relationship before his wife's headstone was even unveiled. She *had* been cheating on him.

But with whom?

"You can't know that for certain," said Pearl. "There are lots of reasons why a man might visit a woman at a hotel."

"Such as?"

I could tell she was pulling the first available theory out of the sky. "Maybe he was a relative."

"She doesn't have any family here. The ones who brought her over are all dead and gone."

It was obvious Pearl was out of examples. We walked in

silence until we entered school property. I could feel Pearl struggling to find a way to change the subject. "That was really nice of Benny, to go with you like that. I wouldn't have expected him to do that."

"You and me both." It still felt like a dream, his being there to help me the day before. Someday, when all this business with Mama was behind me, I'd have time to reflect on what Benny had done. But for now I had to set it aside.

There were much bigger issues demanding my attention.

"Do you think you can find a way to excuse our absences yesterday?" I asked Pearl.

"Sure."

"And maybe filch a handful of hall passes?"

"Why?"

"Benny asked for them."

Pearl shifted her books from one side to the other. "They keep pretty close tabs on those."

"All he needs are two or three."

"I'll see what I can do."

"So tell me about the new note," I said. "Who got it? Did this one have anything in it?"

"Sarah Stein was the recipient. And there was a pamphlet in it from a pro-German group. Pretty awful stuff."

"So I should talk to her and Saul. What about the lockers? Do you want to do another stakeout today?"

"You know what? Let's not worry about it today. You've got a lot on your mind."

"I could use the distraction, Pearl."

Her eyes danced toward the front steps of the building. Benny was there with the other Rainbows, leaning against the banister with a sort of ease that suggested he'd been there for a while. When I saw him, he raised a hand just enough to let me know that he saw me, without alerting his friends to my presence. "Let's talk about it over lunch."

"Okay."

The bell rang. I drifted away with a casual "See you later, alligator" and headed toward first period. On my way there, I passed Paul and Denise. His face was a fright of bruises. He smiled my way, showing off the missing eyetooth his father was so angry about having to replace.

I returned the smile and mouthed "Ow" at him.

As I approached the classroom for Personal Hygiene, Michael Rosenberg appeared. "I was hoping I might run into you. Did you hear about the new note?"

"The one Sarah got. Yeah—Pearl told me about it."

"This was in it." He thrust a pamphlet toward me, deliberately hiding the cover with his hand. I took it from him and caught a glimpse of it before shoving it in my health-and-hygiene book. "How to Solve the Jewish Problem," it read.

I wished I could unsee it, but then I wished I could unsee a lot of things these days.

"We're getting a little frustrated," he said.

"I imagine so."

"If you don't think you can catch whoever's doing this, you need to tell me."

And then what? "No, I'm sure we'll be able to do it. We just need more time."

"Just don't take too much," said Michael. Benny walked by us. Michael waved his way. "Hey, Benny."

Benny returned the "Hey" and kept on walking.

"I didn't know you knew Benny," I said, grateful for the change in topic.

"He works for my dad."

"Oh."

"He's a good guy." Michael winked at me. "But I guess you already know that."

Michael knew about Benny and me? Had Benny said something?

Before I could ask, he said, "I'll see you later," and disappeared down the hall.

I went to Personal Hygiene and opened my book. The page I landed on, unfortunately, was where I'd shoved the pamphlet.

Did Mama distribute these kinds of pamphlets?

Stop it, Iris. Why was I trusting the word of a woman who was so slippery morally that she accepted money in exchange for the truth?

Mama wasn't a Nazi. She couldn't have been. Her devotion last Hanukah, the way she insisted we be observant after Pop was injured, she couldn't have faked that. And there was no way she suddenly lost her faith in the days between when Hanukah ended and her body was found. Which meant that if someone thought she was a Nazi they'd gotten it wrong.

But why?

Because they knew that if they claimed she was a Nazi, the police would have no reason to investigate the crime?

By lunchtime I was all but convinced that that had to be the case. I joined Pearl at our usual table and dug into the day's hot meal of chili with surprising gusto. My appetite was back, even for food that hardly earned such enthusiasm.

"You seem better," said Pearl.

"Do I?" It all seemed so desperately absurd that I had to fight the urge to laugh. Sure, I'd just tell Pearl, *The good news is I'm positive my mother's not a Nazi. The bad news is, she's still dead.*

"Just thinking about something Benny said," I said. "I talked to Michael this morning. He said the group is losing patience."

"I'm not surprised," said Pearl.

I looked toward where Paul was having lunch with Denise Halloway. They weren't alone. Michael was there, too, and a couple of other boys I recognized from the federation. Despite the injuries, Paul was engaged in an animated conversation with the other boys.

"Well, if nothing else good comes out of all of this, it at least looks like the group is banding closer together. If the note-writer was hoping they'd disband, they're sorely mistaken."

"Paul says some people are still on the fence," said Pearl. "But it is amazing what people will do when faced with a challenge."

Denise looked around the room, clearly bored with whatever the federation members were talking about.

"Denise looks like she'd rather be anywhere but that table," I said.

"She's worried about Paul. She kept going on and on yesterday about how stupid it was that he told those boys he was Jewish."

"Why did he tell them that?"

"Pride, I guess. He didn't want to hide who he was."

"Do you think it would've mattered if he hadn't said anything?" I asked.

"Of course not. And even if it did, it's offensive, isn't it? I mean, she's acting like it's his fault that they targeted him. Personally, I think he should break up with her."

I didn't know Denise very well. She seemed nice enough, but there had to be something off about her if she thought Paul hung the stars and the moon. "You really think this is worth him ending his relationship with her?"

"Eh. She's whistle bait. She'll find someone else. And besides, it's not like they're going to get married."

"Because she's not Jewish?"

"No, because he is."

I was confused. "Isn't that what I just said?"

Pearl lowered her voice. "Paul told me her parents don't know. And that they'd never allow her to see him if they did."

I probably should've been shocked, but after living most of my life on the Upper East Side, the situation struck me as par for the course. It was okay to be a Jew among Jews, but you'd best keep it to yourself in a room full of Protestants.

"Hey, Pearl Harbor," called a boy to our right. "I hear it's almost your birthday."

"Bombs away!" said another boy as he chucked a wad of paper in her direction. It missed its target and fell to the floor.

"Ignore them. So how about we do another stakeout this afternoon?" I said.

"I can't."

"Why not?"

She stared at the floor, where the paper missile waited to be picked up. "I promised my mom I'd come home right after school."

"All right. Why don't I do it by myself then?"

She looked lost for a second. "Why don't we just take the day off?"

"Michael's pretty anxious. I don't think he'd appreciate our taking another day off."

Her eyes finally left the floor. "It seems silly, though. After what happened to Paul, the note-writer probably wants to lie low for a while."

"I thought you didn't think that the notes and what happened to Paul were related."

"I don't, but if you didn't want to get caught, you would probably want people to think that the person writing the notes and the people who beat up Paul were one and the same, right?"

It made sense, I guess, but it seemed like Pearl was making an awful lot of assumptions.

"Maybe tomorrow?" I said.

"Sure. Maybe tomorrow."

The afternoon passed slowly but uneventfully. I dreaded going home. I couldn't stomach the thought of being shut out of Pop's office and passing the evening with nothing to do but obsess over what Mama had done in her final days. I thought about trying to angle a dinner invitation to Pearl's. After all, it was the third night of Hanukah. It might be nice to celebrate with her and her family.

I waited for her in our usual after-school meeting spot, but she never showed. After ten minutes and no Pearl, I went back into the school and checked the hall where her locker was located. She wasn't there. I went by the newspaper office and her other haunts, but they, too, proved fruitless. Feeling discouraged, I decided to walk the halls one more time, just in case she hadn't headed home as quickly as she planned. That's when I spied her in the upperclassman hallway, pushing a note through the vents of a locker.

13

PEARL DIDN'T SEE ME. I doubled back and turned a corner, hugging the wall while I caught my breath. Surely I hadn't seen what I thought I'd seen. Pearl couldn't possibly be the one leaving the notes.

Could she?

No. She was just leaving a note for someone completely unrelated to the federation. People did it all the time. Lockers weren't just places we stashed books, lunches, and gym clothes—they were mailboxes where you deposited notes for friends on your way to your next class.

Except this was the end of the day. A day when she'd begged me not to do the stakeout.

Her footsteps started loud and grew faint as she headed down the hall away from me. She'd been in a hurry, that was clear. Was she worried she was about to get caught?

I was being ridiculous. This was Pearl I was talking about, Pearl who insisted on helping out the federation.

More footsteps sounded. I peeked around the corner and spied Judy Cohen, one of the federation members. I willed her to pick up her pace and walk past the locker I'd just seen Pearl at. No such luck. She paused at the door, spun her combination, and pulled it open. It took her only a second to find the note. She let out an audible gasp and then dropped the piece of paper. It floated to the floor, coming perilously close to her feet. She jumped backward to avoid contact with it.

She looked up the hallway, toward where Pearl had exited. I could tell she was about to look in my direction next, so I receded around the corner, out of sight.

This didn't make sense. What would Pearl have to gain by leaving the notes? Clearly she didn't believe what was written in them (just like Mama couldn't possibly have espoused what Anna claimed she had). Was it revenge for being kicked out of the federation? If so, why drag me into it? Why insist that we help them figure out who was behind the notes if she was the one writing them all along?

I headed out of the building and into the cold, dark day. I didn't want to go home, but the idea of confronting Pearl was even less inviting to me.

"Iris."

I turned at the sound of the voice and found Benny standing behind me.

"What are you still doing here?" I asked.

"Detention. You?"

"Tutoring." Why the lie? Pearl. I already felt like I had to protect her.

"Tell Pearl Harbor thanks for taking care of everything yesterday. Another absence would've given me detention until the end of the year. You get those passes?"

"She's working on it."

"You look rattled."

"I'm fine." I realized how hollow the lie sounded. How could I not be rattled with everything that had been going on? "I mean I have a lot on my mind."

"Sure, and who could blame you." He shuffled his feet. One of his shoes had a hole where the leather met the sole. "Where you headed?"

"Home, I guess."

"You don't sound too happy about that."

I shrugged. If anyone knew how unpleasant my home life was these days, it had to be the boy who'd journeyed with me to Yorkville.

"You want to go somewhere for a while?"

With you? I almost asked before realizing that it would be better to hide my surprise. "Sure. That would be swell."

WE WENT BACK to the air-raid shelter. The items we'd used the day before remained where we'd left them. I was surprised no one else used the space, but then I guess if you had the option of being in a nice warm apartment instead of a metal bomb shelter, you'd choose the more permanent residence in a second.

In fact, I was starting to second-guess our decision the minute we arrived. Had it been this cold the day before? Or had I been too upset to notice how I could see my own breath even when the door was closed?

"I have a surprise for you," said Benny. He pulled a small bottle from his pocket. I thought it might be booze and was trying to think of how to politely decline. He unscrewed the top and, instead of taking a swig, poured it into the top of the Aladdin heater. "Can't keep it going too long, but it's something." Within minutes, the heater began to cough a steady stream of warm air. We both moved toward it until only inches separated us from it.

And each other.

"That's great. Really great," I said. "Where did you get it from?" I don't know why I asked. Probably just to make conversation. But the look on his face made me instantly regret it. "Oh," I said. He'd stolen it; that was clear.

I'd been told Benny was a thief, that he was no stranger to trouble, but aside from trolling Harlem dance clubs and skipping class, I'd never seen him do anything wrong. It was unsettling to discover that the rumors were true. And, I must confess, for someone like me who had spent most of her life trying to walk the straight and narrow, maybe it was just a little exciting.

"I brought this, too," he said, pulling a flask from his other pocket. This one was undeniably booze—I could smell it the minute he removed the cap. I'd drunk alcohol only one time before—the first night I went to Harlem—and had gotten in enough trouble with Pop to lose the taste for the stuff for good. But the idea of refusing it now, after responding the way I did to the kerosene, seemed like it would magnify our differences until the inches that separated us became miles. And right then I needed someone in my life that I could be close to.

"Want a tickle?" He offered it to me first and I took it without hesitation. Warmth passed through me, removing the little bit of chill the heater had failed to kill. I took another swig and closed my eyes as the booze took hold of me.

"Better?" he said.

"Warmer."

"I thought for sure you'd turn it down."

"I'm not a hair shirt," I said.

"I didn't say you were."

Was he disappointed in me? Maybe I should've said no, but after the past twenty-four hours I needed something to get me through the day. "I guess you never really know what someone's capable of," I said, echoing Pearl. And how ironic that she'd been the one saying it. Was everyone hiding an awful secret from me?

I returned the flask to Benny and waited for him to partake, but instead of doing so, he replaced the cap and

163

put it in his pocket. "Let me know if you want another swallow."

"You're not having any?"

He shook his head. "I don't touch the stuff."

"Why not?"

"Because maybe then I won't turn out like him."

There was a time when the idea of someone disliking their parents would've shocked me. Oh, my spoiled, rich friends sometimes went on about how they couldn't stand their mothers or fathers, but that was about strict rules, limited allowances, and suffocating expectations. And I knew things would reverse with the next fancy party or expensive gift.

"Do you hate him?" I asked Benny.

"Hate takes too much energy." He rubbed his hands together. Unlike me, he didn't have gloves. I hadn't realized that before. "What about you? If what that woman said is true, would you hate your mother?"

"No," I said without thinking. How could I hate her? She'd always been good to me. Her sex life and political beliefs had nothing to do with me. "Besides, I know it's not true. You should've seen Mama last Hanukah. You can't fake that kind of faith."

His face creased. "She was Jewish?"

"We all are."

Benny made a little sound that I took to be surprise. Did my being Jewish bother him? I couldn't tell. And, honestly?

164

I didn't care. "So why would a Jew go to Yorkville?" he asked.

"She was a German Jew. There was a time when Yorkville was her home." Could she still have felt that way after the war started, though? It didn't seem possible. Sixteen years ago, when Pop was courting her, it was a completely different place. Once Hitler came to power, there'd been a concerted effort to push the Jewish businesses out of the neighborhood. It was hardly a place where she would've felt welcomed. "And besides, Anna said she was with that man. He must've been the reason she went there. I'm pretty sure she was having an affair."

"But why Yorkville?"

"Maybe he was another German. Or maybe they thought they wouldn't be recognized there," I said.

"So she's having an affair and what? She decides to end it and the man kills her?"

I hadn't made it that far in my thinking, but I'd read enough accounts of crimes of passion to know that circumstances like these were usually at their root. "It makes sense, right? And then the man tells everyone she was a Nazi to keep the police from investigating what happened." I waved my glove-clad hands in front of the heater.

Benny took my hand. "You still cold?" he asked.

I was shaking, but it wasn't from the temperature. "A little."

His other hand joined his first, making a sandwich of

mine. Despite my glove, I could feel his warmth radiating through the wool.

I put my other hand into the mix and let him gather both of them in his hold.

"That better?" he asked.

"Much." I kept my eyes rooted on our hands, worried that if I looked right at him I'd be too embarrassed to let him continue touching me.

"Hey."

I looked up at his voice and found him staring at me. Before I could untangle what the look meant, he leaned toward me and kissed me.

It was so much better than that first kiss we'd had weeks before. I'd been tipsy that time, too, and completely taken off guard when he kissed me on the dance floor. This time I was ready to feel his lips on mine, ready when one of his hands left my hold and gently eased into my hair. He tasted like penny candy, Royal Cola, cigarettes, and a flavor I had to imagine was his alone. It shouldn't have tasted good, yet when he started to pull away, I put a hand on his neck and pulled him back.

His skin on mine, his lips on mine—I tried to memorize the sensation. I had plenty of time. This kiss went on for so long that I felt compelled to open my eyes to make sure I wasn't boring him.

I found him staring back at me.

"Oh," I said, and finally released the hold I had on his neck.

"What's wrong?" he asked.

"Nothing." We kissed again and this time I didn't open my eyes and waited for him to be the one to pull away. Heat coursed from my lips to my toes and continued to boil even after he released me. "I'm not cold anymore," I told him.

"Good." His hand left my hair and again took hold of my hands.

We returned to silence and I wondered which of us would be the first to break it. I decided I would be the brave one and jumped right in. "What are you thinking about?"

"Did your mom look, you know, Jewish?"

"Huh?" It wasn't exactly what I was expecting to hear him say.

"I was just thinking how it was in Yorkville the other day. It had to be like that last year, too, right? The way it felt like everyone was watching us. I was just wondering what it had to be like if you were Jewish."

"I am Jewish, remember?"

"Yeah, but not . . . I mean . . . uh, this is coming out upside down. I'm just wondering if she looked more like you or Michael Rosenberg."

"She looked like me," I said. The conversation was making me really uncomfortable, though I wasn't sure why. "I didn't realize you worked for Michael's dad."

"Yeah. He's a nice guy. Both of them are."

"Strangely enough, I'm working for Michael, too," I said.

"At the store?"

"No. At school. As a detective. Michael hired me to find out who's been leaving nasty notes in the Jewish Student Federation's lockers."

"Huh." His hands were no longer touching mine. My fingers bent instinctively, searching for the return of his touch. "What do the notes say?"

"Awful anti-Semitic stuff. It's not worth repeating."

"Are you close to cracking the case?"

"Not really." I thought of Pearl pushing her note through the locker vents. Could I tell on her, even if I knew it was the right thing to do? "I'm starting to think I'm not a very good detective."

If he was listening to me, he didn't show it. "It's getting late," said Benny. "I better bounce before I'm late for work." He stood up and instantly the cold air bored back into my bones.

"Okay. Well, thanks for everything." I leaned into him and gave him a quick kiss. "I'll see you tomorrow?"

"Sure. Tomorrow." And with that, he left.

I MADE IT HOME just before six o'clock. I delayed my arrival long enough to stop off at the five-and-dime and buy some chewing gum. I gnawed on the wad for four blocks, hoping to get rid of the liquor smell on my breath. It was going to be bad enough being yelled at for coming home late; I didn't want to add boozing to my list of crimes.

I entered the house and found Pop's door closed. It was clear he was in there, though, talking to someone. That was fine. If he'd decided that he'd rather have me out of his hair than deal with me, then out of his hair I would be.

"Ah, Iris—is you." Mrs. Mrozenski appeared near the kitchen, a dish towel in her hands. "I get worried."

"I'm sorry," I said. "I had a meeting after school." The lie came too easily and I hated myself for it. What happened to being honest with everyone from here on out? I guess it didn't matter when it was clear Pop wasn't doing the same.

"I hear you go to your aunt's this weekend."

"Yeah. Pop seemed to think it would be a good idea." I nodded toward the closed office door. "Who's in there?"

"I don't know," she said. "Client, I guess. I have food when you ready."

I told her I'd be in shortly, that I needed to wash up first. As soon as she disappeared back into the kitchen, I crouched before Pop's door and peered through the vent. I was half expecting to find Betty, but instead saw what was clearly a man. As I watched, he stood up and turned so that he was facing the door. He looked familiar. I knew I'd seen him before but I couldn't recall where.

They were nearing the end of their conversation. I left the floor and bounced to the sofa. There was nothing on the coffee table to use to hide my interest, so I picked up the photo of Mama and tried to act like I was studying it.

Pop's door opened. The man exited, saw me, tipped his hat, and offered a smile. And just like that I knew where I'd seen him: he was the man I'd tailed the previous weekend, the one whose picture I'd taken after he'd confronted me for following him.

But why was he here?

I didn't know what to say. Had he tracked me down? Was Pop in trouble? Pop appeared in the doorway behind him, a look on his face that made it clear he would've preferred if the man had made a sharp right and never paused in his path. "I'll see you out, Jim," he told him.

They both walked out the door. I dashed after them to

observe what was going on from the small window that butted against the doorjamb. They were on the sidewalk, talking. Both men were smiling. There was something almost collegiate about them, like two old friends who'd spent the afternoon catching up. They shook hands and exchanged some parting words that were impossible to hear from inside the house.

What was going on? This wasn't a confrontation at all.

Rather than returning to the sofa before Pop came inside, I stayed by the door and waited for him. He was startled to see me. I didn't give him a chance to speak.

"You know him," I said.

He was going to play innocent, that much was clear. "What do you mean?"

"That man. Jim. He's the one I followed for you last weekend. You know him."

He didn't say anything. He didn't need to.

"He wasn't a real client," I said. "That wasn't a real job. I didn't mess up and draw attention to myself. He knew I was there all along."

He looked ready to argue with me but something made him decide against it. He showed me his palms as though to let me know that he was giving up. "It was a test."

"You told me that was part of the reason you wanted me out of the business for now."

"You didn't handle it as well as I hoped you might."

I put my hands on my hips. "It wasn't a fair test."

"I'm not going to argue with you about this, Iris."

"What about all those hotel calls I made? Were those a test, too? Is Mickey Pryor for real or just another phantom you have me chasing?"

His face told me everything. All those hours of work, save the filing I did, had been for nothing. "I couldn't put you in the field until I was certain I knew you could handle yourself."

"So why was he here? To give you a full report of what happened?"

"Jim and I had other business to attend to. It's no concern of yours."

I stared him down. This whole thing had been a farce. Pop had never trusted me from the get-go. And here I thought he was shutting me out, when the truth was I'd never been let in to begin with. "Yeah, it's no concern of mine. Just like Mama."

He returned my glare. I thought for a moment that he might tear into me for that, and God help me if he had.

"Iris? Homework?" said Pop.

"Pop? Dinner?" I said, in a snotty voice I didn't regret one bit.

He turned tail and left the room. I was so frustrated that I picked up the photo of Mama and threw it against the wall as hard as I could. I wanted a satisfying smash to underscore my anger, but all I got was a wimpy crunch as the corner of the wooden frame detached and the picture came tumbling out. Instantly I regretted my actions. I fell to my knees to rescue Mama from any further damage and gathered up her photo, the pieces of wood, and the cardboard backing that used to hold it all in place. As I worked to reassemble everything, a piece of notepaper caught my eye. It was a letter that had been wedged between the photo and the frame's backing:

Dear Ingrid,

I know you're angry with me, but please know that I am only thinking of your best interest. We must stop this immediately, for Art's sake as well as our own. I know you're heartbroken at the thought of it, but please think about what we're doing to my brother.

Adam

I gasped and then clamped my hand over my mouth. Adam was the man Mama was involved with? How could that be? And did that mean Uncle Adam was the one who—?

I didn't get to finish the thought. Mrs. Mrozenski called me in to dinner. I shoved the photo under the couch and dutifully followed her into the kitchen.

DINNER WAS VIRTUALLY SILENT. Pop and Mrs. M. made small talk about the weather (cold) and the war (bad) while I shifted food around my plate and tried to feign eating. Pop seemed as oblivious to my lack of appetite as he was to the booze on my breath. Mrs. M. was a bit more wary.

"Something on your mind, Iris?"

Boy, howdy, was there. Pop doesn't trust me. He's covering up that my mom, who may have been sleeping with my uncle, was murdered. My best friend is leaving anti-Jewish propaganda in people's lockers. And the boy I think I love kissed me for the second time today and then got weird and left.

Also, I'm a little drunk.

"Just tired," I said.

"Early to bed tonight," said Mrs. M. "It would be good for you, too, Arthur. You have shadows under your eyes."

Pop did, too. In fact, he looked a lot older to me all of a sudden, which was saying something. "I've actually got to work tonight, but don't worry—I'm getting my rest."

He was probably exhausted from having to do his real casework and make up imaginary tasks for me. Oh, and Betty—don't forget Betty. He had fifteen years on her. Keeping up with her had to take a lot of energy.

Why was I getting upset about that? Mama and Uncle Adam were . . . they were . . .

Pop wiped his mouth, dropped his napkin, and rose from his seat. "In fact, I should head out now. Thanks for the meal. It was delicious, as always. You're in for the night, Iris."

It was an order, not a question. "Where would I go?"

He didn't answer me. Instead, he left the room and I helped Mrs. M. clean the dishes and put them away.

"You have another fight?" she asked me once the front door closed and we knew he was on his way.

"He doesn't want me working for him anymore."

"Why not?"

I shrugged.

"Maybe after Monday he change his mind."

Monday? That was right—the anniversary of Pearl Harbor. I'd forgotten about that. It had to be weighing on him, too. Not that I cared.

"I'm not sure why it would," I said.

"If he knows he is safe now, maybe he think you'll be safe now, too," she said.

It was a nice thought, but I didn't think an anniversary could change how little he trusted me.

I left her alone and went into the parlor. The phone rang and Mrs. M. answered it. The call was obviously for her; after the initial greeting she switched to rapid-fire Polish.

It reminded me of Mama.

I dug the photo out from under the couch and read the note again. How could I have missed it? We saw so much of Uncle Adam in the months before Mama died. We ate at Adam and Miriam's house at least once a week, but Adam was a constant fixture at our house, too. Sometimes Miriam came with him and entertained me while Mama and he sat in the dining room talking in low voices. Other times it was just my uncle, and I was told to occupy myself while they disappeared behind closed doors.

What else could it have been but an affair?

Did Pop know? It would certainly explain why Adam and he were no longer speaking. Maybe he'd gotten as far as I had on the case and decided he couldn't bear to learn any more. It was one thing to lose your wife so brutally, but to find out that your brother might be behind it all—

I shook the idea out of my head and approached Pop's office. He'd left it unlocked, at least, though I was willing to bet he'd triple-checked that the safe was secure. The desk was clean. Whatever notes had been there had been stored away before he'd left the house. I opened the top desk drawer to see if he might have pushed them in there, but it was virtually empty. All it contained were pens, pencils, paper clips, and a business card.

For McCain and Sons, Investigations.

I picked up the card and examined it more closely. Jim McCain's name and exchange were on the card, along with an uptown address for his office. So Jim—if this was the same Jim that had been at the house earlier—was a detective. Why had Pop used another detective to help him test me? The card certainly didn't answer my question, but at least it reassured me of one thing: if Pop did get in over his head trying to do his work without me, he had someone to help him.

I DIDN'T SLEEP. Again. Pop returned in the wee hours of the morning. I heard him pause at my door, but he never bothered to open it to see if I was in there. If he had, I would've pretended I was asleep.

When morning finally came I decided that the best thing I could do was unravel one mystery at a time. I'd start with Pearl and what was really going on with the notes and then worry about Mama and Uncle Adam. But as I arrived at Pearl's house to walk with her to school, my determination to get answers faded. How could I accuse her of something like that? Pearl's whole existence had been reduced to being the school punch line because of the unfortunate coincidence of her first name. Didn't she deserve to have one person in her corner?

Besides, there was a part of me that lacked the courage to accuse my best friend of being an anti-Semite. It was right up there with accusing my mother of being the same. In both cases it was just completely illogical, no matter what the evidence showed.

"Iris," she said, her surprise showing as she left her house and found me waiting for her. "What are you doing here?"

"I got an early start and figured I'd walk with you."

"Is everything all right?"

I shook my head as we started walking. "I'm pretty sure I know who the man was that my mom was seeing in Yorkville."

"Who is he?"

"My uncle." I told her about the note, about how much sense their illicit relationship made in retrospect. She didn't argue with my interpretation of things, though I sorely wished she would. "I don't know what to do."

"Just because they had a relationship doesn't mean he was the man in Yorkville."

"I don't know that I find it reassuring that she may have been seeing more than one man. Besides, the tone of his letter was desperate. He knew it was going to be hard to persuade her to end things. Does that sound like she was seeing more than one person?"

"I guess not." Pearl hummed under her breath, like she was about to say something else but squelched it. We traveled half a block in silence. "Would he have the kind of power to pay off the cops, though?"

I knew Uncle Adam had paid the police for information. Most private eyes relied on bribes, at least the ones who could afford them. And while he wasn't exactly rolling in dough, Miriam was. He could've used her money to buy off the police.

Or Mama's.

That was the piece of the puzzle that still hadn't been explained: what happened to Mama's money. Miriam said Mama had made some bad financial decisions, but wasn't it possible that Adam had gotten access to what she had and used it to buy off the police and Anna Mueller?

"How do you prove it?" asked Pearl after I explained to her what I was thinking.

"I guess I start by confirming it was him. I could show Uncle Adam's picture to Anna and see if she recognizes him." Of course, that meant getting a picture of him. "We could steal one from his apartment this weekend."

Pearl frowned.

"What's the matter?" I asked.

"I'm just wondering why she would keep that letter."

"If she loved him, she probably wanted to keep any memento she could of him."

"But this wasn't a love letter, Iris. He was breaking up with her. Who keeps a letter like that? And why hide it in her picture when she had to know that someday you or your pop might stumble on it."

I shrugged. It seemed like a minor point to focus on. "I'm sure she just put it there temporarily. And I've saved plenty of things that have bad memories attached to them."

"Really?"

"Sure," I said, though I couldn't think of a single instance of my doing so.

"What time are we leaving tomorrow?"

"Right after school. Can you bring your bag with you? My aunt's going to pick us up in a cab."

"We're going to take a cab all the way uptown?" She let out a low whistle. "They must be rich."

My eyes drifted, as they always did, toward the front of the building, where Benny was holding court with the other Rainbows. I kept hoping he might look my way, that we could share a secret, knowing smile, but he remained focused on Suze and Rhona, who were telling him some animated tale.

What had happened yesterday? What had suddenly made him cool off? Had I made a mistake kissing him? Or was it the tangled tale of what was going on in my family that made him lose interest?

Pearl cleared her throat. "Have you talked to him again?"

I hummed a yes. We entered the building and headed toward our lockers. "We kind of spent the afternoon together yesterday. And we kissed. A lot." If her eyebrow had gone any higher it would no longer have been attached to her face.

"Are you going to see him again this afternoon?"

"I don't know. He might have to work." I felt jittery, though I wasn't sure if it was the topic or the little sleep I'd gotten. "It didn't end so well yesterday. I mean, he got really weird right before we separated."

We paused before Pearl's locker. "Why?"

"I'm not sure."

"Well, what did you two talk about?"

"Mama. My being Jewish. He didn't know that, believe it or not."

Pearl worked her combination lock. "Then that's probably what it was."

"You think Benny was bothered that I'm Jewish?"

"Who knows? Either way, I guess it's good that you found
out now, before he really broke your heart."

I didn't have a chance to respond because just then a
note that had been shoved into her locker lost its hold and
fluttered to the ground.

CHAPTER

15

PEARL FROZE AND STARED at the note. When it became obvious that she wasn't going to pick it up, I did. I unfurled the page and looked down at what was now familiar handwriting: "Jews Are Not Wanted Here. Heed the Warning, or Pay the Price Like Your Brother Did."

"Oh, God," said Pearl. She looked like she was going to be sick. If she wrote the note, she was one heck of a performer. But then if she wrote the note, wouldn't it be in her handwriting?

"Why would they target you?" I asked. "You're not even in the federation."

"Maybe they don't know I was kicked out. Or maybe they saw me doing the stakeout and decided I'd earned a warning, too."

Or maybe Pearl knew she was close to being found out and decided the best way to get the heat off her was to turn herself into a victim.

The warning bell rang and Pearl slammed her locker shut. "Here," I said, passing her the note.

She pushed it back toward me. "I don't want it."

"Michael might. Or Paul."

"So everyone can get even more scared and drop out of the federation?"

Nothing was making sense. "It's evidence," I said.

"Then you hold on to it. I'm done."

Naturally Pearl's words stayed with me, especially when I arrived at lunch and found her missing. I approached Paul's table and waited for a break in the conversation before asking where she was.

"She went home with a stomachache," he said, making it clear from his tone that he thought the source of her malady was something else entirely. He looked at Michael and Saul and the three of them started cracking up.

"What's so funny?" I asked.

"I hear her Aunt Flo's visiting," said Saul.

"And that she's decorating the place with roses to get ready for her arrival," said Paul.

"I guess that means both of them will be seeing red," said Michael.

"You, too?" I said. It was universal. Whether you were Jewish or not, all boys thought period jokes were hysterical.

Denise landed an elbow in Paul's ribs, abruptly putting a stop to the hilarity.

"Nice," I said. "Can I talk to you for a minute, Paul?"

"Sure." He left his seat and followed me toward the lunch line.

"It just so happens that your sister is upset."

"About what? Did somebody threaten to bomb her ship?" His missing tooth gave him a slight whistle when he talked.

"No, she got a note this morning that threatened to do to her what was done to you."

"Oh." The news squashed his grin before I did it for him. "Why didn't Pearl tell me?"

I rolled my eyes. "Given your history of sensitivity, I can't imagine why she didn't. She's probably trying to protect the federation. She doesn't want to be the reason the group breaks up."

Paul didn't look so convinced. "They think it's her," he said.

"What?"

"Saul, Natalie, Ira, Sarah, Judy—they all think Pearl's the one writing the notes."

"But you and Michael don't?"

He shrugged. "My sister's an odd duck. I wouldn't put anything past her."

"You've read the notes, Paul. She couldn't write those things. And besides, why would she do it? To break up the group because they don't want her around? If that was her plan, she's failed. It sounds like the only thing the notes have done is convince everyone that the group has to stay together."

"Not everyone. Some people are still on the fence."

"Who?"

"Me for one."

"Seriously?"

"I lost a tooth," he said, pointing at the gaping black hole in his mouth that hardly needed to be highlighted.

"So you think your sister hired someone to beat you up?"

He didn't answer. He had to realize how absolutely absurd the idea was.

"If you honestly think Pearl is behind this, why would you even think about leaving the group? Don't you realize how stupid that sounds?"

"This isn't about me." He turned his head slightly. I followed his line of sight back to the table where the federation was sitting. Denise was staring back at him.

"Denise is making you drop out," I said.

"She's not making me do anything. If I drop out it's my decision. And don't change the subject: we're talking about Pearl."

"Right. So what happens now? Is everyone going to accuse Pearl to her face?"

"We're kind of hoping you could do it for us."

"We? You mean Michael is in on this, too?"

"We're a democracy."

That old chestnut again. I looked toward the federation table. It seemed to me that Michael was making a concerted effort not to look my way. "Forget it. I'm not your lackey."

"No, but you are working for us."

"To solve the case, Paul, not to be your messenger. And I haven't seen any evidence that suggests Pearl has anything to do with this. In fact, she's the one who insisted I take the case."

"Sure," he lisped. "To get back into the federation's good graces. Who better to investigate the crime than the best friend of the criminal? She practically guaranteed that she wouldn't get caught."

"Go soak your head," I said, even though I'd had the same thought myself.

"And we have something better than evidence: we have an eyewitness."

That stopped me. "What are you talking about?"

Paul crossed his arms triumphantly. "Judy Cohen saw her putting the note in her locker."

"No she didn't."

"Are you calling her a liar? You can interrogate her yourself if you like." He raised his arm like he was going to call her over. I caught him at the elbow and stopped him before he could wave.

"That's not necessary. I'm sure that's what she thinks she saw."

"Look, it's your choice, but I'm telling you now: things are going to be a lot easier on Pearl if you tell her the jig is up and get her to stop writing the notes. Get her to go away quietly and they might be willing to forget everything."

"And if I don't?"

"Then things might get a lot harder for her at P.S. 110."

"Let me think about it," I said. "She's going away with me this weekend. If I decide to do this, I'm going to do it then."

"I know you'll do the right thing, Iris."

I skulked away, shaking my head in disgust.

WHEN I GOT HOME that afternoon, Mrs. M. greeted me from the kitchen and broke the news that Pop was planning to be gone for much of the night.

"Where?" I asked.

"He no tell me." Of course he didn't. Despite Pop's planned absence, it didn't escape my notice that the table was set for three people.

"Are we having company?" I asked.

"Betty is coming."

"Again?" I immediately regretted sounding so snotty. "I mean, is everything okay with her? She's been spending a lot of time here lately."

"Oh, she's fine. She have plans tonight in the area. I tell her she should eat with us first."

Plans, hmmm? Could this be Pop's and her attempt to throw me off their trail? Perhaps they thought if Betty showed up to dinner while Pop was out I wouldn't think they were planning on meeting up later.

I called to check on Pearl and got her mother instead. She assured me that Pearl was going to be fine and would still be able to go away with me for the weekend. Betty arrived twenty minutes later, dressed to the nines, further confirming my theory that she had a date with Pop. As Mrs. Mrozenski finished cooking, she hummed a folk song to herself. The humming turned to full-out singing and the singing was soon joined with foot stomping and hand clapping.

Betty rolled her eyes my way. Boy, howdy—did she really think I would help her gang up on Mrs. M.? Seriously?

"Just once," she whispered, "it would be nice if Ma remembered that she's in America now. If I wanted to eat Polish food and listen to Polish music, I'd go to Poland."

I didn't respond. Was she so naïve that she didn't know what was going on in Poland right now?

"I guess it was probably the same with you and your ma," she said. "Crazy accent, crazy food, always telling you how things were done in the old country."

"No, it was nothing like that," I said. "Nothing like that at all."

"Then you were lucky," said Betty.

Over a meal of egg noodles and cabbage, Mrs. Mrozenski interrogated Betty about her day. As soon as she paused for breath, I decided to jump in with questions about her night.

"So where are you going after this?" I asked.

"Just out with some friends."

"Here? On the Lower East Side?"

"I did grow up here, Iris. Most of my girlfriends got hitched and set up housekeeping near here."

"Where will you go?"

"Here and there," she said. Before I could ask another question, she turned her attention back to her mother. "Did I tell you I saw Jenny Delaney yesterday? She's as fat as a house with twins, if you can believe it. And with her husband overseas for the duration." The news of poor Jenny Delaney's stretched abdomen took center stage and Betty's plans for the evening were forgotten.

She stayed long enough to help clean up the kitchen after dinner. Since it was clear that three sets of hands weren't needed, I retreated to the parlor to do my homework and listen to the radio. As soon as the dishes were done, Betty claimed her coat, hat, and pocketbook and said goodbye to her mother.

Once Mrs. Mrozenski was out of earshot, Betty turned to me. "Iris, can you do me a favor?"

"Um, sure." I was expecting a reprimand for asking about her imaginary plans in front of her mother. Instead, she handed me an envelope. "What's this?"

"Can you give it to your pop?"

"Sure."

"Thanks," she said. And then she gave me a wink before walking out the door.

It was a plain white envelope with Pop's name written in her sure, girlish hand. I couldn't believe she was asking me to be her messenger. I was torn between opening the envelope and reading her note, and tearing the whole thing to pieces and never giving it to Pop at all.

In the end, I did neither. I put the note in the back of my health-and-hygiene text and decided I would hand it to Pop when he arrived home. Let him squirm in front of me as I passed him a love letter from his new girlfriend.

Aunt Miriam phoned to confirm what time she would meet Pearl and me after school and ride with us to the Upper East Side. After I talked to her, I retreated to my room to read. The phone rang a second time and I was certain it was Pop checking in, but if it was, he didn't ask Mrs. M. to extend any message to me.

I waited up for Pop until midnight. Just as I was turning off my lamp, I heard him arrive home. I tiptoed down the stairs, with Betty's letter in my hand. He was in his office, kneeling before the safe. A weird sound came from the room. At first I thought he was singing, but as I moved closer to the open door, I realized he was crying.

He was looking at the photos of Mama.

My eyes watered and I silently backed away from the

scene. I could wait until morning to give him the letter. There was no reason to do it tonight.

MY WEEK OF SLEEPLESS NIGHTS finally caught up with me and I overslept the next morning. Pop was still sleeping when I got up for school, and I had exactly ten minutes to get dressed and pack for my weekend.

As I came downstairs, hauling my bag behind me, Mrs. M. greeted me with a piece of toast and a glass of milk.

"Here. You be late."

"Thanks." I gobbled the bread and chased it with the cow juice.

"Have fun with your aunt and uncle," Mrs. M. told me as I threw on my coat and hat.

I told her goodbye and rushed out the door and onto the street. My bag was heavy. In an effort to pack quickly, I'd grabbed too much, uncertain what I was going to need during my time at Miriam and Adam's. Not only did I have clothes, but my camera and Pop's picklocks. I transferred the bag from one hand to the other and tried to double my pace.

School appeared in the distance, but something was strange about it. A banner hung over the front doors. It had been torn in half and its two portions now hung limp and flapping in the wind. "Hitler Is Right," said one half as the breeze lifted and stretched it. The other half was mercifully unreadable, though it was easy enough to guess at its content.

A crowd had formed on the steps, staring up at the torn message. I could see Paul, Michael, Saul, Judy, and Denise among the group. The warning bell rang and the crowd remained in its place, staring at the fabric flapping in the breeze. As I approached, teachers ordered everyone inside and told them to get to class. Reluctantly, the crowd disbanded. By the time I reached the steps, they were gone, giving me a chance to view the other half of the banner unimpeded.

"Death to the Jews," it said.

THE BANNER WAS ALL ANYONE wanted to talk about during first period. Rather than encouraging the conversation, Mr. Pinsky ordered us all to take out our health-and-hygiene texts and read about the importance of washing our hands.

I stared at the page for half an hour but I couldn't tell you what it said if my life depended on it. Get your hands wet and use soap, maybe?

Why had the note-writer escalated things? That was all I could wonder the whole time I sat in class. If the group was right and Pearl was behind it all, how had she managed to hang the banner by herself? That was a feat that required at least two people.

A boy interrupted class with a package from the front office. Mr. Pinsky removed the mimeographed page from the folder and told us all he had an announcement.

"What we witnessed this morning was an outrageous act directed at the Jewish students in our community. Such stunts will not go unpunished. Anyone who knows anything about the perpetrator or perpetrators behind this terrible crime is ordered to come to the principal's office immediately."

While everyone processed what that meant, I absorbed the words it didn't include: the investigation was no longer in our hands. The school was taking over.

I DREADED GOING to lunch and facing Pearl, but I knew it had to be done. I didn't want to run the risk of leaving her alone and having the federation confront her before I had a chance to warn her. As I entered the cafeteria, I scanned the crowd, looking. She wasn't there. I took my seat at our regular table and waited five, ten, fifteen minutes, but still no Pearl. The members of the federation weren't there, either. But Denise was.

"Can I join you?" she asked halfway through lunch.

"Sure," I said. "Where is everyone?" Had they lured Pearl someplace private to talk over their suspicions? God help Paul if they accused her before I could alert her.

"I'm not sure. I heard a rumor that Mr. DeLuca is questioning all the people who got the notes."

"Seriously?"

She removed a compact from her pocketbook and smiled at the mirror. With her index finger she scraped off a tiny scrap of green that was wedged between her teeth. "It's about time. I told Paul he should go to the principal about this days ago."

"Michael seemed to think the principal wouldn't care," I said.

She closed the compact and returned it to her purse. "Maybe about the notes, but the banner is hard to ignore. I heard there was a newspaper photographer taking pictures before they took it down. If something shows up in the papers about this, he's going to have to care."

"You don't sound too happy about that," I said.

Her eyes widened. "Why would I be? It's all so embarrassing. I mean, it's fine that they're Jewish, but do they have to draw so much attention to it?"

"I'm Jewish, too," I said.

She patted the table with her hand. "I know, but you keep it to yourself. That's much more dignified."

My mouth opened so wide it's amazing my chin didn't hit the table.

"I'd better go," said Denise. "Paul might've gone back to the newspaper office to wait out the rest of lunch. See you around."

Not if I see you first, I thought.

I got more of the scoop on what was going on during afternoon classes. Mr. DeLuca had indeed questioned everyone who got the notes. He'd also rounded up the usual campus suspects: Benny, Dino, and a few other boys who seemed to materialize wherever a crime was being committed. As bad as I felt for Benny, that at least meant the federation hadn't yet shared their suspicions about who the culprit was. The school day came to a close and I rushed to Pearl's locker to find out what had happened during her interview. She wasn't there. I headed to the front steps of the building to see if she was waiting for me and saw her at the curb, where she was standing beside a cab with my aunt Miriam.

The federation would have to wait. We were about to go into Uncle Adam's lair.

16

AFTER SPENDING THE ENTIRE DAY obsessing over the federation, I'd almost forgotten about Uncle Adam and Aunt Miriam. As I walked to the curb to join Pearl, I struggled to prepare for the weekend. I needed to get a photo of Adam. What else? It probably wouldn't be a bad idea to search his office. If Mama kept a note from him, it was possible he had held on to letters from her. Fortunately, I had my picklocks packed and ready to use to gain access to his office. But what I didn't have was an excuse to be in the apartment by myself long enough to perform a search.

I paused in my path and coughed into my hand. My body swayed slightly and I reached out to steady myself but found nothing to grasp.

I resumed walking under the gaze of my worried aunt.

"Iris," she said, meeting me halfway. "Are you all right?"

"Just feeling a little . . . woozy," I said. Another cough, hopefully more convincing than the first.

"You poor thing—you sound terrible. How long have you been sick?"

About thirty seconds by my watch. "I woke up feeling a little weird, but I just assumed I was tired."

"I knew this was going to happen. After walking around in that ice storm the other day you were practically begging for a head cold. As soon as we get home, I'll have Lydia make you some hot tea. Come on—let's get you in the cab."

As I climbed into the backseat, Benny came into my line of sight. He hovered halfway between school and the curb and raised his hand in a tentative greeting. I waved back. He mouthed something but I couldn't figure out what he was saying from that distance. I shrugged and he held up both hands with his fingers pinched together like he was dangling something between them.

Whatever Benny wanted, it would have to wait. I had more important things to attend to.

It was a long drive to the Upper East Side. We sat with Pearl between us and, like Fred Astaire to my Ginger Rogers, she immediately fell into step with me.

"You're burning up," said Pearl.

"Is it cold in here?" I said.

"Turn up the heat," Miriam barked at the driver.

"Here, take my coat," said Pearl. She removed it and set it on my lap.

"I'm so sorry," I said. "I don't want to ruin your weekend."

"Nonsense," said Aunt Miriam. "You can't help being sick. Perhaps it's better this way. Adam wanted us all to go to the Pollocks' party this evening, but honestly I'd prefer to stay in. You remember them, don't you, Iris? On Central Park West? Their parties are always terribly dull."

This was not going as I'd hoped. I elbowed Pearl in the ribs.

"Oh!" she said. "I love parties."

"And the Pollocks have such a lovely home," I told her.

"Oh. Well, maybe I'll get to see it another time," said Pearl. She was playing it a little too heavy-handed, but fortunately, Aunt Miriam didn't seem to notice.

"Perhaps Iris will be feeling better in a few hours," she told Pearl. "And then we can go after all."

"You could always go without me," I said, being careful to punctuate the suggestion with another cough. "I wouldn't mind. Honest. I'd hate for Pearl to miss out on something like that."

"We'll see," said Aunt Miriam.

By the time we arrived uptown, my imaginary illness had escalated to uncontrollable shivers that forced me to wrap my arms about myself. As we entered the apartment, Aunt Miriam demanded that I go lie down while she fixed me some tea.

"Thank God that's over," Pearl said once we were alone in the guest bedroom I'd stayed in the previous December. Pearl took in our surroundings with wide-eyed amazement:

furniture that matched, linens that were unstained, wallpaper that didn't curl, rugs that bore no wear from feet passing over them, paintings that were actually worth more than the frames they hung in. "I never thought a cab ride could feel so long. So what's the plan?"

"I decided I should search his office."

"What are you looking for?"

"I'm not sure yet." On the surface it was a lousy plan, but when you examined it carefully . . . it was still a lousy plan. "Maybe he held on to letters from her, something that would explain why she ended up in Yorkville that day and whether or not he was the man Anna saw with her."

"It would seem awfully silly for someone to hang on to evidence from a crime."

I had to agree. Uncle Adam was hardly a stupid man. "Just do what you can to keep them out of the apartment."

"What about the photo?"

I gestured for her to keep her voice down, just in case anyone was listening outside the door. "I'll find one tonight."

"What if they notice—?"

"They won't, Pearl. Okay?" It was snottier than I'd intended, but the enormous task in front of me suddenly felt hopeless. I wasn't going to find anything in Adam's office. He wasn't a foolish man. If he were, an entire year wouldn't have passed without his being caught. And did I really think Aunt Miriam wouldn't notice when I plucked their

portrait off the fireplace mantel and stuck it in my overnight bag? "I'm sorry," I told Pearl. "I'm just overwhelmed
by all of this and don't know where to start. Maybe Pop was
right to test me before letting me loose in the field. I don't
think I'm cut out to be a detective."

"What do you mean by 'testing' you?"

That was right—I hadn't told her about Jim McCain.
"The man I tailed last weekend? It turns out he was a friend
of Pop's. Oh, and it looks like everything else Pop's had me
doing was also a big fat lie designed to keep me busy and
out of his hair."

"Don't be silly. If your pop was testing you, it was to
keep you safe, not because he didn't think you could hack
it. Look at how much you figured out when Tom Barney
went missing—you did that all on your own. If you figured
that out, you can figure this out, too."

I hoped she was right, but I had a feeling her faith in me
was as misplaced as the faith I used to have in Uncle Adam.
"So what happened today?" I asked.

"What do you mean?"

"I heard you were questioned about the notes."

"Oh, that." She rolled her eyes. "It was stupid, really. Principal DeLuca made all of us who got notes come see him
one by one. I honestly felt like he didn't believe me when I
told him about it, and of course I didn't have it . . ."

"Because you gave it to me."

"Right. It's clear he found the whole thing irritating to

have to deal with. Not only did I have to sit through the grand inquisition, I had to miss lunch, too." To demonstrate that point, she pulled a paper sack from her bag and removed her sandwich.

"What about yesterday?" I asked. "Paul said you went home sick."

"I had to. I was too upset after we found the note."

"I'm sorry, by the way."

"For what?"

"For telling Paul about it."

"Oh, that." She rolled her eyes again. "I would've told him sooner or later."

The scent of liverwurst filled the room, making it easy for me to pretend to be nauseated. Pearl pulled apart the sandwich and studied its contents like she'd never seen liverwurst before. "They think I did it." She looked up from her lunch. "The whole federation is certain I'm the one writing the notes."

Here's what I should've said: "That's ridiculous." Here's what I actually said: "Did you?"

She dropped the sandwich back onto its waxed-paper shroud. "Are you serious?"

"No . . . I mean . . . No."

"You are," said Pearl, her disbelief making her eyes water. "You honestly believe I could write those awful things."

"I don't. But I can understand why they do. You were upset that they kicked you out."

"Of course I was. That doesn't mean that I demonstrated it by writing anti-Semitic notes. And if you'll remember, *I'm* the one who told you you should take the case."

I didn't bother to point out that that was the perfect way to distract me from what she was doing. "There were times when you were more than happy not to do the stakeouts," I said.

"Because I was helping you find out about your mother. And even still there wasn't a day that I didn't stand in those halls, waiting—"

There was a knock at the door. I jumped into the twin bed I'd claimed for myself and did my best to look weakened with fever.

"Come in," said Pearl.

Aunt Miriam entered with her maid fast at her heels. The young woman toted a silver tray that she set on the dresser. "Oh, this won't do," she told Pearl. "We can't have you getting sick, too. Let's put you next door, Pearl. Lydia," she said to the maid, "please move Miss Levine's things into the other guest room."

"That's a great idea." Pearl tossed a pointed look my way. "I'd hate to come down with something."

Miriam made note of the liverwurst sandwich with a wrinkle of her nose. "Are you hungry, dear?"

Pearl nodded while trying to return the sandwich to her bag.

"Lydia—please see to it that Miss Levine gets a snack.

I believe there are cookies in the kitchen. Those should tide her over until the party."

"Have you decided to go to the Pollocks', then?" I asked.

"Adam wants to go. He said it would be rude to decline at this point. Frankly, I think it would be odd for him to go alone, don't you?" Aunt Miriam didn't look happy about that, but she was hardly the kind of spouse to tell her husband no when he'd made a decision. "But don't worry—Lydia will be here if you need anything, Iris. And I'm sure we won't be late."

On cue, Uncle Adam appeared. He looked so different from the last time I'd seen him. While Pop was the younger of the two of them and, arguably, the more handsome of the brothers, Uncle Adam had also been an attractive man. Now his face was crisscrossed with lines I'd never seen before, a kind of road map of grief that made it hard to look directly at him.

Had guilt done this?

"You must be Pearl," he said while extending his hand. Pearl took it reluctantly, like she half expected to find it rigged with a buzzer.

"I was just moving Pearl to another room," said Miriam. "I don't think it's wise for the girls to be in such close quarters with Iris sick."

"No, that doesn't seem very smart," said Uncle Adam. Miriam hustled Pearl from the room and exited behind her. I was hoping Uncle Adam would leave, too, but he seemed to have other plans. He closed the door and looked my way. For a moment the veneer of weakness I thought I'd seen in him lifted. I got the impression that just as I was seeing through him, he was seeing through me. "What's bothering you, Iris?"

That my mother was murdered and you may have been involved in it. Oh, and that affair you two were having. That's got me a little rattled, too. "Pearl and I had a fight," I said.

"That's no way to start the weekend." He sat on the bed beside me. The springs groaned beneath his weight. "What are you two quarreling about?"

"I didn't stick up for her when someone accused her of something terrible." I gave him the same pointed look Pearl had given me, though it seemed to go right over his head. "I know it was the wrong thing to do. Pearl couldn't have done something like that."

"I'm sure she'll forgive you. I understand you're not feeling well?"

"Just a little warm and woozy."

He put a clammy hand to my forehead. I recoiled at his touch as though it were dead flesh he was touching me with, not the arm of a living, breathing man. "You don't feel warm to me."

"Your hands are pretty cold."

He rubbed them together as though that would somehow ease my discomfort with him. "I must say I'm disappointed you won't be joining us tonight. The Pollocks were very excited when I told them you were visiting."

"I hope it's not an inconvenience," I said.

"Illness is always an inconvenience, but only to the person suffering it. Are you sure you can't rally and go with us?"

I receded further into the bed. "I wish I could. I really do, but I just feel too awful to go anywhere." I didn't dare fake a cough in front of Adam. He would've seen through it faster than a sheer skirt on a sunny day.

He put his hand on my blanket-covered feet. "I was very surprised when Miriam told me you were coming this weekend. Even more so that Art thought it was a good idea."

I curled up my legs to increase the distance between us. "I think Pop wanted me out of the house for a while."

"Why is that?"

I thought of Pop crying over the photos of Mama, then forced the image out of my head. "He's seeing someone. I think he wanted some time alone with her."

An eyebrow went up. "Really? I had no idea."

"It's kind of hush-hush," I said. "In fact, I don't think he knows that I know, but I'm pretty sure that's why he was so nice about my coming here."

He frowned. "It hasn't even been a year yet."

Was it grief that brought Pop to look at Mama's pictures the night before, or guilt? It seemed incredibly disrespectful for Pop to dive into a new relationship so soon, but weren't the circumstances a little unusual? She'd been cheating on him, after all. With his own brother.

"She's very nice," I said. "She's our landlady's daughter."

He paused a moment too long, drinking me in with eyes that I'd never remembered seeming so cold. "And you feel safe there, Iris? On the Lower East Side?"

"Of course. Why wouldn't I?"

"I just wanted to make sure. We worry about you, you know." He patted my legs through the coverlet. "Get some rest."

"I will. Thanks."

He stood up and started to leave. Right before he reached the door, he paused. "Your mother's death must be weighing heavily on your mind."

I swallowed hard. "Maybe."

"It must be very hard to be here so close to the first anniversary of when all that happened. After all, this is where you heard the awful news."

"It's a little hard." What was he getting at?

"Maybe you even feel guilty being away from your father during this time. Worried that if you have fun without him you're betraying him in some way."

If he thought this weekend was fun for me, he sure didn't know me very well. "I don't think that," I said.

"Okay. But if you did, it would be okay. Being here, away

from him, you're not hurting him. If he can move on with this landlady's daughter, you can, too."

"All right." Another awkward pause as he waited for me to say . . . what exactly? "I think I'd like to take a nap," I said.

He nodded as though to say that while the subject was closed for the moment, he expected to bring it up again. "Sleep well, Iris," he told me, before leaving me alone.

Right then I had the strongest urge to call Pop. I needed to hear his voice and to know that he was all right, that he wasn't in fact spending the whole weekend prostrate before Mama's photos. I left my room and crept into the hallway. I could hear Miriam and Pearl talking in the room beside mine. I tiptoed past them and went into the kitchen, where Lydia was arranging cookies on a platter.

Boy, howdy—Pearl was going to shake when she saw that display of sugar.

"Aunt Miriam said I could use the phone," I told Lydia. Recognizing my need for privacy, she took the platter and left the room. I found a few stray cookies that hadn't made their way onto the tray and pocketed them for later. Then I lifted the receiver and asked the operator to connect me to Pop's office exchange.

"AA Investigations," he said.

I was so relieved to get him that I almost couldn't speak. "It's Iris, Pop."

"Iris! Is everything okay?"

I felt silly all of a sudden. Why was I calling? "Yeah. I

just wanted to let you know that we made it to Adam and Miriam's."

"Good, good." He sounded distracted. Was there someone there with him? Betty, maybe? "Are you having fun?"

I wrapped the phone's pigtail cord around my hand. "I guess."

"I want you to enjoy yourself this weekend. Okay? No feeling guilty for being there and having a good time." Why were both Adam and he talking about guilt? What did I have to feel guilty about? "I have to go." And then he said something he'd never said to me before. "I love you, Iris."

He hung up before I could say the same to him.

The call did nothing to ease my nerves. By the time Miriam came to check on me, I was nauseated for real.

"What can I get for you before we go?" she asked me.

"Nothing, thanks. I just want to sleep."

She turned off the lamp and started to leave.

"Aunt Miriam?"

"Yes, dear?"

I had a hunch about the weekend that I had to follow. "Why did you decide to invite me here?"

"Whatever do you mean?"

I rolled onto my side. "This is the first time you've invited me since we moved to the Lower East Side."

Her hand found the string of pearls around her neck and gently tugged on it. "You know that's not true. I've always told you our door was open."

"I know that, but it's the first time you've invited me for a specific date. Why now?"

She tucked a loose hair behind her ear. "Hanukah, of course."

"But Yom Kippur and Rosh Hashanah are much bigger holidays."

I could see a flicker in her eyes that meant I was onto something.

"Did Pop ask you to invite me?" I asked.

Her eyebrow rose almost imperceptibly. "He and I may have spoken about it."

Her visit to our house that night had been planned? "Why the ruse?"

"I . . . I don't think I know the answer to that, Iris."

"What did he tell you when he asked you to invite me for the weekend?"

"Just that he had some things to deal with this weekend and thought it would be better if you weren't around while he did so. I think he's worried about how the anniversaries are going to affect you. He thought we might be a good distraction. And frankly, I was thrilled when he suggested it. I'm hoping this means that after all that's happened we might be able to be a family again."

She had to have been shocked when Pop called her. And why her, after all? Why not ask Pearl's parents to take me for the weekend? Did he want me out of the Lower East Side so I didn't accidentally run into Betty and him walking arm in arm? Or was there some other reason he didn't want me around?

The tension left her face and she smiled at me. "Get some rest, Iris. We'll be back in a few hours."

I told her I would, though rest was the farthest thing from my mind.

17

THEY WERE OUT THE DOOR at 7:00. At 7:15 Lydia
came to check on me. I assured her I was fine and was planning on spending the evening sleeping. She showed me how
to use the call buzzer to summon her if I needed anything,
then left me alone.

I ate the cookies I'd stolen and let five minutes pass before leaving the room. I could hear Lydia in the kitchen,
fixing herself a snack to accompany her as she listened to
Amos 'n' Andy. I tiptoed in sock-clad feet across the parlor
to the room my uncle used as his office, with my camera
and picklocks in hand. The door was shut and locked. Apparently, Uncle Adam made a habit of not trusting anyone,
including his wife.

I took a deep breath and went to work inserting my picklocks into the keyhole. I tried to pretend it was one of Pop's
practice locks and set about the delicate task of turning the
picks this way and that before they came into contact with

the vital part of the mechanism. With just a few adjustments, the lock sprang open and I found myself facing a dark room.

I barricaded myself behind the door, and stumbled blindly until I located a lamp I'd spied when I first entered. Adam's office seemed like the big brother to Pop's modest space. Instead of a secondhand desk and chair, Uncle Adam had a custom-made piece covered in a leather blotter, and a padded leather throne upholstered in the same deep red. It was hard to believe he ever conducted business in such a pristine room, but then I guess that was kind of the point. This wasn't Adam's only office. He had a storefront space where he met clients. This office was for the more important people, the ones paying a premium for discretion, who couldn't risk being seen going into and coming out of a detective's office. And it was also the place he stored his case files, to ensure they were secure under lock and key. During those few months when I'd stayed with them after Mama died and while Pop was recovering, he'd told me all about it, how there was a certain class of people who'd take you seriously only if you had a business address and another class that wouldn't dare meet you somewhere that advertised what they were up to. So he catered to both to maximize his profits.

Unlike Pop, he wasn't militant in his neatness. There were stacks of papers to be filed, notes he'd scrawled on the backs of envelopes or bills or a menu for a restaurant that delivered its food right to your door. There was clearly a method to his madness, though. You didn't reach Uncle Adam's level of success if you couldn't find what you needed to find. And while he might have lacked the basic skills necessary to create order, he wasn't above hiring someone to create it for him. That task fell to a file clerk who came to the house once a week to make sure notes and other materials made it into the proper folders in his cabinets.

Aunt Miriam used to do the job for him, but at some point he'd decided it was unsavory to have his wife working for him. Or maybe he just no longer wanted her to have the ability to pry into his business.

I started by looking through his desk. This seemed the most likely place for him to store some personal memento of an affair. The drawers were locked, but they took only a skeleton key that the picklocks could mimic with little effort. When the first drawer was opened, I quickly scanned its contents, only to find a collection of office supplies—pencils, pens, and paper clips—that hardly seemed to warrant locking it. The second drawer held stationery, a receipt pad, envelopes, and postage—again, hardly the kinds of things worth the effort of turning a key. The last drawer had a bottle of whiskey, two crystal tumblers, and a gun. There was a box of bullets, too, so light when I picked it up that I had to open it to confirm that there was anything in it.

What kind of gun had been used on Mama?

I took a photo of it just in case.

"Mr. Ackerman?" Lydia's voice tore through the room, interrupting my work. She knocked on the door. "Sir? Are you in there?" Nuts. I hadn't locked the door behind me. She must've seen the light under the door and assumed Uncle Adam had stayed behind. I looked for a hiding place, but there weren't any available, save the space beneath the desk. Moving as quietly as possible, I crouched in the cavern intended for Uncle Adam's legs, and pulled my own stems into my chest. Just as I got into position the door creaked open. "Sir?" She was silent as the empty space greeted her. I held my breath. Could she hear my heartbeat? Feel my pulse as the blood rushed through my veins?

Apparently not. She clicked off the lamp and closed the door.

I counted to a hundred before I got up. Then I removed my sweater and placed it along the bottom of the door so no light leaked through to warn Lydia that something was once again amiss.

With the lamp on I scanned the room, looking for somewhere someone might squirrel away a love letter. There was a bookcase full of phone directories and other tools that helped Adam locate people. I searched under and behind the books but only came up with dust that indicated that not even Lydia was let in here regularly. There were also a series of framed illustrations of Sherlock Holmes and Watson. I lifted each one, expecting to see a safe like in the movies, but the wall was bare behind them. The rug proved a little bit more insightful. Underneath the corner farthest from the door were two magazines depicting naked women.

What's the matter, Uncle Adam? Weren't Mama and Miriam enough for you?

I could feel time ticking away. The only place remaining to check were the cabinets where Adam's case files lived. I picked the lock on each one and opened the first drawer. What was I looking for? A folder with Mama's name on it, perhaps? There was nothing so obvious in any of the drawers. Each file was neatly labeled with the name of the client whose case it represented and cross-referenced with the files for anyone he was being asked to watch on that client's behalf. It was a clever system—one that Pop might be wise to emulate, if he ever let me back into his inner sanctum.

Maybe Adam used a pet name for Mama, or filed her things under a name that held a special meaning for him. I went through the drawers twice, but I didn't see anything that made me think of Mama. Then, on the third pass through, something caught my eye: Rheingold Accounting.

I knew that name. Pop had a client with the same moniker. The file had been in his safe. There had been photos in it that I'd thought might have been of the man he had had me tail before I'd learned I was actually tailing his old friend Jim McCain.

The coincidence was too much. I removed the folder and sat behind the enormous desk to see what it contained.

The file was thick, so thick that it took two hands to lift it. Page after page of notes were inside, all neatly typed, some on onionskin that made it clear that copies of whatever information Adam had put together had circulated among more than one person. Everything was arranged chronologically, and relevant photos, invoices, and other materials were carefully paper-clipped to each day's notes.

Whoever did Adam's secretarial work was pretty impressive. And, I was willing to bet, not fifteen.

I started at the beginning. Those notes detailed a visit on September 14, 1941, from Jude Rheingold and Edgar Valentine, senior partners of an accounting firm on the Upper East Side. They suspected that money was being skimmed out of their accounts. After conducting their own investigation, they identified the culprit most likely behind the theft: Karl Hincter.

Hincter was a controversial hire. He was German but claimed to have left Germany to get away from Hitler. Rheingold suspected he was taking the money he was stealing and sending it home to family still living abroad. He had no proof of this, of course, and had asked Adam to find it.

Hincter, unfortunately, lived in Yorkville.

My heart picked up its pace.

Adam wrote: *I explained to Rheingold and Valentine that as a devout Jew, I cannot easily maintain surveillance in an openly German community, especially since Hincter has an active social life that starts at sundown on Friday and continues into the wee hours of Saturday morning. I suggested to them that they seek another detective, but both are quite passionate in wanting to use me. If I'm going to be able to assist them, I'm going to need to enlist the help of someone who can more easily infiltrate Yorkville, ideally someone who speaks German.*

The next page was a list of names, each one with a red-penciled "no" beside it. I wasn't sure what the list meant until I saw Jim McCain's name on there. Detectives—he had contacted detectives to see if he could get someone to help him. Or at least, some of them were detectives. As I scoured the list, my eyes landed on one name that hadn't been bisected by a red "no": Ingrid Anderson.

I gasped. So there it was: Mama wasn't just having an affair with Uncle Adam. She was working for him.

The next pages were simply a record of her work:

Ingrid has made contact with Hincter and has spent several hours in his company at the Spotted Pig, a dance hall and brewery on East Eighty-sixth Street. She said he was very cordial and eager to talk about his family back home. She turned the conversation to her own desire to help those she left behind and, hopefully, get them out of Europe. His tone changed and he seemed agitated at the suggestion, telling her that he would much rather be in Europe than here, where being a German means constant scrutiny. Ingrid agreed that it was hard and said she finds it particularly difficult since so few of her friends are German. He suggested that she accompany him to a meeting of "like-minded Germans" the next night. She agreed.

It came as no surprise that the meeting Ingrid attended with Hincter was for an offshoot of the German-American Bund, a pro-Nazi organization that we had hoped had been squelched in New York but apparently is thriving underground. Ingrid successfully made it through the meeting, no mean feat given the anti-Semitic content my sister-in-law had to endure. She assures me that she raised no suspicion during the proceedings and that, when questioned about her background, talked of her family back in Germany and described herself as a recent widow who was hoping to find friendship among like-minded individuals. Given her Nordic coloring, a complexion Hitler himself would envy, I believe it's safe to say that no one would have mistaken Ingrid for a Jew. At the end of the meeting she said that an appeal was made for contributions to help fund a number of activities the group had planned over the next several months. While those activities were not enumerated, she suspects that they are talking about terroristic threats.

I found myself holding my breath. How had Mama gotten the courage to go to a group like that? What horrible things did she hear at that meeting, things that were said about people just like us? It must've been so hard to go through each day with the memory of all that in her head. And yet she had. For months, apparently, she'd walked around our apartment like everything was perfectly normal.

No wonder Anna Mueller thought she was a Nazi.

I glanced at the clock and realized I'd been at it for more than an hour and a half. I picked up my pace, skimming the notes as best I could. Hincter eventually confessed to Mama that not only did he work for Jews, he was stealing from them and using their money to fund Bund activities. He found the irony of all this terribly amusing and suspected that it was the fact that he was stealing from Jews that increased his esteem among the Bund members more than the dollar amount he'd given to them.

Mama reported all this to Adam, who relayed it to the clients. They wanted to fire Hincter immediately and begin legal proceedings against him, but Adam encouraged them to wait a little bit. After all, this was no longer about stopping one man from stealing. They might be able to halt an entire sect of the Bund from whatever it was they were plotting.

So Mama continued going to the meetings, and reporting what she'd learned. The problem was, Hincter didn't know anything about what the group was planning to do. While he contributed to their coffers, whatever he had given them wasn't enough to get them to tell him how his money was going to be used. And Hincter didn't seem to care. It was enough to know he was helping, and besides, it wasn't his money to begin with. The person Mama needed to get close to was an S. Haupt, who was the leader of the organization.

Thus far, wrote Adam a few weeks later, *Ingrid's attempts to get close to Haupt have been unsuccessful. She believes he may be suspicious of her and is concerned that she has been followed on more than one occasion. She has mentioned these concerns to Hincter, who confirms that it's a modus operandi for new members of the Bund to be tailed to verify that they are who they claim to be. Ingrid is, naturally, quite concerned. While she has not been attending synagogue or any other activity that might raise suspicion, I have been to her home several times and she has taken Iris to and from school on a daily basis. I have suggested she discontinue escorting her daughter for the time being and try to restrict her activities to those of a wealthy widow living on the Upper East Side.*

I looked at the date: November. I remembered it well. Mama abruptly stopped accompanying me to Chapin. She also started shopping more, going to lunch more—both activities she used to claim bored her silly.

Ingrid's attempts to get close to Haupt are finally paying off. She had a private audience with him in which she gushed about her desire to help the Bund. Haupt talked to her about making a financial contribution to the organization and seemed very aware of her personal finances, though fortunately he seems, as of now, unaware of my brother's existence. Ingrid concluded the conversation by saying that she would be interested in making a substantial contribution, but was not content in being a silent partner like Hincter. If she was going to be funding the Bund, she wanted to be part of the conversation about how the money was going to be used. Haupt agreed to talk to the other group members about this, but cautioned that they may be unwilling to welcome a woman's insight about their plans.

Another week passed, and Adam wrote, *Haupt has contacted Ingrid and invited her to a meeting on December 8, this one of just the most crucial members (no Hincter, etc.). I have suggested that we might want to contact the authorities before proceeding any further.*

(Later the same day.) I have been advised that this is a matter for the Office of War Information, not the local police. Repeated attempts to contact the OWI have failed to put me in touch with anyone of authority.

Then, on December 8: *In light of the attack on Pearl Harbor, Ingrid has canceled her meeting with Haupt. Understandably, she is too distressed to pretend all is well. She told him she's concerned that Pearl Harbor means that even more Germans will be targeted by the local authorities and wants to lie low for a few days.*

A few days later Uncle Adam noted that Haupt had been trying to contact Mama about her financial contribution. He wrote: *I have advised her that if she wishes to cease contact at this point, I completely understand. She said she'd like to think about it. Right now her main concern is Art and the severity of his injuries. I have a meeting set up with Rheingold and Valentine to find out how much money they might be willing to commit to "give" to Haupt under the auspices of Ingrid.*

A week passed before Uncle Adam recorded any other notes. It was now the last week of December and I could feel time ticking away as the remaining span of Mama's life could be measured in hours. How did I spend those days? I was off from school, hanging around friends, ignorant of everything but that Mama's mood had changed and Pop was soon going to return from Hawaii. And I wasn't happy about that, not because of his injury, God help me, but because of the changes his return would spell for me. More rules, perhaps. Less of Mama to keep to myself. A militant household where discarded boots and misplaced drinking glasses would no longer be tolerated. I remember thinking I had to cram as much living as possible into the weeks before he came home, and so I seized every opportunity that presented itself.

And then the last of Adam's notes, dated December 26, 1941. The message was brief: *Rheingold and Valentine have decided they are not comfortable putting up money to catch Haupt. The case is closed and they will now proceed with prosecuting Hincter based on the evidence we were able to secure against him.*

An invoice was attached, indicating Adam had been paid in full.

So what had happened between December 26 and when Mama was found on the first? Had Adam decided he wanted to pursue the case anyway and strong-armed Mama into continuing to help him? Did he manipulate her into putting up her own money in order to secure Haupt's trust?

I tried to recall what I knew firsthand from those five

days. Mama had deposited me at Adam and Miriam's on the Monday before New Year's. She had to go out of town, she said, and so I would be staying with my aunt and uncle until she returned. I remember being excited about staying with them and not initially questioning Mama's absence. They kept me busy, but insisted I stay with one of them at all times, an arrangement I found bothersome after the weeks of freedom I'd just enjoyed. I thought Mama would be gone a day, but then it stretched to two, then three. I asked Adam and Miriam when she was coming back and was told that they weren't sure, it was a family matter, nothing for me to worry myself over. I began to suspect she'd gone to Hawaii to bring Pop home. It made the most sense, after all. She'd been so worried about him, and I knew he was due to return to New York at the beginning of the New Year.

But it made no sense that no one would've told me that, unless something terrible had happened to Pop and they couldn't tell me where Mama was until they knew for certain what his prognosis was.

That was right. I'd forgotten about that, so marred was my memory of that week by Mama's death. As those days stretched on and Mama didn't return, Adam and Miriam grew more anxious. And they were curiously careful with me, planning elaborate meals and outings to help fill my time. I convinced myself that they were delaying telling me bad news about Pop. I was certain he had died and Mama had gone to claim his body, and she'd asked them not to tell me until she returned and could break the news to me herself.

And I was a little relieved, because if Pop was dead, maybe everything wouldn't be changing after all.

How could he have gone from someone who mattered so little to me to someone who'd become my everything?

I closed my eyes and took myself back to that awful New Year's Day. While everyone was celebrating the arrival of 1942, I was sitting in this very office across from Uncle Adam as he told me that my mother had killed herself. I could hear the words in my head as clearly as the day he'd spoken then, but try as I could, I couldn't see his face. Why the lie? He had to know that Mama had been murdered. Was he worried that I couldn't handle the truth?

Or was he worried that the truth would lead back to him?

The front door opened. I jumped at the sound and froze as my aunt's voice rang out, instructing Pearl to leave her coat in the foyer. I closed the folder, made sure no stray pages had escaped, and shoved it into the file cabinet, not bothering to make sure it went back exactly where I'd found it. There was no way I could leave the office as long as they were in the parlor, so I turned off the lamp, retrieved my sweater, grabbed my camera and picklocks, ducked down, and once again hid in the space beneath the desk, hoping it wouldn't take long for the three of them to disperse and go to bed.

"I should check on Iris," said Aunt Miriam.

I swallowed a yelp. Just when I thought I was going to be caught for sure, Pearl spoke up. "I'll do it."

As soon as Pearl was gone, Adam lowered his voice. "She's an odd girl."

"But a good one," said Aunt Miriam. "I'm glad Iris made a friend."

"Didn't you find it strange how she kept pleading to stay longer at the Pollocks' tonight?"

"She doesn't get out very much, Adam. The poor girl wanted a chance to see how the other half lives. Who can blame her? Besides, you seemed to be enjoying yourself."

"You weren't?"

"I didn't say that." She paused. There was an uncomfortable tension in the room that I couldn't read, but which reminded me of their phone call the night of the ice storm. "Beverly Pollock certainly looked nice tonight, don't you think?"

"I can't say I noticed."

Pearl returned to the living room. "Iris is asleep," she said.

"Oh," said Miriam. "I hope she's feeling better."

"Hard to tell," said Pearl. "But she's snoring up a storm."

"Would you care for some tea, Pearl? Maybe a late-night snack? We still have cookies."

"Thank you, but I'm quite full from dinner." That had to

225

be killing Pearl, turning down a perfectly good cookie. I owed her big time. "You don't need to entertain me. I'm sure you're both exhausted."

"Perhaps we should go to sleep. Will you attend shul with us in the morning?"

"Yes, I'd love to," said Pearl.

"Then we'll see you in the morning. Good night, Pearl."

My foot had fallen asleep. As I attempted to shake it back to life, I hit the side of the desk. The wood reverberated like a drum until it seemed like it had swallowed all other sounds.

No one said anything in the parlor. Had they heard me in the study?

"Would you mind if I stayed in here and read for a little while?" asked Pearl.

"Of course not, dear," said Aunt Miriam. "Make yourself at home."

Adam and she left after that, and I could hear Pearl rustle around in the parlor. Once I was certain that she was alone and no one was going to suddenly reappear and engage her in conversation, I grabbed my sweater and the picklocks, left my hiding place, and sneaked out of the office.

Pearl started as I appeared. I put a finger to my lips and gestured for her to follow me back to my room. I don't think I breathed until we were behind the closed door.

"I'm sorry about before," I said.

"It's all right."

"No, it's not. But you need to know why I said what I did. I saw you putting something in Judy Cohen's locker."

The little color in Pearl's face ran out. "Oh."

"I didn't tell anyone, but apparently Judy saw you, too."

She took a deep breath. "I saw the note poking through the vents, so I pulled it out and read it and then stuck it back in the locker."

"Did you see who put it there?"

She rubbed her eyes with both hands. She was clearly exhausted. "No. I was hoping it was just a note from a friend, because I knew Michael was going to be steamed that we'd missed whoever it was again."

It was amazing how much better I felt after hearing this. "I didn't think you could do something like that—"

"Would you have turned me in?"

"What?"

"If it was clear that I was the one writing the notes and putting them in the lockers, would you have turned me in?"

I couldn't tell what answer she wanted to hear, so I told her the truth. "I guess I would've wanted to know why you were doing it first. Then I would have decided."

"But why should it matter? Would you give anyone else the benefit of the doubt if they were doing something as awful as writing those notes?"

The answer was clearly no. If it was anyone but Pearl,

I wouldn't have hesitated before giving their name to Michael. "Probably not."

"Then you shouldn't give me the benefit of the doubt, either. Because even though you're my friend, what I was doing was inexcusable." She was pleading with me and I didn't understand why. The point was moot since she hadn't left the note.

"Okay, if I'm ever positive I've caught you doing something awful, I'll turn you in."

"Even though we're friends."

"Why are you being so weird about this?"

"I'm not being weird." She leaned toward me and for the first time I could see that she wore a gold chain around her neck, half-hidden by the dress she'd worn to the Pollocks'. There was a Star of David dangling from it. Had she always worn that? "That's how it starts, isn't it, Iris? All these awful things in the world? We don't stand up for the people being hurt because the ones doing the hurting are our friends or our family and we can't believe that they don't have a rational explanation for why they did this awful thing. Because what does it say about us that we could be friends or relatives with someone like that? But here's the thing: if we turn a blind eye and allow ourselves to believe that it's okay for them to be doing these things, before we know it, we'll be doing those things, too."

For the first time in our friendship, Pearl had made me speechless. She was right, absolutely. Even though our lives seemed small and unimportant, deciding to tolerate some-thing we'd normally run from, because we liked the person doing it, was what made it easy for evil to creep into our world.

It was how someone like S. Haupt had convinced a bunch of lonely Germans to follow him and how he'd persuaded everyone to lie about how Mama died.

"I promise you, Pearl. Whether it's you or someone else, I won't let you get away with something I think is wrong."

She looked like the weight of the world had just left her shoulders. "Did you get the photo of your uncle?"

"No, but I don't think it's necessary. I'm pretty sure he's not the murderer."

She brightened further. "That's good news, right?"

"Not exactly. I'm still pretty sure he's the reason my mother is dead."

"How?"

I wasn't sure where to start. There were so many things floating through my head: the murder called a suicide, the good German labeled a Nazi, the sister-in-law coerced into losing everything. And poor Pop left in the dark because Adam didn't want to admit how badly he'd messed up.

I decided to tell Pearl everything. Starting with how Anna Mueller had told me my mother was a Nazi.

She listened in rapt silence as I rushed through the story, painting it in broad strokes, giving details only when I thought they were necessary. I don't know how long I talked, but by the end of my tale of what I'd read in the file, my voice had grown hoarse.

"You thought your mother was a Nazi?"

"Not really. For a second, maybe, but then I realized how foolish that was."

"Why didn't you tell me?"

"It didn't strike me as the kind of thing I should tell people, you know?"

She nodded, and I was relieved that this wasn't going to turn into another argument, especially after the strange conversation we'd just had. "So you don't know what happened after he wrote his last notes?" she asked.

"Only what he told me last year about her committing suicide," I said. "And we know that wasn't true."

"Then how do you find out?"

That was the question, wasn't it? I'd gleaned everything I could from the file. There was only one person who could fill in the missing part of the story and that was my uncle.

I told Pearl this and she nodded solemnly. "What about your aunt?"

"I don't think she knows everything. I just can't believe she would've stayed by his side if she did." Or at least, I didn't want to believe she could. I had a feeling that after this weekend, whatever relationship Adam and I had would be over for good. I didn't want to lose Aunt Miriam, too, not when I felt like I'd just gotten her back.

"So how do you get your uncle to spill?"

"I don't know yet."

While I mulled over my options, Pearl told me about the party they'd gone to. It was a typical Upper East Side Hanukah celebration, replete with good food, music, and fun games. Pearl thought she'd be bored, but between the lavish apartment and the pedigree of those in attendance (college professors, artists, writers, and musicians) she found herself wishing the night wouldn't end.

"So you had fun?"

Pearl sat cross-legged on the bed. "I guess. It would've been more fun if you'd been there."

There was a hitch in her voice that hinted there was something she wasn't telling me. "Is something wrong?" I asked.

She bit her lip. "I saw something tonight."

"And?"

Another bite, hard enough to leave the impression of teeth on her skin. "I'm sure I misinterpreted it."

"Tell me and I'll tell you what I think."

"It was something between your uncle and the woman who was hosting the party. Mrs. Pollock."

I still wasn't getting it.

"They were kissing," said Pearl.

"Like a hello kiss?"

"More like a *this way to my bedroom* kiss."

A chill went through me. He was doing it again. "Did he see you?"

"No. And I don't think it went any further than that. But from the way they were acting, I don't think it was the first time."

Did Miriam know? Her remarks to Adam implied that she was uncomfortable about *something*. How could he do that to her?

"You look really upset," said Pearl.

"I'm just surprised." I shouldn't have been, though. After all, if he'd cheated on my aunt once, it wasn't a leap to think he'd do it again. And again. "I keep learning all this stuff about Adam that makes me dislike him more and more."

"More than when you thought he might be a murderer?"

"In some ways, yes." For all my relief in realizing that, given the facts, it wouldn't have made sense for Adam to have killed Mama, I still hadn't forgiven him for putting her in a dangerous position to begin with. At least it wasn't Mama I was learning these things about. There was some consolation there. Her misdeeds, if she'd committed them, were done.

We said good night and Pearl went to her room. How could I get Adam to tell the truth about what had happened? Just asking him wasn't likely to do it. If Pop could cut me off with nothing more than a stern "I'm not talking about this now or ever," there was no reason my uncle couldn't do the same. I needed leverage, a reason to make him tell me what I needed to know.

I almost woke up Pearl when the idea hit me: Pearl had given me the perfect leverage. And now I was going to blackmail my uncle into telling me the truth.

I would've felt relieved that I had a plan, if I hadn't realized just then that I'd left my camera under Adam's desk.

18

I HAD NO CHOICE: if I was going to get the camera back, I had to do it then, while everyone was in bed. I left the guest room and headed back toward the front of the apartment, picklocks in hand. There was no reason to panic, I assured myself as I crept down the dark hallway. I'd gotten into the office relatively easily before. I could be in and out again in under five minutes.

I kept my hand on the wall to help me find my way in the dark. As I left the hallway and entered the parlor, the darkness abated enough that I could make out the furniture with relative ease. Where was the light coming from? It took me only a second to find out: it was leaking from beneath Adam's closed office door.

Had I left the lamp on, too? I couldn't believe I'd forget something so obvious. In fact, I was almost relieved when I heard someone moving around behind the closed door since it meant, more likely than not, that they were the one who turned the light on. That relief went out the window as soon as I realized that it also meant there was no hope of going into the office and getting my camera.

I retraced my steps and went back to the guest room, praying that Adam had no reason to look under the desk for at least the next twenty-four hours.

MIRIAM WOKE US AT 8:00 and instructed us to get dressed for synagogue. I thought about continuing to cry sick so that I could go back into the office, but I needed to figure out a way to get time alone with Adam without any chance of Miriam being in earshot. The camera could wait.

My plan fell into place on the way to shul. As we walked, Aunt Miriam proposed that we have lunch at the Plaza Hotel afterward, an experience Pearl had never had before. Pearl oohed and aahed at the prospect, cementing our plans for the rest of the day.

The weather was clear and cold, the sun adding a welcome warmth each time we left the shade of the awnings that lined the businesses we passed. I paused twice on the brief journey, complaining that I still felt a little weak from being bed-bound the day before.

We arrived at the synagogue, covered our heads, and took our places, Pearl, Miriam, and me on the women's side of the congregation, Adam on the men's. As I settled into a service I hadn't heard in almost a year, I began to doubt my strategy.

Was it possible Pearl had misunderstood what she'd seen? No, I couldn't believe that—Pearl was a reliable witness, I was certain of it. But what if Miriam already knew and my threat did nothing but reveal to Adam that I'd been snooping in his office? If I didn't play this right, I might lose whatever chance I had to find out what had happened.

If I were able to get Adam to fess up, what would I do with the information? I certainly couldn't go after Mama's killer. And Adam had proven himself unwilling to do so. That meant that if I were going to do anything, I would have to tell Pop.

And what would Pop do with the information?

I shook my head and tried to focus on the words of the cantor. I was getting ahead of myself. Adam might not know much more than what brought Mama to the Yorkville hotel room. He and Pop might be on equal footing, and that meant there would be no reason to share what I'd learned with anyone but Pearl.

Service ended and we met Adam in the lobby, where a pamphlet entitled "This Is Your Job" was being distributed. Inside, it invoked the anniversary of Pearl Harbor as a good time to start committing yourself to the war effort by participating in salvage activities. After being introduced to various friends of Adam and Miriam's in the congregation, we headed out into the brisk day and started toward the Plaza Hotel.

We hadn't gone half a block when I feigned being woozy.

"Are you all right?" asked Miriam.

"I think . . . no," I said. "I don't think I can make it to lunch. I'm so sorry."

"Don't apologize, Iris. You can't help being ill." Miriam put a hand to my forehead and I waited for her to declare that my temperature was perfectly normal, as Adam had the day before. "We'll all go home."

"But Pearl was so looking forward to the Plaza," I said.

Pearl did her best to look simultaneously disappointed by the change in plans and concerned with my health. "It's all right."

"Couldn't you all still go?" I said. "I could wait here until you're done."

"Don't be silly," said Miriam. "You need to be in bed."

"I'm not sure I can make it all the way back to the apartment." This was the kicker: it was still the Sabbath and Miriam was devout enough that I knew she wouldn't take a cab home. Adam, on the other hand, tended to be less Orthodox in his practices, as his business often demanded. I looked up at my uncle, hoping he would make the suggestion to escort me back so I didn't have to.

He wasn't picking up on my unspoken plea.

"I don't want Pearl to miss out on the Plaza," I said again. "She's never been before, and who knows if she'll ever get another chance."

"I was kind of looking forward to it," said Pearl.

"They have the most amazing tea cakes," I said.

Miriam shifted her weight from foot to foot. Her desire to be a good hostess to Pearl was conflicting with her need to mother me. She turned to Adam. "Maybe you could take Iris back to the apartment and then meet us at the Plaza."

"She can't walk that far," said Adam. He wanted his wife's permission to take a cab. He could have an affair with another woman without a second thought, but violating the Sabbath required consent.

Miriam rolled her eyes. "Then take a cab. It's not like you haven't done that before."

Adam hailed a taxi and agreed to meet them for lunch, provided I didn't get sicker during the journey. I knew what that meant: he had no intention of joining them.

Yeah, well, I had no intention of his leaving me alone, either.

I got into the back of the car with him and feigned continued weakness as we pulled away from the curb and headed home. Miriam watched as we departed, a worried look pulling her face long and lean. I felt terrible about lying to her yet again. Hopefully Pearl would see to it that she enjoyed lunch without spending the whole meal concerned about me.

It was a small price to pay to get the truth out of Adam.

We reached the apartment and my uncle opened my door and helped me up to the curb. The doorman, recognizing my fragile state, helped us into the building and summoned the elevator.

"Almost there," said Adam as each floor clicked by. These were the first words he'd spoken directly to me that day.

"I'm sorry you had to miss lunch."

"No worries. I have work to do, though your aunt Miriam would have a fit."

"Working on the Sabbath? I can't imagine she'd forgive you for that."

He winked at me. "It will be our little secret, right?"

The rage that had been building up inside me since reading my uncle's notes was reaching its peak. So now I had to be complicit in his lying to my aunt? We reached our floor and I hung back while Adam unlocked the door and let me in.

"I guess you'll want to lie down for a while," he said. "Perhaps after a nap, we should call a doctor."

"Perhaps," I said as I removed my coat. I was losing my nerve. It would be so easy to go back to the guest room and lie down and forget about all of this for a few hours. But then where would I be? Back where I started with nothing to show for it. "Could I talk to you for a minute, Uncle Adam?"

He looked at the mantel clock. Did he seriously just do that? "Of course. Why don't we sit?" He took his place in a large leather wingback chair and waited for me to do the same.

"I'd rather stand," I said.

"I thought you were ill."

"And I thought my mother committed suicide. It looks like both of us have been misled."

I'M NOT SURE how long I stood there waiting for him to respond to my pronouncement. However much time passed, it was enough for my legs to grow rubbery.

"What did your father tell you?"

"Nothing. I found out on my own. And last night I learned that Mama was working for you."

He wordlessly stood up and walked into his office. I thought that might be his way of dismissing me, but moments later he returned with my camera in his hand. "I'm assuming you would like this back?"

"Thank you," I said, taking the Brownie.

"I found it under my desk. The first rule of breaking in is to never leave anything behind, the second is to return everything to the way you found it. In the future, I recommend relocking drawers and cabinets after you open them. And since I'm dispensing advice, while it was very clever of you to bring along a distraction, you might want to teach Pearl the art of subtlety if you decide to continue employing her."

"Thanks, but I'm not here for your praise. Or your advice. I want to know what happened to Mama."

He returned to his chair and clasped his hands. "You read the file. You know everything I know."

"Your notes stopped on December 26. I want to know

what happened between then and when her body was found."

He sighed heavily. "You and me both, Iris. I'm afraid there's nothing to tell you. She asked us to watch you—we thought she wanted some time alone to get ready for your father's return—and then on New Year's Day we were contacted by the police and told she was dead."

"Why did they call it a suicide?"

"Because that's what it looked like. The police make do with the information they have available to them."

I stepped toward him, cutting the distance between us in half. "But that's *not* what it looked like. I've seen the crime-scene photos. It was clearly a murder. And even if it wasn't, you could've told the police what you knew. At the very least, you could've put them in touch with the Office of War Information. Why didn't you?"

"Because it wouldn't have made any difference."

"I think it's because you didn't want anyone to know how desperately you'd failed, Uncle Adam. You forced Mama to meet with Mr. Haupt and to turn over her money to gain his confidence. When things went terribly wrong you didn't want to be blamed for it, so you let the suicide story stand, only Pop was too smart to buy it."

"Is that what your father thinks?"

"I don't know what's in Pop's head. I figured this out on my own."

"You're a very clever girl, Iris, but I'm afraid you've made a leap of logic. I may have made mistakes, but I certainly didn't force your mother to do anything. Nobody could."

Even though his expression hadn't changed, I knew he was lying. He had to be. "She was in love with you. She kept that letter from you, the one where you begged her to end the affair."

He laughed, God help him. He sat there and laughed at me. "Your imagination is getting the best of you. Your mother and I were colleagues only. There was never a romantic relationship between us. Now, I suggest you go to bed and at least pretend, for your aunt's sake, that you haven't been lying to her this entire weekend." He stood up and headed toward his office again.

I followed him. "She should be used to it by now."

"What was that?" He paused at the doorway.

"Pearl saw you last night. Kissing Mrs. Pollock."

He couldn't have been more surprised if Mama had just walked into the room. "She misunderstood, that's all."

"Who am I going to believe, my uncle with his history of telling tales, or my best friend, who's never done me wrong?"

Pink tinged his cheeks. "All right. Things have been strained between your aunt and me. This past year has been difficult for all of us . . ."

I crossed my arms. The room suddenly seemed unbearably cold. "And it's bound to get more difficult when Pearl tells Aunt Miriam what she saw."

Rage lit his eyes. For the first time in my life, I was afraid of my uncle. "What do you want from me?"

I could feel tears wanting to appear, just like they had the day I'd tailed Jim McCain. To steel myself against them, I focused all my energy on clenching my toes. "I want the truth. About Mama. If you give me that, then Aunt Miriam doesn't need to be the wiser."

"I've told you the truth."

I grabbed his sleeve to show him that I wasn't going to back down. "No, you haven't. Why did she go to see Mr. Haupt? Why didn't you do anything to help her? You had to have known she was in danger when she didn't come home after a day passed. Why did you let the police call it a suicide?"

He closed his eyes tight and I could tell he was squelching whatever impulse he had to strike out at me. When he opened them I saw resignation: he had been cornered and he knew there was no way out but the truth. "All right," he said. "I'll tell you why she did it: because of you."

My voice faltered. "What do I have to do with it?"

"Haupt knew about you. He followed your mother. He saw her taking you to school. After Pearl Harbor, her desire to help with the case waned—your father was the only thing she was thinking about. She didn't want to upset him."

"Why would she worry about that? Did Pop know she was working for you?"

"It was his idea."

I was shocked, so shocked that I couldn't hide it. Pop had known she was doing this all along?

"Why don't you sit down, Iris."

I did as he said before my legs gave out entirely.

"I can tell you're surprised," said Adam. "I was in the habit of writing to your father about cases, getting his opinion when things were difficult. He'd always been an excellent investigator. When things took a challenging turn and I realized I couldn't continue the case without assistance, I wrote to him asking for ideas about who could help me. Name after name turned me down, and when it looked like I was never going to find someone to assist me, Art suggested that your mother might be able to help. She'd worked with us a handful of times before. She was very clever, your mother. Extraordinarily observant. And so seemingly innocuous that she could get anyone to tell her anything. And of course her familiarity with Yorkville and being a fluent German-speaker would be a tremendous boon. At the time we thought it was nothing more than an embezzlement case, and knowing how bored your mother was, your father saw no harm in letting her tail Karl Hincter to find out what he was using the money for."

"But what about once you found out he was funding the Bund? How did Pop feel about that?"

"He saw danger. A lot of danger. And he demanded that your mother stop participating in the case. I didn't know that at the time—he didn't let me in on the argument until he began to fear that she wasn't listening to him. That was when he asked me to step in and tell her that I didn't need her anymore."

"But you didn't."

Adam leaned toward me. "No, I did. Think what you want of me, Iris, but I always had the utmost respect for your father. If he didn't want Ingrid involved anymore, then I had to heed his request. I begged her to stop. When she refused my visits and calls, I wrote her a letter telling her that she needed to stop for your father's sake." The letter. It wasn't a lover ending an affair; it was an employer firing his assistant. And she'd saved it as proof, if she got in over her head, that it wasn't Adam's fault. He'd asked her to stop working, just like Pop told her to. Her choice to continue was her own. "Your mother refused to listen, though, and continued meeting with Hincter and Haupt. So I went to the Office of War Information, hoping they might take over the case. I thought by doing so, she'd be content knowing things would be followed to the end and we could obey your father and discontinue conducting the investigation on our own. Of course, it didn't work out so well. The OWI needed more information before they would agree to act, and your mother was determined to give them what they needed. But then Pearl Harbor happened and she finally realized that the last thing in the world she needed to be doing was upsetting your father. So she stopped working on the case. Haupt kept contacting her, though. We had dangled enough money in front of him that he was determined to get your mother's financial support. And I imagine he was very concerned that he had let her in on as much of their plans as he had. She kept putting him off and telling him it was a bad time to meet. Then, on Christmas, a package was delivered to her containing photos of you. The note that accompanied the images made it clear that if she didn't turn over the promised funds your safety could not be guaranteed."

The photos. Pop had the photos. I'd seen them in the safe, only I thought they were new surveillance photos, not pictures of me taken back when I was at Chapin. Did Pop know what they meant and what role they'd played, or were they, like the crime-scene photos, just another piece of the puzzle he was hoping to put together?

"I told her she should go to the police or the OWI and get their assistance. Before she could, a second package arrived containing another photograph: this one of Hincter. He'd been killed. The message was clear: if she didn't do as Haupt asked, Hincter's wouldn't be the only blood on her hands. She agreed to meet him in Yorkville on December 28 and to bring with her the money she had pledged. Unfortunately, by this point Rheingold and Valentine had decided they couldn't risk losing any more money, so she withdrew her own funds. And she asked Miriam and me to take you in and make sure of your safety until her return."

That explained their odd behavior that weekend, how

my every move was monitored. What would I have done differently if I'd known what Mama was up to? Would I have tried to stop her? "Shouldn't the meeting have only taken a few hours, though?"

"She needed more time to convince Haupt that her . . . enthusiasm was genuine. She called us not long after the appointed meeting time and told us that she was going to spend a few days with some friends, which we knew was code meaning that she would be with Haupt. She claimed all was well and she wanted to make sure that you were cared for in her absence." Mama had called? They'd never told me that. What I wouldn't give to have heard her voice for myself, one last time. "We didn't like the change in plans, but from her tone it sounded as though she didn't believe she was at risk. Her hope all along was to ingratiate herself with Haupt, get the information she needed for the OWI to take the case, and then leave."

"And the money?"

"She assumed from the beginning that it would be easy to retrieve it. Honestly, she didn't care. I think that if she could've gotten Haupt arrested and ensured your safety, she would've gladly lived the rest of her life as a pauper."

It was all so impulsive and risky. And why? Because of me. Because Mama was terrified they would do something to hurt me. "When did you know things had gone wrong?"

"We were never comfortable with any of it, but by New Year's Eve we were in a panic. I talked to the OWI again, but their energies were being directed at potential threats leveled against the Times Square celebration—they couldn't do anything to assist me until the New Year. I went to Yorkville myself and tried to find her, but I didn't know where to look and no one wanted to assist someone who clearly didn't look like they belonged. So we waited and hoped that all was well, even though we knew it most likely wasn't."

"Aunt Miriam knew about all of this?"

"Oh yes. There was no way I could've suffered through all of that without her."

Then why betray her now? I almost said, but I bit my tongue. "What do you think went wrong?"

"I'm not sure. It may have been a trap from the very beginning. Ingrid knew they had been following her before Pearl Harbor. I'm sure it must have continued well into December. After your father was injured, she grew careless. She started going to synagogue." We both did. "My guess is they found out she was a Jew and killed her for it."

Poor Mama must've been so scared. And so angry that she allowed herself to walk into an obvious setup. But then that was how she was: for all her intelligence, she was a woman ruled by her allegiance to Pop and me. She would've done anything to protect either of us.

"Why did you let the police declare her death a suicide? They had to know it wasn't."

"Stefan Haupt was a very powerful man, Iris. He had plenty of police in his pocket. I'm certain that he paid them off to prevent any scrutiny that might come his way. It was terrible to let people believe the lie, but I didn't know what else to do. If I told people the truth and it got back to Haupt that someone had knowledge of what really happened, he would know that your mother wasn't the only one aware of what he was up to. That would put you back in danger, and perhaps Miriam and myself. So I let the lie stand, hoping that Haupt would believe that any danger he was in had died with Ingrid." He ran his hands through his hair, and I saw for the first time how all of this must've eaten at him over the past year. "If there is any consolation, the OWI did shut down that branch of the Bund before they were able to do anything."

"Because of Mama?"

"In a sense. Hincter kept detailed notes about the meetings, which were discovered after his murder, including a list of who Haupt's followers were. Haupt was forced to go underground and the authorities were able to gain enough information from those included on the list to prevent a number of bombings and other events the group had been planning."

I let it all sink in. Mama was a hero. If she hadn't worked for Adam, if she hadn't gotten close to Haupt, if he hadn't killed Hincter to force her hand, many more people might be dead. It was a comfort, I guess, that her death did some good in the end, though I'd be lying if I said that I would've gladly sacrificed her for all those unnamed lives.

Besides, Haupt was still out there.

"How much does Pop know?"

Uncle Adam swallowed hard. "You must understand how fragile he was when he came home. I wanted to protect him."

"How much, Uncle Adam?"

"He knows your mother continued her involvement in the case, but he doesn't know why. I told him about Karl Hincter when the case began, and he knew the Bund was involved, but we never told him about any of the other parties. As far as your father is concerned, I insisted that your mother keep working on the case, even after he begged me to make her stop."

"Why? Why let Pop believe it was all your fault? Why not just tell him the truth?"

"I know your father, Iris. If there was a chance that he could have exacted revenge on Haupt, he would've done it in a second, even if it meant killing himself in the process."

19

THE OFFICE TELEPHONE RANG and Adam excused himself long enough to take the call. I was grateful for the reprieve. My world had been turned upside down and I needed to figure out how to reorient myself.

Adam was protecting Pop. Mama had been protecting me. And somewhere, out there, Stefan Haupt walked the streets a free man despite being a murderer.

Adam hung up the phone and joined me, this time with a glass of liquor in his hand. I had half a mind to ask him for my own snifter. "I take it you're going to tell your father about all of this," said Adam.

"Don't you think he should know that you weren't to blame?"

He swirled the amber fluid until it kissed the lip of the glass. "This isn't about what he thinks of me. I'd love to have Art back in my life, but you have to consider what he'd do with this information."

But there was a good chance Pop already did know. After all, he had the crime-scene photos and the surveillance photos of me. "Let me think about it," I said.

He took a sip of the booze. "And your aunt?"

"You said she already knows everything."

"I'm referring to what your friend Pearl saw."

Oh, *that*. "A deal's a deal," I said. "You told me what I needed to know, so I won't tell Aunt Miriam anything."

"Thank you, Iris. I know you've been put in a very unfair position and I apologize for that."

So he wasn't the devil I'd imagined him to be in my mind—he was just a flawed man whose betrayal was much more personal than I'd originally feared. Was there hope for Pop and him? I hoped so, though honestly that was the least of my concerns right now.

"I think I want to go home, Adam."

"Your aunt will be heartbroken. She had so much planned for you this weekend."

"She already thinks I'm sick. I'll come another weekend and make it up to her. But for now, I really want to be in my own house with my own thoughts. I can't stay here and pretend everything's all right."

He considered this for a moment. I hadn't intended it as a threat, but I think he took it that way: bow to me again, or I just might forget my promise to keep Miriam in the dark.

"All right. Shall we wait until Miriam returns with Pearl?"

I hated to abandon Pearl without an explanation, but my

need to see Pop was so powerful that my heart ached. "No," I said. "I want to go now. That way I don't have to look into Miriam's eyes and lie to her again."

HE AGREED TO SEND me home in a taxi by myself. I arrived at the Orchard Street house, tipped the driver with money Uncle Adam had given me, and hauled myself and my bag up the steps. My stomach grumbled with hunger and I realized I hadn't eaten anything since the cookies I'd stolen from Lydia. The weakness I was starting to feel was real.

I unlocked the front door and entered the house, half hoping to find Pop and Betty in a lover's clutch on the sofa. Unfortunately, the only thing there was the newspaper.

"Pop?" I called out as I walked from room to room. He wasn't downstairs, so I headed up. "Pop? Mrs. Mrozenski?" The bedrooms were empty, each bed crisply made. It looked like Pop's workmanship—the corners he learned at the Naval Academy. There was no reply as I paced the upper hallway. Where were they?

Betty's. Maybe Pop went to Betty's.

I picked up the phone and asked for Betty's exchange. As the operator connected me, I hummed a prayer for Betty to pick up. "Hello?" she said.

"Betty? It's Iris Anderson. I just got home and the house is empty. Do you know where your mom and my pop are?"

"I don't have a clue about your pop, but Ma's right here. Do you want to talk to her?"

I told her yes. There was a murmur of background noise before Mrs. M. came onto the line. "Iris. Is everything all right?"

"I came home early and was worried when I found the house empty. Do you know where Pop is?"

"No. I not see him since yesterday, when he tell me how sick Betty was."

Betty was sick? She sounded fine to me. "Right. How is Betty?"

"She's much better now, but your pop, he is worried yesterday and tell me to come to stay with her."

What was Pop up to? Why would he want Mrs. M. out of the house, too? "Okay, thanks."

I hung up and went back to the parlor. That day's newspaper had been folded so that the front page faced up, though it was clear someone had been through its contents. That meant Pop had been there at some point that morning. Amid the latest war news was an article entitled "Pearl Harbor Bared." The brief piece warned that in tomorrow's *Times* there would be a detailed pictorial look at the events of Pearl Harbor as a way of commemorating the anniversary. I set the paper aside and went into Pop's office, looking for a clue as to where he may have gone. The desktop was wiped clean, the top drawer contained the same assortment of office supplies and the lone business card I'd found in it before. The bookcase to the left of the desk was neat and dust-free. The only thing that seemed slightly out of place was a glass. A quick whiff told me that it had contained liquor.

So Pop had been drinking. That was his right. A man could drink in his own home. Alone.

So why was my stomach clenched in fear?

I spun in the office chair, hoping the change in perspective could lift my anxiety. As I completed my rotation, my eyes landed on the open closet. It wasn't the only thing ajar. The safe was open, too.

I perched before it and studied the contents. It looked like he'd been through it in a hurry. The once neat pile of folders was smeared into a fan, making it hard to see if anything was missing on first glance. Hard, but not impossible. One thing was clearly gone: Pop's gun.

So Pop had been drinking. And his gun was missing. And he'd sent Mrs. Mrozenski and me away for the weekend. No, he hadn't just sent me away: he'd sent me to my next of kin. And he'd read the paper that day where the subject of the Pearl Harbor anniversary was front-page news. And just days before, I'd caught him crying before the safe as he looked at the photos of Mama. And he'd been consulting with another detective, perhaps with the intention of passing his clients on to him. And when I last spoke to him he'd told me to have fun and said that he loved me.

Wait—what was I thinking? Pop wouldn't . . .

The doorbell rang. I jumped at the sound. Once I

registered where it was coming from and what it meant, I left the office and entered the foyer. Fear weighted down each footstep until it felt like I was slogging through snow. What if it was the police coming to tell me that Pop was dead? How would I ever recover from that?

"Iris? It's me."

It wasn't the police; it was Pearl. "Oh, thank God," I said as I opened the door. She was alone. The taxi that had escorted her from the Upper East Side pulled away from the curb and disappeared.

"What's the matter?"

Did I dare say it? It was such an absurd thought, and yet try as I might I couldn't get it out of my head. The words came out in such a rush that it seemed like they'd converged into one single word, with the same stark meaning. "IthinkPop'sgoingtokillhimself."

"Slow down. Start from the beginning." She came in and deposited her bag next to mine. I took a deep breath and filled her in as best I could about what I'd discovered since arriving home.

"That doesn't mean he's going to commit suicide."

"How would you interpret it, Pearl? He sent me away for a reason. I know he called Aunt Miriam and asked her to invite me to stay with her this weekend. And he got Betty to lie to her mom to get her out of here. All week I've been thinking that he didn't care about Mama, or anything but this new relationship with Betty, but that wasn't it at all.

He didn't want me to know what he was planning on doing." I was beyond distraught. When I believed Mama had killed herself, there had been no warning signs, no way I could've stopped it. But this time there had been ample cues I should've caught and didn't.

"But why would he leave the safe open?" asked Pearl.

Boy, howdy—was that really the one detail she was going to latch onto? "Because he was in a hurry and forgot to close it."

"But why would he be in a hurry? If he's killing himself, what's the rush?"

Strangely, that irritated me. It was like she was criticizing Pop for not going about killing himself in the right way. "Who knows what's in his head? Maybe he was worried I'd come home early and wanted to leave before that happened."

Pearl put her hands on my shoulders. "Listen to me, Iris—if he took his gun and left so fast that he forgot to close the safe, he did it because he was in a hurry and needed the gun to protect himself. The only other time he left the safe open was when you found the photos of your mother, right? He wouldn't make that mistake again unless he had to go somewhere fast."

She had a point there. "Maybe. But where would he be going?"

"Tell me what your uncle said," said Pearl. "How did he respond when you confronted him?"

I sat with her in the parlor and gave her the rundown on what Adam had told me.

"So now you know who killed her, and why. I'm so sorry, Iris. Will you tell your pop?"

Assuming he's alive, I almost said. "He needs to know that Adam's not to blame. I don't know if I should give him Stefan Haupt's name, though. He might—" An icy finger ran down my spine. Without explaining myself, I left the sofa and rushed into Pop's office.

Pearl followed fast on my heels and hovered behind me as I knelt before the safe. Why hadn't I put it together before? The man I'd met on the street outside the house at the beginning of the week had told me to tell Pop that Stefan said hello, and right after that was when Pop started acting so strange. It couldn't be a coincidence—it had to be the same Stefan, and that meant Pop knew a lot more than Uncle Adam thought.

Pearl crouched beside me. "What are you looking for?"

"I'm not sure yet." I pulled out the folders and rifled through them. A photo of me slid out and landed on the floor in front of us.

"Why is that photo in there?" asked Pearl.

"That's one of the pictures Haupt used to lure Mama to him," I said. "Pop got hold of it somehow."

Pearl frowned. "But isn't that Suze's skirt?"

I stared at the eight-by-ten. Pearl was right: this wasn't a picture of me in my Chapin uniform on the Upper East

Side. I was wearing a skirt Suze had loaned me to go dancing in Harlem, which hadn't happened until months after we moved to Mrs. Mrozenski's house. And there wasn't just one photo: others had been added to the safe since my last visit, each one capturing a closer and closer view of me as I left school, walked with Benny, and met Pearl at the corner of her street.

"Oh no," I said.

"Haupt took them, didn't he?" asked Pearl.

I nodded, unable to speak. It was happening again. Stefan Haupt was using me to lure one of my parents to him. Pop hadn't abandoned trying to track down Mama's killer. He'd been working on it all along and was close, too close, to pinning the crime on Haupt. "Pop's in trouble," I told Pearl.

I found the Rheingold Accounting folder that had the pictures of the man I didn't know in it. I flipped over the photos and found them stamped "Courtesy of McCain and Sons, Investigations." So Jim McCain had been helping Pop with surveillance. That explained how Pop had been investigating Haupt without my knowing about it. I flipped past the photos and perused the notes in handwriting I didn't recognize. It was the same kind of report Pop often made and had been teaching me to make after a tail: where the person had been, what time they'd been seen there, who had accompanied them. Pages of notes tracking Stefan Haupt's movements over the past few weeks.

But the handwriting was too florid and feminine to be Jim McCain's.

Wait a minute—I knew that writing.

I rose to my feet and went to my overnight bag, where I'd stored schoolbooks I might need for over the weekend. I removed an envelope stashed at the back of my health-and-hygiene text, the one containing the note to Pop from Betty.

The handwriting matched.

20

I TORE OPEN THE ENVELOPE and removed not a love letter, but another page of notes written in Betty's prim hand, detailing her most recent job tailing Stefan Haupt:

It looks like you're right: the German-American Bund is still alive and well and being run covertly by Haupt. The meeting location he suggested looks like it's his headquarters. I surveyed the place and I have to tell you, I don't think it's safe. Even if he's on the up and up, there are too many entrances and exits to guarantee there won't be someone else hidden there waiting to do you harm.

Pearl read Betty's notes over my shoulder. "So that's where he's probably gone, right? To meet with Haupt."

I nodded. What had I done by holding on to this? Would Pop have postponed the meeting or suggested another location if he'd seen Betty's note?

"Any idea where?" Pearl asked.

I shook my head. "Haupt must've suggested a meeting spot when he sent the photos."

"So they could be anywhere," said Pearl.

It was funny how Manhattan could seem so small to me at times, and at others inconceivably big. This was one of the moments when the number of places someone could disappear to on our tiny island boggled my mind.

I flipped idly through the textbook, as though the answer were hidden among its articles on hand-washing and sanitary food preparation. In a sense it was, because as I journeyed through the chapters, I landed on the pamphlet that had been included with Sarah's note. I hadn't looked at it very carefully when Michael gave it to me, but now I examined it. Part of it was in English and part of it was in German. "Amerikadeutscher Volksbund," it said at the top of the pamphlet, identifying who was authoring and distributing this material.

Amerikadeutscher Volksbund. I'd read that somewhere else.

"The White Swan," I said.

"Where?"

"The hotel where Mama was found. There were notes there from German-American Bund meetings in the lobby. And it was evident someone was still living or working there. That must be Haupt's headquarters now." I'd been in Haupt's lair and hadn't even realized it. Had he seen me there? Were there more photos showing Pop how close I'd been to danger?

I ached at the thought of Pop trying to climb into one of the windows and navigate that enormous space. Betty had been right: it was a meeting place that favored Haupt. If he intended to hurt Pop, Pop didn't stand a chance of getting out of there alive.

"Should we call the police?" asked Pearl.

"It won't do any good. What if we got the same cops who'd helped cover up Mama's murder?" We could try to contact the OWI. They were looking for Haupt, but would they believe a fifteen-year-old girl who claimed to know where he was? And even if they did, would they act before it was too late for Pop? They certainly hadn't sprung into action when Mama was the one in danger.

"We should call your uncle," said Pearl. "He'll know what to do."

She was right; Adam was the only one who could save Pop now. I picked up the telephone and asked for his exchange. Lydia answered and quickly relayed the bad news: neither Adam nor Miriam was home.

"Would you like to leave a message?" she asked.

"Yes. Tell him my pop's in trouble. I think he's gone to the White Swan to meet with Stefan Haupt." I hung up the phone. I wanted to cry, but I wouldn't let myself. There was no time for it.

"Come on," said Pearl. She pulled me into the parlor and grabbed our coats.

"Where are we going?"

"To Yorkville, of course."

I pulled back from her. "Think about what you're saying, Pearl. I couldn't drag you kicking and screaming there last week."

"That was last week. Someone's got to help him, right? If we don't go, if we don't do something, you're always going to wonder."

She was right. I might not be able to save Pop, but at the very least, I owed it to him to try.

WE POOLED OUR MONEY and came up with enough for the subway but little else. It was the first time since moving to the Lower East Side that I genuinely regretted being poor. We ran to the station and waited a good half hour before a train arrived to ferry us uptown. As the subway lights flickered on and off, I imagined Pop getting closer and closer to his end. Why hadn't I given him that stupid letter from Betty? If I'd done so, maybe he would've thought twice about doing this. He wouldn't have walked into an ambush trying to protect me.

"It's going to be okay," Pearl told me every few minutes, but the words had lost their power. How could things possibly turn out okay? What was my life going to look like in the days to come? Would I move in with Adam and Miriam,

264

a strange, sad shadow that they tried dutifully to cheer up? I didn't want to be part of their world anymore. I just wanted Pop.

After an eternity, we arrived at our stop. We rushed up Eighty-sixth Street while I tried to get my bearings. People stared at us as we jogged side by side, two Jewish girls who belonged in this neighborhood about as much as a klezmer band. Then I saw it on our right, the abandoned building with only the outline of letters still on its sign. The front door was barred, and the window Benny and I had entered had new boards nailed over it. Pearl and I went to the rear of the building, where a network of fire escapes snaked up the side. Someone had already entered this way—the second floor's ladder had been extended.

Pearl didn't hesitate before starting up the ladder. I followed suit and we made it to the second-floor platform and paused. The window facing the fire escape was open, or rather the glass was broken out of it. Sheer curtains danced in the winter breeze.

Pearl climbed through the window and I did the same. Broken glass crunched beneath our feet. We were in a corridor. The only light came in through the window we'd just entered, but it was enough to see that we were alone.

"Now where?" whispered Pearl.

"I'm not sure." I listened hard for the sound of anyone else in the building. Footsteps crossed the floor above us.

The third floor, where Mama died. "Up one more," I whispered. If they were up there, what would we do? In all our urgency to get here, we hadn't come up with a plan. It wasn't like either of us could wrestle the gun from Haupt's hand. Our only hope would be to create a distraction that would give Pop, if he was still armed, a chance to fire first.

Assuming we weren't already too late.

"Where are the stairs?" asked Pearl. I pointed toward where I remembered the stairwell being. Once inside it, we plunged into total darkness. Had it been like this when I was here with Benny? I didn't think so, but maybe I hadn't noticed because I'd felt safe in Benny's company and had no reason to fear anything but the lingering evidence of what had happened to Mama.

We held each other's hand as we crept up the stairs, taking our time so that we didn't make too much noise or stumble in the dark. It seemed to take forever to go up a single flight. A tiny bit of light illuminated the third-floor landing door, and we went toward it with muscles so tense they ached with every step.

The door creaked as we opened it. To my ears it sounded like a gunshot. We paused with it halfway open and waited to see if anyone had heard us. Once a minute had passed and no one came running, we went into the hallway.

"There," I whispered, pointing a finger toward the end of the hall at room 3C, the room Mama had died in. The door was closed, just as it had been the day Benny and I had been there. We started toward it when something stopped Pearl. I was about to ask her what was the matter when she put a finger to her lips and turned toward me.

I froze and heard what had stopped her: a male voice was coming from the room.

The voice was low and indistinct. I strained for some clue as to who was talking but we were too far away to tell.

"Is it them?" whispered Pearl.

"Who else would be here?"

Pearl closed her eyes as though by doing so she might be able to hear more clearly. After pausing for a few seconds she opened them. "What do you want to do?"

I'd hoped *she* would have a plan. "Let's get closer and make sure Pop's in there." The room next to 3C was open. We could go in there, put our ears to the adjoining wall, and listen for Pop's voice. "If he is in there, we'll have to create a distraction."

We slowly made our way toward the adjacent room. With every step floorboards groaned as though they were determined to give us away. After a few feet we paused to confirm we hadn't alerted them to our presence. Then, just as we were about to cross the threshold, a gun fired and ruined everything.

Pearl and I looked at each other before dashing into room 3D. We pressed ourselves against the wall that faced the hallway to make sure no one could see us. As we got into position, the door to 3C banged open and footsteps pounded past us. A second door opened with a boom and heavy footsteps made their way into the stairwell and down the stairs.

"Oh, God," I whispered. We were too late. If we'd moved a little faster, if I hadn't been so hesitant, we might have been able to stop him.

Pearl grabbed my hand and pulled me out of our hiding place and into the hallway. The door to 3C was starting to close on the rebound from being thrown open. Pearl pushed her body against it and we rushed into the room to see what, if anything, could be done to save Pop. He lay on the bed, his blood commingling with the stain made by Mama or some other crime that had happened in the months since her death. I could feel myself starting to crumble and I knew it was a matter of seconds before I would lie limp on the carpet beside him. As I began my descent, I grabbed on to his legs to let him know that I was here and would remain here in his final moments. Through the fabric of his pants, two good legs stiffened beneath my touch.

It wasn't Pop; it was Stefan Haupt.

I stared at him for what seemed like an eternity. Pop had shot him in the face, leaving the body completely unidentifiable. Pop hadn't just won; he hadn't intended for Haupt to live beyond this day.

Haupt struggled to breathe. A gurgling sound came from his throat and his chest convulsed three times.

"Iris, he needs help. He's going to die."

"He's going to die regardless of what we do." His face looked like freshly ground meat. Had there ever been a creature more pathetic than Stefan Haupt in those moments? I don't think so, but as vulnerable as he appeared, he also terrified me. This was the man who'd killed my mother and who knew how many other people. The man who threatened to kill me not once but twice, and who would be gladly celebrating right now if it was Pop lying across that bed. I couldn't forget that. He didn't deserve my mercy. Not after what he'd done.

Sirens sounded in the distance. Had Pop called the police, or had someone on the street heard the gunshots?

"We should go," said Pearl.

"Not yet."

I stepped toward him. "Do you know who I am?" I asked.

He didn't respond, of course. He didn't have the capacity for speech anymore.

"I'm Iris Anderson. Ingrid Anderson was my mother. Arthur Anderson is my father." There was so much more I wanted to say. How he'd taken away the one person who mattered the most to me. How he'd caused me to lose faith in her. How he'd almost destroyed my life irrevocably. But I knew he wouldn't care. Whatever had twisted his heart and convinced him that it was okay to hate someone based on their race wouldn't care about a sad little Jewish girl like me.

The sirens grew closer. Stefan gurgled again and a line of blood mixed with spittle dripped from what was left of his mouth. A rattle sounded in his throat, then his chest went still.

Pearl took me by the hand and pulled me from the room. We made it to the second floor and climbed out the window and onto the fire escape. The metal reverberated beneath our footfalls as the police pounded at the front door, trying to get in.

We hit the ground and kept running.

21

I EXPECTED SOMEONE to yell for us to stop, or to grab our collars, but all of the attention was on the White Swan, not the two of us. "Which way do you think Pop went?" I asked Pearl.

She shrugged as we both surveyed the street before us. The only path that made sense was back the way we came, assuming Pop was headed home. If he'd decided to hide out and lie low, he could be anywhere.

"We should go," said Pearl.

"We need to find him," I said.

"He's got a good ten minutes on us. I say we head back to your house. If he's not there yet, he will be soon."

I reluctantly agreed and followed her down Eighty-sixth Street. "Do you think they can link this to Pop?" I asked as we rounded the corner, putting the White Swan, and all of Yorkville, behind us.

"I doubt the police would do anything if they did. Haupt

was a Nazi, right? Your pop could claim he was just defending himself. After all, Haupt did threaten you." She slowed her pace. "You don't look relieved."

"Should I be?" I asked.

"Your pop made it out of there safe and the man who could have killed him won't be hurting anyone else anymore. That sounds like a reason for celebrating to me."

It did when she said it. But I couldn't get Haupt out of my mind. Despite knowing about the evil things he'd done and being painfully aware that there were probably many more misdeeds I'd never know about, all I could see was his ruined face as he lay dying. Pop had done that to another human being. Whether he deserved it or not, Pop had served as judge and jury and taken another man's life.

I didn't like knowing that, even as I understood the necessity of what he'd done.

We boarded our train and started the journey home. As we got farther from the Upper East Side, I began to relax. It was over; really, truly over. Pearl was right: Pop was safe, and Haupt had received his punishment.

We exited at the Lower East Side and started homeward. The sun set in the distance, throwing a pale pink light over the darkening street. "Thank you," I told Pearl. "For everything. For coming with me to Uncle Adam's. For going to Yorkville. For making me see that we had to help Pop. I don't know what I would've done without you."

"You would've done fine," said Pearl.

"Do you want to come back to the house with me?" I asked as we approached Orchard Street. After all, Pearl was supposed to be with me until Sunday.

"No, I think I'll go home and take a nice long nap. What are you going to do?"

"Wait for Pop. Then I might hug him for three or four years."

"Sounds like a good plan."

We parted ways and I approached the house. From the sidewalk I could see lights on in the parlor. I rushed up the stairs and heard the chirp of Mrs. M. as she sang to herself in the kitchen. I turned left, toward the office, but it was empty.

"Iris?" said Mrs. Mrozenski. "You are home? You are hungry, maybe?"

"Famished," I said. "I thought you'd still be at Betty's."

"A friend called wanting to go out tonight. She say she fine. She don't need me no more. Is okay. I sleep in my own bed tonight."

"Where's Pop?"

She shrugged. In her hand was a coffee mug that she was drying with a dish towel, no doubt Pop's from that morning. "Working, maybe? He no home when I arrive."

The phone rang, startling both of us. Mrs. M. answered it and, after a quick conference, passed it my way. "Is your uncle."

I'd forgotten about Uncle Adam. He had to be frantic

after getting my message. "Hello?" I said. Mrs. M. gestured that she'd be in the kitchen.

"Iris! Is everything all right? Lydia told me—"

"It's fine," I said. "It turns out I was wrong." I'm not sure why I lied. To protect Pop, I guess. If word got out that he'd done what he had, I didn't want anyone to know, not even Uncle Adam.

"Why did you—?"

"Overactive imagination," I said. "After our conversation today, I got a little paranoid, that's all."

"So Art's there?"

"Yep. He's in with a client. Nasty divorce case." Would he ask to talk to him? Probably not, though I couldn't be too careful.

"That's a relief. And you're sure everything's okay?"

"Absolutely, Uncle Adam. Everything's aces. Thanks again for everything."

I hung up and was surprised to find my heart racing. Why couldn't I relax? Everyone was all right, even if I hadn't seen Pop with my own eyes yet.

I ate a generous dinner with Mrs. M. and then forced myself to go to my room. Where was Pop? I could understand him wanting to lie low for a while, but this seemed excessive. If he didn't come home, what would I do? Call Uncle Adam back? Track down Jim McCain? Hope the police might be able to lend me some help? I paced the floor of my room until the creaking of the boards beneath my feet started to drive me mad. I moved to my bed and sat upright, facing the window. Even though it was freezing out, I left the pane raised so I could hear the comings and goings on the street below me. I'm not sure how it happened—perhaps my exhaustion had reached its limit—but my body gave up on me and I fell into a deep sleep. I awoke with a start to the sound of a cat wailing in the alley. I got up, confirmed the source of the noise, and then tiptoed down the hall to see if Pop was in his room.

Please let him be there, I prayed as I opened his door. *I'll do whatever You ask of me from this moment forward, just let Pop be okay.*

He was sprawled across his bed, sleeping so heavily, he was snoring.

I smiled at the sight, returned to my room, closed the window, and fell back asleep.

I SLEPT UNTIL ALMOST NOON, when hunger pains finally forced me out of bed. When I came downstairs, Pop was sitting in the parlor reading the newspaper. The "Pearl Harbor Bared" story took up most of the front section, and he studied each picture carefully, as though he were looking for someone he expected to see hiding in the background of each photo.

"Morning," I said.

"Morning."

I left him and went into the kitchen, where I made myself

several pieces of toast smeared with the oily margarine that was quickly replacing butter because of rationing. I rejoined Pop with plate in tow and set it on the table between us. He acknowledged my offering with a nod and claimed a piece for himself.

"I was surprised to see you here," he said. "I thought you were staying at Miriam and Adam's."

"I didn't feel good yesterday, so I came home." I sat in the rocker and picked up the comics page.

"You look like you're feeling better."

"Yeah, whatever it was passed. Mrs. M. said Betty was sick, too. Maybe I caught it from her."

If he was aware of my little dig, he didn't show it.

"Speaking of which, I forgot to give you a note from her. It's on your desk." I'd resealed her letter in another envelope, hoping Pop wouldn't find it strange that she hadn't written anything on the outside of it.

"Thanks. I found it." He turned the page and stared at a cartoon of a sword-wielding Uncle Sam.

"Were you working on a case yesterday?"

"Hmmmm?" He continued staring at the paper.

"I was worried when you didn't come home last night."

He licked his fingers and turned another page. "I was supposed to meet with a client uptown."

"Supposed to?"

"He was a no-show. So I decided to make the best of a bad situation and do a little surveillance for another case."

How could he be so calm after everything that had happened the day before? Was it possible that it hadn't hit him yet, or was this relief from knowing Stefan Haupt was gone for good?

I put aside the comics and retrieved the local section from the pile on the coffee table. Most of it contained listings about the ways in which Pearl Harbor would be commemorated the next day. Any number of blood drives, convocations, and moments of silence were planned across the city. And then, near the back of the section, I found a brief article mentioning that an unidentified body had been found in Yorkville.

Body. He was definitely dead, then. Deep breath.

I looked at Pop again. He was staring at an article called "The Truth About Pearl Harbor."

"Didn't they tell us the truth before?" I asked.

"Depends on your interpretation," he said. "Right after it happened, Secretary Knox made some statements that don't seem in line with what we now know to be true."

"Like what?"

"He didn't make it clear how extensive the damage really was. He tried to minimize things."

"Why did he do that?"

He folded the page in half. "To reassure people, I imagine, though I think the American public would've rather had the truth."

Just like Pop would've rather had the truth about Mama. "But the truth is out now, right?"

"Some of it. I'm sure there will be many other things we'll learn about what really happened in the years to come."

I wasn't that interested, to be honest, but I was so happy to be sitting in my living room, talking with Pop, that I would've asked him questions all day if I could guarantee that he'd sit there with me. "Like what?"

"If I had to guess, I'd say we knew the attack was coming."

"Seriously? If that was the case, why wouldn't we have stopped it?"

He traded that section for another. "We may not have been able to. Or maybe we wanted an excuse to enter the war and knew this would unite the American people in their desire for revenge. In fact, that might be why Secretary Knox downplayed things. Things weren't supposed to get that out of hand."

"But people died."

Pop nodded. "Collateral damage. It's an ugly side of war, Iris, a cost of doing business, if you will. Sometimes people have to die so that many more won't." I thought of Mama and Karl Hincter, whose deaths may have prevented thousands of others from dying at Haupt's hands. "Something needed to happen to rally the American people and, unfortunately, the only thing that would do so was an attack on our own soil."

"Do you think it was the right thing to do?" I asked the man who had shot someone the day before.

"I don't think anyone cares what I think."

"I do." I chewed my lip, trying to steel myself for my next question. "Have you ever killed anyone?"

He didn't look up from the paper. "No. I didn't serve in combat."

I shouldn't have been surprised that he lied, but it still bothered me that there was nothing in him that showed any regret for what he'd done.

The house phone rang and I could hear Mrs. M. leaving the kitchen to answer it. She paused after greeting the caller, then said, "Iris. Is for you."

I left Pop and took the receiver from Mrs. M. I didn't even get out a hello before a voice barked at me, "WHAT IS PEARL HARBOR UP TO?"

I was so confused by the question that I didn't even try to figure out whose voice was on the line. "What?"

"Give me that," said a female voice that I finally could put a name to—it was Suze. "Iris, I'm sorry we're calling like this—"

"Don't apologize to her," said the first voice. Rhona. It was Rhona. "I want to know what the story is and I want to know now."

"Cool it," said Suze. "I'm sorry, Iris. She's upset about Benny."

"What about Benny?"

"You haven't heard?"

"Heard what? I just woke up." Suze repeated this

279

information to Rhona, hoping it would calm her down. It had exactly the opposite effect.

"While you were lying on your lily whites," said Rhona, nearly breathless with rage, "Benny was being kicked out of school."

"I don't understand—Benny was expelled? For what? And what does Pearl have to do with it?"

Suze wrestled the phone from her again. "Pearl pinned the banner on him, and all those letters the Jewish Federation has been getting."

"You've got this wrong. Pearl wouldn't do that."

"I wish I was wrong, baby girl. My kid sister is pals with Judy Cohen's sister. She gave her the whole scoop."

"I told him to stay away from that icky," said Rhona in the background. "Every time he's messed with her something bad has happened."

"I'm so sorry," I said, because I was, even if this wasn't my fault.

"Sorry?" said Rhona. "How's sorry going to help Benny? You know what happens to boys who are eighteen years old and no longer in high school? They get drafted, that's what. Thanks to your friend Pearl Harbor, Benny could be staring down the Krauts in less than a month."

"Close your head, Rhona," said Suze. "Look, Iris, you know he wouldn't do something like that—"

Rhona broke in again. "You know what? Let's just go to that fat cow's house and make her take it back." The operator's voice came on the line, telling Rhona she needed to drop in another dime if she wanted to keep talking. "She's going to be sorry she ever messed—" Rhona's voice disappeared and the dial tone came on the line.

What was going on? Benny had been kicked out of school for writing the letters? And Pearl was the one who turned him in?

And now Rhona was on her way to Pearl's house.

I ran upstairs and threw on some clothes. When I returned to the parlor, Pop was waiting for me. "Whoa, where's the fire?"

"I forgot about a test," I said. "That was Pearl on the phone. She wants to study."

"Can't you study here?"

Was he still being overprotective? Seriously? "Pearl's babysitting her cousin," I said so fast that I didn't have time to register the lie. "She's kind of trapped at home."

He looked at his watch. "Back by five, okay?"

"Okay," I said, then I grabbed my coat and ran out the door.

22

I RAN ALL THE WAY to Pearl's house, trying to make sense of my conversation with Suze and Rhona the whole way there. Surely they'd gotten something wrong. This had to be a silly rumor that had gotten legs when Benny couldn't be found that morning. Or maybe it was a prank, albeit a strange one. I banged on Pearl's door, momentarily worried that Rhona was already inside, doing her worst. But after ten seconds, the front door creaked open and Paul appeared.

"Hey, Iris—"

I cut him off before he could say anything else. "I need to talk to Pearl. It's kind of important."

"She's in her room."

"If anyone else comes by looking for her, tell them she's not here."

"Why—?"

"Just do it, Paul," I barked. I blasted past him and took

the stairs two at a time. The Levines lived in half of a narrow brownstone. Paul's and Pearl's bedrooms were upstairs, as was the house's only bathroom. Pearl was on her bed as I entered her room, reading a book amid a tangle of unmade sheets and yesterday's clothes. As I arrived she looked up with a grin that quickly vanished when she saw the look on my face.

"Rhona and Suze are on their way over here. They said you had Benny expelled."

"They expelled him on a weekend? Wow, I didn't think they'd do that."

I wasn't expecting her to confirm it. "You really did turn him in? Why?"

"Because, like you said at your aunt and uncle's: the right person needs to be punished, no matter how much it hurts."

That's what she'd been getting at? "But Benny couldn't . . . he wouldn't . . ."

Pearl removed her glasses and rubbed her eyes. Dark circles made moons in the flesh beneath them. "I'm sorry, Iris, but I saw him putting letters in the lockers. In fact, I was so bewildered by it that I fished the letter out of Judy Cohen's locker to make sure it wasn't something else that he was leaving her. But it wasn't."

"Maybe he was doing the same thing you were doing, looking at something someone else had placed there."

"This was the second time I saw him do it. The first time

was the day you two went to Yorkville. He was slipping a note into Saul's locker that morning."

"But you have to be mistaken—"

"The handwriting matches." She opened her bedside drawer and pulled a folded page from it and passed it my way.

Iris,
Sorry I had to run off the other day.
Can I make it up to you this weekend?
                                        Benny

So that was what his pantomime had meant when I was leaving school on Friday: Did you get my note?

"He gave this to you to give to me?" I asked as I took in the scrawl that I recognized from the locker notes.

Pearl nodded. "If I had any doubt, any doubt at all, I wouldn't have turned him in. I wouldn't do that to you."

I sank onto the bed beside her. I knew she was telling me the truth, but that didn't mean it hurt any less. "But I don't understand why he'd do it."

"I don't either, but you said he seemed strange when he found out you were Jewish."

Did he? Looking back, it wasn't my being Jewish that seemed to bother him, but the fact that I knew about the letters that the federation had been receiving. And why would he be upset about that unless he was the one who was sending them?

Pearl closed her book and shifted until she was sitting cross-legged. "The Rainbows have a reputation for a reason. They start fights, they steal, they skip class."

"But that's gossip. Maybe this is the first time Benny's done anything wrong." I knew that wasn't true, though. I'd seen evidence of petty theft with my own eyes.

"You probably don't want to hear this," said Pearl, "but Paul told me that Michael caught Benny stealing food from the A and P a couple of weeks ago. Michael swore Paul to secrecy, but you know my brother."

"But Suze said he wouldn't do something like this," I said.

"Suze is his friend. Of course she's going to say that. And he's just been expelled. It's not like he's going to jail or something."

No, but he could be facing a much worse fate. If he were still in school, at least he could avoid being drafted for a few months, not to mention how his father was likely going to take the news.

"We have to be missing something here, Pearl. We've got to have this wrong."

She leaned back on her arms. "This isn't like your mom, Iris. Sometimes rumors about people are true."

I LEFT PEARL'S HOUSE and started down Delancey, hoping the cold winter air might clear my head enough to

285

either accept Benny's guilt or come up with a way to exonerate him. I couldn't be mad at Pearl, even though I desperately wanted to be. Given the information she'd gathered, Benny was the obvious culprit. I would've thought so, too, in her shoes. But that was the point: I wasn't in her shoes, I knew him better than that.

Or I thought I did. Was I becoming one of those people who became blind to the wrong happening right around them because they so desperately wanted to believe that someone they cared about was good?

"Iris!" called a voice. Nuts. It was Rhona. I quickened my pace. "I see you, girl detective. Don't you think you can outrun me."

I stopped and turned toward her.

"Where's Pearl Harbor?" she said. Suze and Maria were with her, pleading with her to slow her pace.

"I don't know," I said.

"Did you talk to her?"

"No." I fought to keep my voice calm. "She wasn't home."

Rhona squared her shoulders and stood directly in front of me. She was taller than me and sturdy in a way that I hadn't yet become. I had no doubt she could hurt me if she really wanted to.

"Step off, Rhona," said Suze.

"You're both going to pay for this," said Rhona. "This is on you, too."

"Let me talk to her," said Suze. Maria pulled Rhona

away while Suze did the same to me. "You've talked to her, haven't you?" Suze asked in a hushed voice once there was half a block between Rhona and us.

I nodded, almost imperceptibly.

"What's the news, baby girl?"

"There were witnesses," I said.

"More than one?"

I shrugged, unable to lie to the one person who'd always been nice to me. "Do you think Rhona will really hurt Pearl?"

"She's upset. She's protective of Benny. You know that. And she's already lost one boy who meant the world to her. Just get to the bottom of this, okay? No one even knows where Benny is. We don't need another Rainbow disappearing."

"I'll do what I can," I said, though I knew they weren't going to be happy with any of the answers I turned up.

Rhona was starting to raise her voice again, though I couldn't hear what she was saying.

"You better scat, pussycat," said Suze.

While Suze and Maria distracted Rhona, I ducked into the A&P. There, behind a display of Bisquick, I hid until I could no longer see them through the front windows.

"Iris?" said a male voice. "What are you doing?"

It was Michael Rosenberg. He had on a white apron that was smeared with juice from fresh produce.

"Hiding," I said.

He looked amused. "I think the coast is clear."

"Benny isn't working today, is he?"

"He's off. But don't worry—Pearl's already taken care of everything." So he thought I was there to interrogate Benny.

I moved away from the Bisquick toward a pyramid of canned peas. "I guess they're going to expel him, huh?"

"Believe it or not, they already did. Judy Cohen's father called Principal DeLuca last night and demanded that something be done immediately." So that explained why swift action was taken. "And at tomorrow's convocation DeLuca's going to formally apologize to the federation."

That was good news for the federation, though I hated to think how the gossip mill was going to twist and turn this story come lunchtime.

"I know this must be hard for you," said Michael. "Paul told me you two were close."

"Not that close, apparently." As sick as I was at the thought of Benny taking the rap for this, I couldn't help but want to divorce myself from him. The federation could think what they wanted about my level of devotion, but I couldn't stand the thought that they might assume I shared any of the sentiments in those letters. "Just so you know, I had no idea—"

Michael raised his hand to stop me. "Of course you didn't. No one thinks that."

"Good." I didn't know what else to say to Michael. I was embarrassed, not just about what Benny had done, but that

Pearl was the one who discovered it. "I guess your pop's going to fire him, huh?"

"No," said Michael. "We're keeping him on."

"Seriously?"

Michael cleared his throat and leaned toward me. "My old man believes that everyone deserves a second chance."

"Does he know how awful those letters were?"

"Look, I know this may not make sense, but he likes Benny. In fact, I like Benny. I'm not sure why he did it, but the last thing we want to do is retaliate. If he really thinks badly of Jews, we want to see if we can't change his mind by showing him a little kindness."

"That's generous of you."

Michael pushed his glasses up in a way that reminded me of Pearl. "I don't know how much you know about Benny, but the kid's had a hard life. His dad got canned for being a drunk and now Benny is the only one bringing in money. He needs this job, now more than ever. I couldn't sleep at night if we took that away from him."

I have to say, Michael's charity impressed me, even if I wasn't convinced we had our man.

"Of course," Michael continued, "you only get one second chance. If he does something like this again, I doubt we'll be so forgiving." He eyeballed the pyramid of peas and adjusted a can so that its label faced forward. "Speaking of second chances: I told everyone that Pearl's been helping you with the case. Believe it or not, some of them actually

289

thought she could be the one writing the notes." I stopped myself from saying that, according to Paul, Michael had been one of those pointing the finger at her. "Anyways, I think there's a good chance that we're going to let her back into the federation."

"That's swell," I said.

"And while I know you're not interested, the invitation is extended to you as well. In my opinion, you don't have to demonstrate your faith outwardly to be devout. What we do when we know no one is watching is more important than what we do when they are."

"That's a good philosophy." It was such an interesting way of describing faith, not just in God, but in people. "Maybe that's why I have such a hard time believing Benny is capable of doing something like this: I'd never witnessed him do something bad. He just never let me see that side."

"Or maybe you just never wanted to see it."

Ouch. As hard as it was to hear, it was certainly possible that it was the truth.

A woman knocked her shopping basket into the pea pyramid, sending cans tumbling to the ground.

"I'd better go," I told Michael. "It looks like you have work to do."

I LEFT THE A&P and headed toward Benny's building. If Suze was right and no one knew where he was, there was a good chance he was hanging out in the air-raid shelter. The temperature fell as I walked, the sky rippling with snow flurries that seemed determined to fall by the most circuitous route possible. I'd rushed out of the house without gloves, and now I shoved my frozen fingers in my pockets and forced them to bend to increase my circulation. As the temperature dropped, so did my spirits. I might have been wrong about Mama and Uncle Adam doing bad things, but that didn't mean I was wrong about Benny, too. Like Pearl said, he had a history of misbehavior that I was well aware of. Doing something like this wasn't out of character.

I arrived at the air-raid shelter and found the door closed. From inside came the gasp of the Aladdin heater. I knocked four times: two short, two long.

Benny opened the door a crack. "I'm surprised to see you here."

"I wanted to hear the truth from the horse's mouth."

He pushed the door open wider and I took in his father's handiwork. His left eye was hidden in a mass of purple bruises. His right cheek was stained yellow and brown.

"Did you write the notes?" I asked.

"What do you think?"

I thought of what Pearl had said. She wouldn't have come forward if she wasn't certain. "I think if you did, you must've had a good reason for it."

He pulled his pack of cigarettes from his pocket. "So you think I'm guilty, too?"

"I didn't say that."

"You didn't have to." He lit a cigarette and shoved the crumpled pack back into his pocket.

"What happened to your face?" I asked, even though I knew the answer.

"Principal DeLuca visited us this morning. The old man doesn't like surprises."

It was funny how both he and Michael called their pops "the old man," and yet, based on their descriptions, they couldn't be more different.

"He must be pretty steamed that you were expelled."

"Nah, otherwise he would've blackened both eyes. I've still got a job, right? That's all that matters to him."

I tried not to stare at the damage to his face, but the bruises were so vivid that it was impossible to look at anything else. "Can I get you something for your eye?"

"No, thanks. I can always use snow if it starts to sting." He sat back down and wrapped himself in a blanket he'd left on the bench. "What happened with your uncle?"

He was changing the subject and I knew it, but I was grateful for the shift. I sat beside him and told him the tale of my weekend with Adam and Miriam and how things had resolved the night before.

"And you're okay with how your pop handled things?"

"He didn't exactly have a choice, right?"

"He could've just injured the guy and let the police deal with it. There's no hope of the truth about your mother coming out now. If the guy's dead, he can't confess to what he did."

Benny gave voice to something that had been bothering me: Pop got his revenge when he killed Haupt, but what did Mama get? There were still people who thought she was a Nazi and many, many more who thought she'd killed herself. He could've kept us safe and vindicated her if he hadn't responded so brashly.

Benny offered me the flask he'd had the other day. It felt lighter to me, a lot lighter, in fact. I took a swig, but instead of handing it back to him, I held on to it.

"You still didn't answer my question," I said.

"Do I really need to? You've made up your mind."

"Pearl saw you putting notes in the lockers."

He flicked ash into an empty can of pork and beans. Had he stolen that from the A&P? "And she couldn't have been mistaken, huh? Or made the whole thing up because she was jealous that her best friend had someone new to occupy her time?"

Would Pearl act that way? No, not the Pearl I knew. But then the Benny I knew couldn't write those letters. "Your handwriting matches," I said. "Pearl couldn't be mistaken about that."

"And here I was starting to think you were the one person who believed in me," he said.

"I do believe in you."

"Then you never would've asked me if I'd done it to begin with."

I hugged myself against the cold. It wasn't just the room that was chilly; Benny's manner was doing a fine job of sucking any hint of warmth from the air. "What are you going to do now?"

"Work. Wait to get called up. I'm eighteen, so it's only a matter of time before that happens. Hopefully I'll be able to take out a few Krauts and Nips before they do the same to me." He rubbed his hands together.

"That's a pretty dim future."

"What do you expect from someone like me?" He leaned his head against the wall and stared at the ceiling. "You'd better go, Nancy Drew."

I stood up, biting back the urge to tell him that he could've been so much more than he was letting himself become. As I turned to go, he took my hand. I thought he was going to pull me back to him, but his fingers slid from my grip and wrapped around the flask. I let go of it and him and left.

23

I TRUDGED HOME IN THE GATHERING SNOW, feeling just as bad as I had in the days before I visited Miriam and Adam. Was Benny innocent? How was that possible? Pearl had seen him. I didn't doubt that for a moment. She had seen him putting those notes in the lockers. Twice. And there was no mistaking that handwriting.

I stopped in my path. He may have written the notes and put them in the lockers, but what if someone else had put him up to it?

I turned tail and headed back to the air-raid shelter. I slid the last few feet to the door and pounded on it with my bare hands.

It wasn't necessary. The door was unlocked. Under the force of my knocks it swung open, revealing an empty space.

I stepped back and peered at the building Benny lived in. I had no idea which apartment was his. In the distance the bells at Our Lady of Sorrows began to sound the five o'clock hour.

I needed to get home. Benny would have to wait until morning.

I made it home ten minutes later. As I entered the house, I waved to Pop, who was seated in his office with the phone to his ear. As he returned my wave, he gestured for me to close his door. It latched with a sickening thud.

It seemed I'd hurried for nothing.

Would I ever work with him again? I wasn't sure if I wanted to. It turned out I was a terrible detective, just like I feared. I had gotten so many things wrong in the past week, misread so many signs and clues. It was embarrassing that I could be born into a family of detectives and have so little common sense and basic skill at my disposal.

I stood before his closed door and strained to hear his side of the phone conversation, but his voice was too low to make out. Just when I was about to abandon my eaves-dropping, he started to laugh.

How could he possibly find something funny after he'd killed a man?

What I'd seen in Yorkville came rushing back to me. When it came to working cases for unscrupulous people, Pop sometimes operated under a different morality—after all, he was being paid to do what they asked, not pass judgment. He seemed to conduct himself more carefully in his private life, though, and encouraged me to do the same.

Being honest, respecting authority, saying thank you—these were all things he believed were important. So why did he choose to act like one of his clients when he faced down Stefan Haupt? Why not, as Benny suggested, shoot to disarm him and then let the proper authorities determine his punishment?

I couldn't come up with any reason other than that it was easier.

After a quiet dinner of kasha with lard and onions, I spent a miserable evening in my room, trying to unsuccessfully distract myself with comic books and *True Romance* magazine. I kept waiting for the phone to ring and for Rhona to demand to know if I'd talked to Pearl, but it remained silent. No doubt she'd pounce on me at school the next morning. What would I say then?

What could I say?

Just before I was about to call it a night and turn out my light, there was a knock at the door.

"Come in," I said.

Pop entered the room, looking strangely out of place among my girlish things. "I wasn't sure if you'd be sleeping."

"Not yet."

"What's on your mind, Iris?"

"What do you mean?"

He sat on the edge of my bed. "You were so quiet at dinner. It's obvious something's bothering you."

I couldn't tell him everything that was on my mind, but

perhaps I could share part of it. "I'm just thinking about this boy I know. I found out he did something really terrible and I can't wrap my head around it. I never would've thought he was capable of something like that."

He rubbed his chin, where that day's growth of beard was starting to create a shadow. "The two things aren't mutually exclusive, are they? People who do awful things can also be kind and generous. No one is all bad or all good. And sometimes, though we may not understand it, people have reasons for the things they've done, even the awful things."

Was it possible Pop knew that I had been brooding over what he'd done to Stefan Haupt? "Isn't that just making excuses, though? If you've done something awful, can your reasons for doing it ever justify it?"

He smoothed my quilt with his hand, pressing out the wrinkles in the fabric. "It's not about justifying or forgiving someone, Iris. A bad thing is still a bad thing. But it gives you a reason, and once you have a reason, maybe you can prevent it from happening again."

I tried to tune my head to what he was saying, but all that came back was static. "Thanks, Pop," I said.

"Get some sleep." He looked down at his hands and it became apparent that there was something he wanted to tell me. "I might be gone for a few days. There's a big case upstate that I've gotten involved in. The money's too good to pass up, I'm afraid."

"When are you going?"

"Tomorrow."

Still he didn't meet my eyes. Maybe he was more bothered by what had happened to Haupt than he'd let on. Or maybe he was just worried about possible retribution.

"I could go with you," I said.

"Not this time, Iris." He bent my head forward and kissed me. "When I come back, let's talk about the business again and how you can help me. All right?"

I stared at his face, a face that was, mercifully, still whole, and wondered how he ever thought things could go back to how they used to be. "Sure, Pop," I said. "That would be swell."

I DISTRACTED MYSELF with *True Romance* until my eyes grew too heavy for reading. Despite the light subject matter of the magazine, as I dozed, my mind seemed determined to go to dark places. In my dreams I was back at the White Swan with Pearl, listening to the gunshot and the sound of what we thought was Stefan Haupt running from the scene. We went into 3C, and just before I was able to verify that Pop wasn't the one who was shot, the gun would fire again and I'd be back at the beginning, breathlessly worrying if Pop was dead.

I awoke with a jolt after the dream had restarted for what must've been the fifth time. I couldn't bear to experience the worry that we'd been too late again, that Pop would be dead, that our trip had been in vain. Each time it felt so hopeless. Why did my mind insist on going back there again and again?

Was I missing something? Was this my brain's way of conflating the anniversary of Pop's injury with what happened at the White Swan, or was something else afoot?

BEFORE I LEFT for school the next morning, I combed the paper, looking to see if they'd identified Stefan Haupt, but there wasn't even a mention of the body in Yorkville. Pearl was waiting for me at the corner. From the look of the snow accumulating on her shoulders, she'd been waiting for a while.

"Hi," she said shyly, like this was our first encounter since I'd moved to the Lower East Side.

"Hi." We started toward school, both of us bent into a powerful wind that ruffled our hair and sent the snow into our mouths and eyes. "I think we should hold back until the first bell."

"Why?"

"Rhona's on the warpath. Until I figure out how to handle her I think it's best if you lie low."

Pearl nodded her consent and slowed her pace.

"There was nothing about Stefan Haupt in this morning's paper," I said.

"I know. I looked, too."

"Why do you think that is?"

Pearl removed her glasses long enough to wipe them free

of snow. "Maybe they couldn't identify him? After all, he was shot in the face."

That could've been deliberate on Pop's part. If the police couldn't identify the victim, it would be that much harder to track down a killer. Besides, this was a personal victory, not a public one. He didn't need anyone else to know that Haupt was dead.

I had to change the subject, before that wretched bloody face moved into my brain and set up camp. "I talked to Benny," I said.

Pearl put her hands in her pockets and buried her chin in her scarf. "And?"

"And I wonder if it's possible that there's more to the story.

"I told you what I saw." Her words were clipped, her tone defensive.

"I know. And I believe you. I believe he wrote those notes and put them in the lockers. But what if someone made him?"

"Like who?"

"I'm not sure yet." We walked in silence, both of us weighing the possibilities in our heads. "I talked to Michael, too. He said the federation wants you back."

"Really?"

I nodded. "They're impressed with what you did and they want to give you a second chance."

Her face flushed despite the cold. "Wow. I didn't expect that."

"Are you going to take it?"

"I don't know."

P.S. 110 came into view. Another banner hung above the main entrance, unreadable from this vantage. Could it be more anti-Semitic vandalism, perhaps proof that someone else had been behind this all along?

With each step, the sign became clearer. This wasn't another threat to the Jewish students, just a reminder: "Remember Pearl Harbor." Like we could forget.

PERSONAL HYGIENE. Again. Mr. Pinsky droned on about the role of sanitary fairs in the nineteenth century while the students around me giggled at the concept that people used to throw their poop out the window.

But as compelling as disposing of fecal matter during Victorian times could be, it wasn't where my mind was. It was buzzing around Benny and Pearl.

Michael had given both of them a second chance. But that wasn't accurate, was it? The notes weren't the first bad thing Benny had done that Michael knew about: according to what Paul told Pearl, Benny had also stolen from the store.

Was it possible that while Michael knew Benny was stealing, his father didn't?

The notes and the banner were a public act, one that Mr. Levine was bound to hear about from customers in the neighborhood. Michael would've had no choice but to tell him about that.

Michael had to know his father would forgive Benny for all of that, just like he had to know that he would've given him another chance if he'd known he was stealing. So why tell him about one crime, but not the other?

Leverage. Michael could have used the thefts as leverage. After all, Benny probably didn't know what Mr. Levine would do if he knew he was stealing. That information was Michael's alone.

Michael knew that Benny's dad was out of work and that Benny was the family's only source of income. He knew Benny would've been desperate to keep his job. And if Benny were fired, the fact that he was a thief could keep him from getting another one.

So Michael dangles this carrot in front of Benny and tells him his lips are sealed, as long as Benny does him this one little favor . . .

Wait a minute—what was I thinking? That Michael made Benny leave the notes? How on earth did that make sense?

"Don't forget," said Mr. Pinsky as class wound to its completion. "After lunch everyone will be convening in the auditorium for our 'Remember Pearl Harbor' convocation. We ask that you treat this somber occasion with respect and demonstrate the maturity we know you young men and women are capable of displaying."

And that's when it hit me: Michael had done it to force the federation to band together at a moment when it seemed like the group was doomed to fall apart, and to force the school to recognize what was happening to the Jews in Europe. He needed Benny's help because he knew he couldn't write the notes and plant them himself. He may not have ever anticipated our figuring out who was behind the crimes. And if we did, Michael may have assumed that we'd never come forward if we knew Benny was behind it.

But that didn't stop him from letting Benny take the fall.

24

I TOLD PEARL THAT I WANTED both of us to eat lunch with the federation at their table that day.

"Why?" she asked.

"If you're back in their good graces," I said, "I want to see them grovel a little and congratulate you on a job well done. Besides: safety in numbers. If we're with the federation, hopefully Rhona will keep her distance."

As we started our meals under the weight of heavy praise from the federation, I could feel Rhona's glare from across the room. I did the best I could to ignore her and focus on the matter at hand. When we reached a lull in the conversation, I smiled sweetly and said to no one in particular, "There's one thing that's still bugging me about all of this."

"What's that?" asked Judy Cohen.

"That banner was a two-man job. Who was helping Benny?"

"Probably one of the other Rainbows," said Ira.

"Hmmmm, maybe," I said. "Where do you think he got the ladder from? I mean, they would've had to use a ladder to hang something up so high."

"The firemen had ladders in the school all week," said Paul. "Benny probably stole one."

"Right," I said. "I understand Benny's real good at stealing things." I looked at Michael as I said it and I could see that he knew what I was getting at even as it went over everyone else's head. "Wouldn't you guys love to find out who was helping him? You know, so that everyone gets punished?"

"Of course," said Natalie.

"I bet I could get Benny to tell me." I looked sideways at Pearl, who was no doubt very confused. "Maybe if I threatened to get him fired from the A and P, he'd tell me anything I asked." I thumped my fingers on the table and frowned. "I'd better go," I said. "I've got some studying to do." I left their little group and hurried out of the cafeteria. It was only a matter of minutes before Michael appeared, his face flushed, his brow damp.

"Looking for me?" I said as he approached the journalism office.

"Who told you?"

"Not Benny, if that's what you're worried about. I figured it out myself."

"Who else knows?" he asked in a hushed tone.

"No one, though I wouldn't be surprised if Pearl put it

together. She's a smart cookie despite what her brother thinks." I clucked my tongue at him. "That's pretty low, Michael, letting Benny take the rap for everything."

"I didn't expect that he'd get caught."

I wagged a finger in his face. "I don't doubt it, but he did and now you have to do something about it."

"Do you have any idea what the consequences will be if the truth gets out that I did this? Anytime anything happens to a Jewish student from here on out, people will claim it's a lie they made up for sympathy or who knows what. Think about what that means, Iris."

He was right—this was going to have a devastating effect not just on Michael, but on every Jew at P.S. 110. But I couldn't think about that. Not when Benny had been expelled. "You should've thought about that before you started this little scam."

"Please," begged Michael. "There has to be some other way."

I showed him my empty palms. "Sorry, nothing's coming to mind." I turned to leave and found Pearl standing behind me. From the look on her face, she'd been there for most of the conversation.

"Please, Pearl. You've got to help me," said Michael.

"Forget it," I told him. "If Pearl hadn't come forward about Benny, you would've been more than happy to let her take the fall. Come on." I pulled Pearl away and walked as if there were a hatchet man fast on our heels.

"He's right, you know," she said as we turned the corner. "This is going to be awful for the group."

"That's not our fault."

"And Benny's still going to look guilty. Even if he was forced into it, everyone's going to say that Michael and he worked together. That's not going to get him back into school. Especially if Michael denies that he blackmailed him."

I had thought that telling the truth would exonerate Benny, but it would be easy to see the charges sticking even after everyone heard about Michael's role.

Benny was behind the eight ball either way.

"I'll figure out another way to help Benny," I said. The bell rang. Instead of everyone pouring out of the cafeteria and returning to their homerooms, they proceeded to the auditorium. Pearl and I got caught up in the flow and rode the wave into the convocation. Still holding her hand, I pulled her to the front, where we claimed two seats in the second row.

As soon as everyone was seated, Mr. DeLuca came onto the stage and the music teacher played a somber procession of American anthems. The lights dimmed and a projector whirred to life, showing us images from newsreels from the past year. There were the ships at Pearl Harbor smoking just after the attack. There was President Roosevelt calling us to war. There were the lines of men fighting to be the first to enlist and seek revenge. As the early days of our involvement in the war flashed before us, I thought back to what I'd been through during those initial weeks: both what I thought was the truth and what I learned had actually been going on.

As the film came to an end, the lights in the room returned to their full brightness. "Before we continue with this somber anniversary, I wish to make an announcement," said Principal DeLuca. "As you all know, our Jewish students have been targeted by the most profane kind of cowardice over the past week, a situation that did not become evident to me until a banner containing the most vile language was hung in front of the school. I am pleased to say that over the weekend we were able to identify the culprit behind all of this."

My body tingled with anticipation. It was now or never. I would stand up and announce that Mr. DeLuca had it all wrong. Benny may have written the notes and helped hang the banner, but the scheme was all Michael Rosenberg's.

"While the culprit has been punished, I think it is only fitting that we acknowledge those students who have suffered through these attacks and make it clear that P.S. 110 is committed to protecting and nourishing the Jewish Student Federation. I understand that their president, Michael Rosenberg, would like to share a few words with you about the plight of the Jews in Europe. Michael?"

Michael appeared from the wings and crossed toward Mr. DeLuca as the student body greeted him with a smattering of applause. He was obviously nervous. Did he know where I was sitting? Did he know that as soon as he started talking, I was going to stand up and tell everyone the truth about him?

"Thank you, Principal DeLuca," said Michael. "Today marks the anniversary of the first of many tragedies we—"

"Stop!"

Everyone turned my way, only I wasn't the one standing up and yelling for their attention. Pearl was.

"Take your seat, Miss Levine," said Mr. DeLuca.

"I'm sorry, but I can't let this lie go on," said Pearl. "Benny Rossi isn't the person who was writing the notes." She paused and met Michael's eyes. "I was."

A gasp rose from the audience. Had she really just said that?

I grabbed on to the sleeve of her shirt, but she shook herself free and stepped out of my reach. "The federation kicked me out and so I wrote those notes as a way of getting back at them. And then I was worried I was going to get caught, so I pinned them on Benny. I'm so sorry," she said to Michael, whose mouth was so wide its size could rival the Holland Tunnel. "I didn't mean those awful things. There's no excuse for my writing them. None at all."

And then, either because she realized what she'd just done or she was a much better actress than I'd given her credit for, she burst into tears and ran from the room.

I went after her while Principal DeLuca attempted to

get the audience under control. I followed her down the hallway and into the journalism room.

"What was that?" I asked her once the door was closed behind us.

"I'm sorry, Iris—I couldn't let you do that to them. Not to the federation, and not to Benny."

"Why do you care so much about the federation, Pearl? They kicked you out. And not just because you're friends with me. Did you know they—?"

"I know the truth," said Pearl. "They think I'm weird. And you know what? Maybe I am."

"But that doesn't mean you have to take the fall for them."

She shrugged. "I'm already walking around this school with a target on my back. What's it matter if it gets a little bigger?"

The door whined open and I turned, expecting to find the principal ready to haul Pearl away. It was Michael.

"I can't thank you enough, Pearl," he said.

"You'd better be thanking her." I poked him in the shoulder with my index finger. "You listen to me and you listen to me good: those so-called friends of yours, including her brother, are going to be saying some pretty nasty things about Pearl. Put the kibosh on it, got it? She might be willing to take the fall, but it's your responsibility to save her from the repercussions. Otherwise, I come forward with the truth. And that includes whatever punishment DeLuca hands out for this. If you can get Judy Cohen's father to make the principal expel Benny on a weekend, you can get her dad to convince DeLuca that Pearl doesn't get anything more than detention for this. Got it?"

Michael nodded. He looked afraid, and I had to admit that thrilled me a little. *I* had done that. *Me.* And I wasn't done. I'd get Benny to do the same with the Rainbows. They didn't need to know the details of why Pearl was confessing, but they did need to know that they couldn't punish her for it.

By the time I was done, everyone at the school wouldn't just remember Pearl Harbor, they'd respect her, too.

PEARL WENT TO THE OFFICE after the convocation. I waited for her until she was done. She said it was a bad scene, full of tears on her part, and stern words from Principal DeLuca, but she weathered it well. I have to admit I was impressed. After everything she'd done over the past week, from running the investigation to going with me to Yorkville, Pearl had proven herself to be the bravest person I knew.

"There was one thing I didn't admit to," said Pearl.

"What's that?"

"Sending those boys to beat up Paul. I couldn't confess to that, you know? He may be an idiot at times, but he's still my brother and I didn't want people to think I was capable of doing something like that to my own flesh and

312

blood." Pearl paused to tie her saddle shoe. "I wonder if he'll ever forgive Michael for that."

"I don't think he needs to. I'm pretty sure Michael didn't arrange for Paul to get beaten up."

Pearl stood up and dusted off her knees. "You still think that was unrelated?"

"Hardly. I think Denise set that up. She was thrilled when the letters first appeared and everyone started weighing in on whether to stay in the group. When the letters had the opposite effect on Paul, she decided to try a more persuasive approach."

"How do you know that?"

"I don't, but based on the few conversations I've had with her, I wouldn't put it past her."

Pearl consciously avoided each crack in the sidewalk, making her steps strangely staccato. "Do you think I should tell Paul?"

"Do you think he'd listen to you after what you just confessed?"

"Probably not."

I mimicked her weird stride. "Then there's your answer."

I escorted Pearl home, just in case Rhona was lurking about. After seeing her inside, I went to tell Benny the good news. He was in the air-raid shelter again, though he didn't respond to my knock. I opened the door and found him asleep on the bench, the blanket wrapped twice around him for warmth. As I entered, he jolted awake, clearly confused about where he was.

"I'm sorry about yesterday," I said as his eyes focused on me. "You're right—I should've believed in you. I realized after I left here that there's no way you would've written those letters on your own."

"So what do you want? A cookie?"

I was shocked by his tone, but I tried not to show it. "Good news, though: you're off the hook." I told him about what had happened that afternoon, how Pearl had taken the rap for him. I also laid out my conditions for keeping quiet about what had really happened.

I expected a smile or, at the very least, a thank-you. What I got was a shrug.

"That's it?" I said. "Didn't you hear a word of what I just said?"

"I heard you. They're letting me back in and you want me to tell everyone to be nice to Pearl Harbor. I got it."

"Don't call her that."

"Easy, Nancy D."

"And don't call *me* that, either. I thought you'd be a little more enthusiastic about this."

"Why? At the end of the day, none of it really matters—everyone knows who and what I am. Including you. So Pearl took the fall for me—big deal. That doesn't mean my hands are clean."

"Michael blackmailed you. You had no choice in the

matter. You're a good person that was forced into doing a bad thing."

He cut his face with a sardonic grin. "That's what you want to believe. That's not the truth."

"You helped me. You went to Yorkville with me. You brought me back here when I had nowhere else to go."

He shook his head as he pulled out the flask from under the blanket. "You think I didn't want to get something out of that? I knew you were friends with Pearl Harbor. I knew she had access to everything in the office, including the attendance records and the hall passes."

"Don't call her that," I said again.

"And if going with you to Yorkville didn't convince you to do what I asked, maybe holding you while you cried would do the trick. Don't be so naïve, Nancy D. You never get something for nothing."

"You're lying. I know you're lying." My eyes were starting to water with rage. I mashed one hand into the other, but the pain did nothing to squelch my tears. "Don't you understand what Pearl did for you? When word gets out that she's the one to blame for all this, a lot of people are going to be nasty to her, including your friends."

"What do you want me to do about it?"

"Help her out. You owe her that much."

"How do you figure that? I don't remember asking her for a favor."

I stared at him, unable to reconcile the Benny who'd

helped me earlier in the week with the angry boy before me. "Why are you acting this way?"

"This is how I am. Take it or leave it."

"No it's not. You're kind. You don't drink. You do the wrong things for the right reason."

He laughed at me, but there was no joy in the sound. "Boy, do you have a lot to learn. Remember how you lied to my friends and me about who you really were when your pop was poking around a few weeks ago? Well, guess what— the shoe's on the other foot."

I left the shelter and rushed away from his building, hot tears squeezing from the corners of my eyes. By the time I made it to Orchard Street, I could barely see a foot in front of me from crying so hard.

That was probably why I didn't notice the man standing on the front stoop.

"Hello, Iris."

It was the man who'd been there the week before, the one who'd said Stefan said hello. Instinct told me to run, but my feet were too slow. Before I could move, he'd wrapped a hand around my wrist and opened his coat just enough to show me a gun.

A scream died in my throat. I'd seen enough movies to know what he was telling me: if I made a peep, he would shoot me.

"Do you know who I am?" he asked.

I shook my head, afraid that even answering out loud would cause retribution.

"My name is Mr. Haupt and I'm an old friend of your mother's."

This was Stefan Haupt? But what about the man at the White Swan?

"It looks like my name is ringing a bell," he said. "That's good to know. Where is your father?"

"I-I don't know," I said.

"That's a pity. I was hoping that we could resolve this without involving you. He did something very foolish over the weekend. He killed an associate of mine, who was hoping to do the same to him. Had he taken his punishment like your mother did, there would've been no reason for me to come here like this. Is your landlady home?"

I nodded, because it was more likely than not.

"Then I guess we go to Yorkville and wait for your father to find us." He pulled me off the stoop and toward a car parked at the curb. I looked toward the house, hoping Mrs. M. might see me, but the blackout blinds were already drawn. I tried to go limp in his arms, but he was far stronger than me and, even without my help, was able to pull me the ten feet from the house to his automobile.

Just when I thought all hope was lost, a voice called out my name. "Iris!" Haupt turned to look, and I saw my opportunity and wrenched free of his hold. I stumbled and slid across the street, landing behind a mailbox. A gun fired and I was certain that it was Haupt trying to cut me down in my path, but when I peered around the mailbox to see where he was, I found him crumpled behind the car. His blood mingled with the new snow, turning the road scarlet.

Who had done that?

I looked toward where I'd heard my name being called and spied Benny frozen in his path. Benny had shot Haupt? But if he'd had a gun, it was no longer in his hand. I looked the opposite way up the street and saw Pop limping toward Haupt's body, his revolver clutched against his body.

It was Pop. Pop had shot him.

I left my hiding place and ran to him. He caught me, fighting to maintain his balance on the slick sidewalk. "You're okay?" Pop asked, four or five times, until I began to think it wasn't a question, but a chant: You're okay. You're okay. You're okay.

"Yes. I'm fine." My tears returned, only now they weren't for Benny and his lies.

"Thank God. I'm so sorry, Iris. I followed him from York-ville. I figured he was coming to try to ambush me at home. I never imagined that you'd arrive here when he did."

"It's all right," I said.

Haupt stirred on the ground. His gun had fallen beside him, and he stretched his arm as far as he could to try to reach it. Pop left me and, with his own gun extended, approached Haupt. I cringed, waiting for a second shot to fire and for the light to go out of Haupt's eyes. Instead, Pop kicked Haupt's gun into the road, then lowered his own weapon to his side.

Sirens exploded in the distance as the police, roused by our neighbors, rushed to join us. As the first red light pulsed down the street, I took in Benny, who had finally reached my side.

"What are you doing here?" I asked.

"I wanted to tell you that I'll do what I can to call off Rhona. And I wanted to say I'm sorry. I didn't mean what I said." He took in the scene as the cops pulled to the curb and retrieved Haupt's gun. "What just happened?"

"I think you just did something good without expecting anything in return."

He rubbed his chin. "Huh. Who would've thought I was capable of that?"

Me, my heart sang. *Me!*

AFTER THE POLICE had come and taken Pop's statement and hauled Stefan Haupt to the hospital, Pop and I retreated to the parlor with the cups of cocoa Mrs. M. had made for us. Despite the warmth of the fire and the sweet milk, I couldn't stop shivering. Pop wrapped the afghan around my shoulders, and still I shook.

"That was the man who killed Mama, right?" I asked between chattering teeth. I needed to hear it from him, that things were really, truly over and that the right person had finally been captured.

"Yes. That's the man."

"You've been trying to find him for a while?"

Pop wiped away his milk mustache with the back of his hand. "I had hoped to. And then a few weeks ago he came looking for me."

"And you hired Betty to work for you?"

He nodded. I didn't need to hear any more, about how he needed someone to do the footwork that he himself couldn't do, how he took a risk by putting Betty in a similar position to the one Uncle Adam had put Mama in.

The chattering moved through my body, sending my legs into convulsions. I was worried I would never be warm again.

"You're in shock," Pop said. "It'll pass, I promise."

"Why didn't you kill him?" I asked.

"Don't worry, Iris—he's not going to bother us again. His friends on the force worked the uptown beat, not the Lower East Side."

"I know, but—" How to articulate what I was thinking? If Haupt was here today, who did Pop kill at the White Swan? "Would you have killed him if I wasn't there?"

Pop frowned. "Of course not. All I ever wanted was for him to be captured and punished. It was the only way anyone was going to learn the truth about what happened to your mother."

"But if he'd pulled a gun on you first, would you have killed him then?"

He put his arm around my shoulder and rubbed my upper arm through the afghan. "I think I know what you're getting at. This isn't war, Iris. At war, yes, I would've killed him without thinking. But I'm not a soldier anymore. In the civilian world the only reason you use a gun is to maintain control. You don't have to kill anyone to do that, but sometimes you do have to wound them."

The shivering was waning. I relaxed against Pop. "Where were you on Saturday?"

"I told you—I was supposed to meet with a client who didn't show, so I did some surveillance work instead."

I found a loose thread on the afghan and pulled at it. "The safe was open. It looked like you left in a hurry and forgot to close it. And your gun was gone."

He paused for a long time. I thought he was formulating another lie, but he surprised me when he finally answered. "Haupt contacted me. He wanted to meet me at the hotel where your mother was killed."

"And what happened when you did?"

"Nothing. I didn't go."

"Why?"

Another pause, and I knew he was struggling with the best way to tell me the truth. "I was pretty sure I was headed into an ambush. Part of me didn't care. I must've started down Eighty-sixth Street four or five times before changing

321

my mind and walking away. I just couldn't do that to you."

I hugged the blanket closer. "You didn't even go into the White Swan?"

"It probably makes me sound like a terrible coward, doesn't it? In the end, though, it was the right thing to do. Someone was killed there."

"Who?"

"The hotel owner. A man named Mueller." Anna Mueller's ex-husband, the man Benny and I had met the day we broke in. His was the face ruined by the bullet, the body lying unidentified in the morgue.

I'm sure my relief at the news that Pop never went into the White Swan must've shown. The more I thought about it, the more sense it made. After all, how would Pop have made it up the fire-escape ladder? Why hadn't I heard his distinctive footsteps when the killer ran away? How had he managed to make it out of the building so quickly?

It was what my dream the night before had been trying to tell me.

And yet, if Pop didn't kill Mueller, who did? I knew it couldn't be Haupt: he said himself that he thought Pop was the one who'd killed his associate. So then who? Who else knew that danger was waiting for Pop at the White Swan?

Uncle Adam.

"You look like you still have something on your mind, Iris."

I twisted the loose thread around my index finger, cutting the blood off until the flesh turned purple. "Mama's death isn't Uncle Adam's fault," I said.

"Iris—"

"No, listen to me, Pop. He tried to get Mama to drop the case."

"It's nice of you to defend your uncle, but he's admitted what he did."

I left his side and approached the radio, where Mama's photo still sat. I removed the note from inside it and passed it to Pop. "Read this. Adam lied to you. It was Mama's choice to meet with Haupt, not his. If you can show Haupt mercy and he's the one who actually killed Mama, Adam deserves that and so much more. Please. Think about it."

Pop read the note in silence. When he was done, he shoved it into his pocket, wiped his eyes dry, then went into his office to call his brother.

POP IS LETTING ME work for him again. I'm no longer being subjected to tests, but I am being limited to office work until he's certain that there are no associates of Stefan Haupt's out there lurking about. He's also met twice with Uncle Adam, though I'm not sure things will ever be completely resolved between the two of them. Michael and

Benny kept their promise and did their best to defend Pearl from the federation and the Rainbows. The rest of the student body hasn't been so kind, but Pearl is holding up surprisingly well.

Pop and I celebrated our first Christmas with Mrs. Mrozenski and Betty. Mrs. M. gave me a new frame for Mama's picture as my gift and I gave her the *Betty Crocker Cook Book of All-Purpose Baking.* We spent New Year's Eve morning at Mount Hebron cemetery. It was the first time I'd been there since Mama's funeral, when I'd tossed a handful of dirt on her coffin right after it was lowered into the grave. Pop, Mrs. M., Betty, Uncle Adam, and Aunt Miriam were with me, along with Pearl, to witness the unveiling of Mama's tombstone and to eulogize the woman I so desperately missed.

The day was clear, cold, and beautiful, if a winter day in New York can be such a thing. As we recited the mourners' Kaddish, birds that should've flown south weeks before joined us with their own sad song.

It was the second tribute to Mama that week. Days before, the *Times* ran an article describing the long, tangled history of Stefan Haupt and the trail of murder he'd left in his wake. While the police and the OWI refused to speak on the record about any specific crimes of which he was accused, the reporter quoted a number of unnamed sources who were aware of Mama's involvement in the case and how Haupt had wielded his power to cover up her murder.

It wasn't enough to remove the "suicide" label from her death certificate, but at least it proved to everyone that it was still possible to be good *and* a German. To some people, Mama will always be the woman who killed herself when her husband and daughter needed her, just like to some people Pearl will always be the girl who wrote those awful notes. The important thing is that those who matter most know the truth.

As we pulled the sheet from Mama's headstone and revealed the Hebrew words that paid tribute to her life, I felt like we were finally removing a shroud that had covered her for the past year. It was so good to have her back again, to be able to remember her as she really was. And I know I'm not the only one who felt that way.

When the service was over, one by one we placed a rock on her headstone. I was the last one to do so. As I balanced my stone on the curved surface, I whispered at the earth beneath my feet, "You don't have to protect me anymore, Mama. Pop will keep me safe."